David Arnold lives in Lexington, (lovely) wife and (boisterous) son. Previous jobs include freelance musician/producer, stay-at-home dad, and preschool teacher. He is a fierce believer in the power of kindness and community. And chips. He believes fiercely in chips. *Mosquitoland* is his first novel. You can learn more at davidarnoldbooks.com and follow him on Twitter @roofbeam.

Praise for *Mosquitoland*:

'At times heartwarming, heartbreaking and hilarious, but always maintaining a distinctly innocent brilliance'
USA Today

'[A] sparkling, startling, laugh-out-loud debut novel'
Wall Street Journal

'A stunning debut. . . mesmerizing'
Kirkus Reviews, starred review

'[A] captivating first novel… illuminating'
Washington Post

'A breath of fresh air… [a novel that] bucks the usual classifications and stands defiantly alone'
Entertainment Weekly

'Arnold never lets up on the accelerator of life's hard lessons. . . *Mosquitoland* has pizazz – lots and lots of it'
Booklist, starred review

'There is no shortage of humor in Mim's musings, interspersed with tender scenes and a few heart-pounding surprises. Mim's triumphant evolution is well worth the journey'
Publishers Weekly

MOSQUITOLAND

DAVID ARNOLD

headline

First published by Viking Juvenile, USA.

First published in Great Britain in paperback in 2015 by
HEADLINE PUBLISHING GROUP

Cataloguing in Publication Data is available from the British Library

ISBN: 978 1 4722 1890 2

Typeset in Guadri LT Std

Printed and bound in Great Britain by
Clays Ltd, St Ives plc

Headline's policy is to use papers that are natural, renewable and recyclable products and made from wood grown in well-managed forests and other controlled sources. The logging and manufacturing processes are expected to conform to the environmental regulations of the country of origin.

HEADLINE PUBLISHING GROUP
An Hachette UK Company
Carmelite House
50 Victoria Embankment
London EC4Y 0DZ

www.headline.co.uk
www.hachette.co.uk

For Stephanie and Winn,
the whys behind my whats

JACKSON, MISSISSIPPI

(947 Miles to Go)

... 1 ...

A Thing's Not a Thing until You Say It Out Loud

I AM MARY Iris Malone, and I am not okay.

… 2 …

The Uncomfortable Nearness of Strangers

September 1—afternoon

Dear Isabel,

As a member of the family, you have a right to know what's going on. Dad agrees but says I should avoid "topics of substance and despair." When I asked how he propose I do this, seeing as our family is prone to substantial desperation, he rolled his eyes and flared his nostrils, like he does. The thing is, I'm incapable of fluff, so here goes. The straight dope, Mim-style. Filled to the brim with "topics of substance and despair."

Just over a month ago, I moved from the greener pastures of Ashland, Ohio, to the dried-up wastelands of Jackson, Mississippi, with Dad and Kathy. During that time, it's possible I've gotten into some trouble at my new school. Not trouble with a capital *T*, you understand, but this is a subtle distinction for adults once they're determined to ruin a kid's youth. My new principal is just such a man. He scheduled a conference for ten a.m., in which the malfeasance of

Mim Malone would be the only point of order. Kathy switched her day shift at Denny's so she could join Dad as a parental representative. I was in algebra II, watching Mr. Harrow carry on a romantic relationship with his polynomials, when my name echoed down the coral-painted hallways.

"Mim Malone, please report to Principal Schwartz's office. Mim Malone to the principal's office."

(Suffice it to say, I didn't *want* to go, but the Loudspeaker summoned, and the Student responded, and 'twas always thus.)

The foyer leading into the principal's office was dank, a suffocating decor of rusty maroons and browns. Inspirational posters were plastered around the room, boasting one-word encouragements and eagles soaring over purple mountain majesties.

I threw up a little, swallowed it back down.

"You can go on back," said a secretary without looking up. "They're expecting you."

Beyond the secretary's desk, Principal Schwartz's heavy oak door was cracked open an inch. Nearing it, I heard low voices on the other side.

"What's her mother's name again?" asked Schwartz, his timbre muffled by that lustrous seventies mustache, a hold-over from the glory days no doubt.

"Eve," said Dad.

Schwartz: "Right, right. What a shame. Well, I hope Mim is grateful for your involvement, Kathy. Heaven knows she needs a mother figure right now."

Kathy: "We all just want Eve to get better, you know? And she will. She'll beat this disease. Eve's a fighter."

Just outside the door, I stood frozen—inside and out. *Disease?*

Schwartz: (Sigh.) "Does Mim know?"

Dad: (Different kind of sigh.) "No. The time just doesn't seem right. New school, new friends, lots of . . . new developments, as you can see."

Schwartz: (Chuckle.) "Quite. Well, hopefully things will come together for Eve in . . . where did you say she was?"

Dad: "Cleveland. And thank you. We're hoping for the best."

(Every great character, Iz, be it on page or screen, is multidimensional. The good guys aren't all good, the bad guys aren't all bad, and any character wholly one or the other shouldn't exist at all. Remember this when I describe the antics that follow, for though I am not a villain, I am not immune to villainy.)

Our Heroine turns from the oak door, calmly exits the office, the school, the grounds. She walks in a daze, trying to put the pieces together. Across the football field, athletic meatheads sneer, but she hears them not. Her trusty Goodwill shoes carry her down the crumbling sidewalk while she considers the three-week drought of letters and phone calls from her mother. Our Heroine takes the shortcut behind the Taco Hole, ignoring its beefy bouquet. She walks the lonely streets of her new neighborhood, rounds the sky-scraping oak, and pauses for a moment in the shade of her new residence. She checks the mailbox—empty. As always. Pulling out her phone, she dials her mother's number for the hundredth time, hears the same robotic lady for the hundredth time, is disheartened for the hundredth time.

We're sorry, this number has been disconnected.

She shuts her phone and looks up at this new house, a house bought for the low, low price of Everything She'd Ever Known to Be True. "*Glass and concrete and stone,*" she whispers, the chorus of one of her favorite songs. She smiles, pulls her hair back into a ponytail, and finishes the lyric. "*It is just a house, not a home.*"

Bursting through the front door, Our Heroine takes the steps three at a time. She ignores the new-house smell—a strange combination of sanitizer, tacos, and pigheaded denial—and sprints to her bedroom. Here, she repacks her trusty JanSport backpack with overnight provisions, a bottle of water, toiletries, extra clothes, meds, war paint, makeup remover, and a bag of potato chips. She dashes into her father and stepmother's bedroom and drops to her knees in front of the feminine dresser. Our Heroine reaches behind a neatly folded stack of Spanx in the bottom drawer and retrieves a coffee can labeled HILLS BROS. ORIGINAL BLEND. Popping the cap, she removes a thick wad of bills and counts by Andrew Jacksons to eight hundred eighty dollars. (Her evil stepmother had overestimated the secrecy of this hiding spot, for Our Heroine sees *all*.)

Adding the can of cash to her backpack, she bolts from her house-not-a-home, jogs a half mile to the bus stop, and catches a metro line to the Jackson Greyhound terminal. She's known the where for a while now: Cleveland, Ohio, 947 miles away. But until today, she wasn't sure of the how or when.

The how: a bus. The when: pronto, posthaste, lickety-split.

And . . . scene.

But you're a true Malone, and as such, this won't be enough for you. You'll need more than just wheres, whens, and hows—you'll need whys. You'll think *Why wouldn't Our Heroine just (insert brilliant solution here)?* The truth is, reasons are hard. I'm standing on a whole stack of them right now, with barely a notion of how I got up here.

So maybe that's what this will be, Iz: my Book of Reasons. I'll explain the whys behind my whats, and you can see for yourself how my Reasons stack up. Consider that little clandestine convo between Dad, Kathy, and Schwartz Reason #1. It's a long way to Cleveland, so I'll try and space the rest out, but for now, know this: my Reasons may be hard, but my Objectives are quite simple.

Get to Cleveland, get to Mom.

I salute myself.

I accept my mission.

Signing off,
Mary Iris Malone,
Mother-effing Mother-Saver

RETRACING THE STICK FIGURE on the front of this journal makes little difference. Stick figures are eternally anemic.

I pull my dark hair across one shoulder, slump my forehead against the window, and marvel at the outside world. Before Mississippi had her devilish way, my marvelings were wondrously unique. Recently they've become I-don't-know-what . . . middling. Tragically mediocre. To top it off, a rain of biblical proportions is absolutely punishing the earth right now, and I can't help feeling it deserves it. Stuffing my journal in my backpack, I grab my bottle of Abilitol. Tip, swallow, repeat daily: this is the habit, and habit is king, so says Dad. I swallow the pill, then shove the bottle back in my bag with attitude. Also part of the habit. So says I.

"Th'hell you doing in here, missy?"

I see the tuft first, a tall poke of hair towering over the front two seats. It's dripping wet, and crooked like the Leaning Tower of Pisa. The man—a Greyhound employee named Carl, according to the damp patch on his button-down—is huge. Lumbering, even. Still eyeballing me, he pulls a burrito out of nowhere, unwraps it, digs in.

Enchanté, Carl.

"This is the bus to Cleveland, right?" I rummage around in my bag. "I have a ticket."

"Missy," he says, his mouth full, "you could have Wonky's golden fuckin' ticket for all I care. We ain't started boarding yet."

In my head, a thousand tiny Mims shoot flaming arrows at Carl, burning his hair to the ground in a glorious blaze of tuft.

Before one of these metaphysical Mims gets me into trouble, I hear my mother's voice in my ear, echoing a toll, the chime of my childhood: *Kill him with kindness, Mary. Absolutely murder him with it.* I throw on a girlish smile and my mother's British accent. "Blimey, that's a lovely uniform, chap. Really accentuates your pectorals."

The Leaning Tower of Tuft calmly chews his burrito, turns, points to the open door. I throw on my backpack and ease down the aisle. "Seriously, old chap. Just dynamite pecs."

I'm out the door and into the squall before he can respond. I don't suppose that's what Mom would have meant by murdering with kindness, but honestly, just then, that was the only me I could be.

Flipping my hoodie over my head, I cross the station lot toward an awning, hopping a half-dozen rising puddles. Underneath the canopy, seven or eight people stand shoulder to shoulder, glancing at watches, rereading papers, anything to avoid acknowledging the uncomfortable nearness of strangers. I squeeze in next to a middle-aged man in a poncho and watch the water pour over the edge of the awning like a paper-thin waterfall.

"Is that you?" says Poncho Man, inches away.

Please don't let him be talking to me, please don't let him be talking to me.

"Excuse me," he says, nudging my JanSport. "I think your backpack is singing."

I sling my bag around and pull out my cell. The dulcet tones of Stevie Wonder's "I Just Called to Say I Love You" echo off the walls of our little canvas-and-water prison. Stevie only croons when Kathy calls, altogether negating the sentiment of the lyrics.

"That's sweet," says Poncho Man. "Your boyfriend?"

"Stepmom," I whisper, staring at her name on the LCD screen. Kathy preloaded the song to be her "special ring." I've been meaning to change it to something more appropriate, like Darth Vader's "Imperial March" or that robotic voice that just yells *"Warning! Warning!"* over and over again.

"You guys must be close."

Singing phone in hand, I turn to face this guy. "What?"

"The song. Are you and your stepmother close?"

"Oh yeah, sure," I say, summoning every sarcastic bone in my body. Leaving the phone unanswered, I toss it in my bag. "We're tight."

He nods, smiling from ear to ear. "That's terrific."

I say nothing. My quota for conversations with a stranger has officially been met. For the decade.

"So where're you headed, hon?" he asks.

Well, that's that.

I take a deep breath, step through the mini-waterfall and into the rain. It's still falling in sheets, but I don't mind. It's the first rain of autumn, my favorite of the year. And maybe it's this, or the adrenaline of my day's decisions, but I'm feeling reckless—or honest, maybe. Sometimes, it's hard to tell the difference.

Turning toward Poncho Man, I notice his eyes are wet and

shiny, but it's not from crying or the rain. It's something else entirely. And for a split second, I have the peculiar sensation that everyone and everything around us has dissolved. It's just the two of us, cursed to face one another amid the ravenous elements of this bus station for all of forever.

"You know," I yell over the rain, breaking the curse. "I'm sixteen."

The other people under the awning are staring now, unable to ignore the uncomfortable nearness any longer.

"Okay," he says, nodding, still smiling with those glassy eyes.

I push a clump of sopping hair out of my face and pull the drawstrings of my hoodie tight around my head. "You really shouldn't talk to young girls. At bus stations. It's just creepy, man."

Soaked to the bone, pondering the madness of the world, I stomp through puddles to the doors of the Jackson Greyhound station. Next to Gate C, a short man in a tweed hat hands me a flyer.

LABOUR DAY SPECIAL

FOUR $DOLLAR-FIFTY GENERAL TSO CHICKEN

WHY U PAY MORE? DROP BY! WE FAMOUS!

The flyer is a domino, the first, tipping over a row of memories: a blank fortune knocks over Labor Day traditions, knocks over Elvis, knocks over fireworks, knocks over the way things used to be, knocks over, knocks over . . .

From a thousand miles away, I feel my mother needing me.

This is a thing that I know, and I know it harder, stronger, fuller than I've ever known any other thing.

Four days until Labor Day.

Ninety-six hours.

I can't be late.

… 3 …

Northbound Greyhound

September 1—afternoon

Dear Isabel,

So I'm bored. On a bus. Stuck next to an old lady who keeps leaning over like she wants to start up a conversation. To maintain sanity, I shall write.

Labor Day is Reason #2.

Now, I know what you're thinking. *Really, Mim? Labor Day?* And rightfully so. What's so special about the first Monday of September that the government would shut down the country in its honor? Honestly, if it weren't for school closings and extended happy hours, I'm not sure anyone would know it exists.

But I would.

One Labor Day, six or seven years ago, Mom stood up in the middle of dinner and asked if I'd like to go for a walk. Dad kept his head down, toying with the food on his plate. "Evie," he whispered without looking up. I remember laughing because it looked like he was giving his food a name. Mom said something about the digestive benefits of exercise after eating, grabbed my hand, and together we walked out the door, down the hushed streets of our subdivision. We laughed and talked and laughed some more. I loved it when she was like that, all young and fun and eager to keep being young and fun, and it didn't matter what happened the day before or the day after, all that mattered was the Young Fun Now.

Such a rare thing.

Anyway . . .

That's when we found it. Or rather, *them*. Our people.

They lived on Utopia Court, if you can believe it—a little cul-de-sac tucked in the back of the neighborhood. When we turned the corner, it was like stepping through Alice's looking-glass, only instead of the Jabberwock and a Red Queen, we found revolutionaries and idealists, people who damned the Man, people who refused to bow to suburban mediocrity. While the rest of the neighborhood watched TV or played video games, that little cul-de-sac set off explosions for the ages.

They understood the Young Fun Now.

Every Labor Day, Mom and I came back for more. We took part in their pig roasts, lemonade stands, and beer buckets, their loud stereos and rambunctious kids, their flag wavings and fireworkings and food gorgings. We did so with gumption and hunger and thirst, knowing full well it would be another 364 days before those offerings came back around. (That first year, we went back for Memorial Day—*bupkis*. Nothing. Like an empty baseball stadium. Same with Fourth of July. I guess Utopia Court was more like Narnia than the looking-glass in that respect. It was never where—or rather, *when*—you thought it would be.)

Bottom line: in the face of suburban mediocrity, Utopia Court provided an honest-to-God mutiny, and we loved every mutinous minute.

So there's the setup.

Now for the teardown.

Last year, just as the fireworks were picking up steam, Mom set down her beer and began saying thank-yous and good-nights. Something was wrong—we'd never left so early. But I didn't argue. What mattered to her mattered to me. Reluctantly, I followed her back to the other side of the looking-glass. We admired the fireworks from a distance, holding hands as we walked (yes, I held hands with my mother, but then, nothing about our relationship has ever been traditional). Suddenly, Mom stopped dead in her tracks. This image—of my mother's silhouette against a black sky backdrop, as majestic fires exploded all around—is a memory I have tucked in my back pocket, one I can pull out and examine at will, to remember her like that forever and ever and ever and ever and ever . . . infinite forevers. "Mary," she whispered. She wasn't looking at me, and I could tell her mind was somewhere I could never be. I waited for whatever it was Mom wanted to say, because that's how it used to be with us. There was no need for prodding. For a few minutes, we stood there on the quiet sidewalk, stuck between mutiny and mediocrity. As the distant fireworks dwindled, our sidewalk became darker, as if Utopia's pyrotechnics had been the city's only source of light. Just then, Mom let go of my hand, and turned. "I was lovely once," she whispered. "But he never loved me once."

Her tone was familiar, like the lyric of some dark-eyed youth singing tragic clichés. But Mom was no youth, and this was no cliché.

"Who?" I said softly. "Dad?"

She never answered. Eventually, she began walking toward our house, toward mediocrity, away from the glorious mutiny. I followed her the rest of the way in silence.

I remember this like it was yesterday.

I remember because it was the last time we held hands.

Signing off,
Mary Iris Malone,
Mutineer Extraordinaire

"NOW THOSE ARE some interesting shoes. Where does a person get shoes like that?"

I guess I've held the old lady off for as long as possible. "Goodwill," I say, stuffing my journal in my backpack.

"Which one?"

"I don't . . . really remember."

"Hmm. Very strappy, aren't they? And colorful."

The old lady is right. Only the eighties, with its fuchsia-infused electro-pop, could have produced high-top footwear of such dazzling flamboyance. Four Velcro straps apiece, just in case. There's a whole platoon of unworn sneakers in my closet at home, Kathy's attempts to replace more pieces of my old life. "My stepmother hates them," I say, leaning back in my seat.

The old woman wrinkles her forehead, leans over for a better look. "Well, I'm quite taken with them. They've got pizzazz, don't you know."

"Thanks," I say, smiling. *Who says pizzazz?* I look down at her white leather walking shoes, complete with three-inch soles and a wide Velcro band. "Yours are cool, too."

What starts as a chuckle ends in a deep, hearty laugh. "Oh yes," she says, lifting both feet off the ground. "*Très chic, non*?"

I'll admit, initially, I'd been wary of sitting next to an old lady: the beehive hairdos, the knit turtlenecks, the smell of onion soup and imminent death. But as the bus had been packed, I'd had very limited options when it came to a seatmate; it was either the old lady, the glassy-eyed Poncho Man, or a three-hundred-pound Jabba the Hutt look-alike. So I sat. Beehive hair? Check. Knit turtleneck? Check. Nothing to rile the geriatric gestapo. But her smell . . .

I've been trying to place it ever since I sat down. It is decidedly un-geriatric. It's like . . . potpourri, maybe. Abandoned attics, handmade quilts. Fucking fresh-baked cookies, with . . . a hint of cinnamon. That's it exactly.

God, I love cinnamon.

The old lady shifts in her seat, accidentally dropping her purse to the floor. In her lap, I see a wooden container no larger than a shoe box. It has a deep red hue and a brass lock, but what stands out most is the way her left hand is holding it: white-knuckled and for dear life.

I pick up her purse and hand it to her. Blushing, she replaces it on top of the wooden box. "Thank you," she says, offering a handshake. "I'm Arlene, by the way."

Her crooked fingers point in all directions, withering under a spiderweb of bulging veins and rusty rings. Not surprisingly, her hand is soft in mine; surprisingly, it is quite pleasant.

"I'm Mim."

She raises the same hand to adjust her beehive. "What an interesting name. *Mim*. Almost as interesting as those shoes."

I smile politely. "It's an acroname, actually."

"A what?"

"My real name is Mary Iris Malone. Mim is just an acronym, but when I was younger, I thought it was acro*name*, which made total sense."

"Acroname. How clever," says Arlene.

"Mary was my grandmother's name."

"It's quite lovely."

I shrug. "I guess. It doesn't really . . ."

"Match the shoes?" she says, nudging me in the ribs.

Arlene is turning out to be a surprise-a-minute, with her Velcro shoes and phraseology, all *pizzazz* and *très chic, non*. I wonder if she'd be so likable if I unloaded on her—just told her everything, even the *BREAKING NEWS*. I could do it, too. Those bright blue, batty eyes are just begging for it.

"So what's in Cleveland?" she asks, pointing to my backpack. The corner of an envelope is sticking out of a side pocket, its return address clearly visible.

Eve Durham
PO Box 449
Cleveland, OH 44103

I tuck the envelope away. "Nothing. My . . . uncle."

"Oh?" says Arlene, raising her eyebrows. "Hmm."

"What?"

"I was just thinking—*Eve* is an interesting name for a man."

Like a priest during confession, Arlene doesn't meet my eyes. She folds her hands across the purse in her lap, looks straight ahead, and waits for me to tell the truth. We've only just met, but things like time hardly matter when dealing with a familiar spirit.

I turn, look out the window as the dense forest zooms by in a blur, a thousand trees becoming one. "My parents got divorced three months ago," I say, just loud enough for her to hear over the hum of the engine. "Dad found a replacement at Denny's."

"The restaurant?"

"I know, right? Most people find breakfast." Arlene doesn't laugh at my joke, which makes me like her even more. Some jokes aren't meant to be funny. "The wedding was six weeks ago. They're married now." My chest tightens at the sound of my own words. It's the first time I've said it out loud. "Eve is my mother. She lives in Cleveland."

I feel Arlene's gentle touch on my back, and I'm afraid of what's coming. The catchphrase monologue. The sermon of encouragement, imploring bravery in the face of a crumbling American family. It's all in the manual. Adults just can't help themselves when it comes to Words of Wisdom.

"Is he a good man?" she asks. Arlene, it would seem, has not read the manual.

"Who?"

"Your father, dear."

Through the window, I see the ocean of trees, now in slow motion: each trunk, an anchor; each treetop, a rolling wave; a thousand coiling branches, leaves, sharp pine needles. My own reflection in the window is ghostlike, translucent. I am part of this Sea of Trees, this landscape blurred.

"All my sharp edges," I whisper.

Arlene says something, but it's muffled, as if from an adjacent room. The hum of the bus dissolves, too. Everything is quiet. I hear only my breath, my heartbeat, the internal factory of Mim Malone.

I am six, reading on the floor of our living room in Ashland. Aunt Isabel, visiting from Boston, is sitting at my father's old rolltop, writing a letter. Dad pokes his head in the room. *"Iz, I need my desk back. You done?"* Aunt Isabel doesn't stop scribbling. *"I look like I'm done, Bareth?"* Dad rolls his eyes, flares his nostrils. *"What's a bareth?"* I ask, looking over my book. Aunt Isabel smiles, her head still bent over her letters. *"That is,"* she says, pointing to my dad. I look at him quizzically. *"I thought your name was Barry?"* Aunt Isabel shakes her head. *"You thought wrong, little lamb."* I love all her nicknames, but Dad is not amused. *"You writing a novel there, Iz?"* She doesn't answer. *"Isabel, I'm talking to you." "No, you're not,"* she says. *"You're making fun of me."* Dad sighs, mutters something about the futility of correspondence, leaves the room. I go back to my book for a few minutes before asking, *"Who are you writing to, Aunt Isabel?" "My doctor,"* she says. Then, setting her pencil down, she turns to me. *"Writing sort of . . . rounds off the sharp edges of my brain, you know?"* I nod, but I don't know; with Aunt Iz, I rarely do. *"Tell you what,"* she says. *"When I go back to Boston, you write to me. You'll see what I mean."* I consider this for a moment. *"Do I have sharp edges, too, Aunt Iz?"* She smiles and laughs, and I don't know why. *"Maybe, little lamb. Either way, you should write. It's better than succumbing to the madness of the world."* Here she pauses, glances at the door where Dad had just been standing. *"And cheaper than pills."*

Sound returns. The steady hum of the bus engine, and Arlene's voice, warm and wet. "Are you all right, Mim?"

I keep my good eye on the passing landscape. "We used to make waffles," I say.

A brief pause.

"Waffles, dear?"

"Every Saturday. Dad mixed and whisked while I sat on a wobbly stool and smiled. Then I poured the mix into the waffle maker and . . ."

Another pause.

"Yes?" says Arlene.

"What?"

"You stopped in the middle of a sentence, dear."

Aunt Isabel's last line echoes in my head. *Cheaper than pills . . . ills . . . ills . . . ills . . .*

I turn, set my jaw, and look Arlene squarely in the eyes. I choose my words carefully, devoting attention to each syllable. "I think my dad is a good man who has succumbed to the madness of the world."

At first, Arlene doesn't respond. She looks concerned, actually, though I can't be sure if it's due to my answer or my behavior over the last few minutes. Then . . . her eyes flash, and she nods. "So many do, my dear. So many do."

We ride in silence for a while, and I don't know about Arlene, but it's nice to sit that close to someone and not feel the incessant need to talk. The two of us could just be. Which is what I need right now.

Because I am Mary Iris Malone, and I am not okay.

… 4 …

Abilitol

I BEGAN MY sessions with Dr. Wilson just over a year ago. His many framed degrees assured everyone that he was an actual doctor, and not, as I feared, a professional clown.

"Tell me what you see here, Mary."

"That's not my name, Doc. Or . . . didn't my parents tell you?"

The doctor's lips curled into a coy smile. "I'm sorry. *Mim*. Tell me wha—"

"Wrong again," I whispered.

Dr. Wilson looked to my father for help, but that well had dried up long ago. "Okay, then," he said. "What is your name?"

"Antoine," I said, straight-faced.

"Mim, that's enough," said Dad. "Answer Dr. Wilson's questions."

Most girls my age had long ago stopped telling the truth, and simply started saying what everyone wanted to hear. But sometime during middle school, or maybe even before, I'd made a choice about the kind of kid I was going to be, and more importantly, the kind of kid I *wasn't* going to be.

"Mim?" prodded Dr. Wilson. "Can you tell me what you—"

"Where's your bear, Doc?" I interrupted.

"I'm sorry. My what?"

"Wait—don't tell me you're a bear-less doctor."

Dr. Wilson furrowed his brow and looked to my father.

"Dr. Makundi's waiting room had a"—Dad sighed, as if he'd rather say anything other than what he was about to say—"it had a life-sized grizzly. Stuffed."

"Did it?" said Dr. Wilson. His smile had a certain juvenile quality I recognized immediately.

He thinks he's better than Dr. Makundi.

I picked up the ink splotches and leafed through them one by one. "Penis, penis, penis . . . Wow, is that a labia?"

"Mim, God, please," said Dad.

I slapped the cards down on the desk, then held up both middle fingers. "Tell me what you see here, Doc."

Dad stood, looked to my mother, who sat quietly with her hands in her lap. She wasn't smiling, but she wasn't frowning either.

"It's okay, Mr. Malone," said Dr. Wilson, motioning for him to sit. Then, turning to me, he said, "Remember what we talked about, Mim. Remember the importance of verbally expressing *exactly* how you feel. Sometimes a thing doesn't seem real until we say it out loud."

I rolled my eyes. "I feel angry and—"

"Start with your name," interrupted the doctor, holding up his hands. "Your full name, please."

"I am Mary Iris Malone."

"Go on," he whispered.

I lowered my voice, because as I'd learned some time ago, a whisper was louder than a scream. "And I am not okay. I'm angry. And bored. And I think Dr. Makundi is a hundred thousand times better at being a doctor than you are."

Wilson's smile was infuriating. "And what about the voices, Mim? Have you had any episodes lately?"

"You make it sound like, I-don't-know . . . epilepsy or something. Like I'm drooling and convulsing all day." I picked up an inkblot card. "And aren't inkblots, like, completely medieval? What's next, a lobotomy? Shock treatment? God, it's like *Cuckoo's Nest* in here."

Wilson nodded, unfazed. "We can be done with the inkblots if you'd like."

"Yes, I'd like. Very much, I'd like."

Pushing his chair back from his desk, Wilson opened a drawer and pulled out a stereo that looked as if it'd been shot from a cannon. He thumbed through a book of CDs. "How about some music? You like Vivaldi?"

"Makundi had Elvis."

"I'm afraid I only have classical."

Shocker. "Fine. Bach, then. Cello Suite Number One?"

He shuffled through the CDs, pulled out a Bach double disc. "I'm fairly certain the first cello concerto is on here."

"Suite," I corrected.

"Yes, it is," he mumbled, "very sweet."

"Blimey, you're an idiot, Doc."

Dad sank back in his chair, buried his head in his hands.

Admittedly, he'd been hanging by a very thin thread, but this seemed to do him in.

Dr. Wilson asked a few more questions and jotted down some notes while I studied his office. Cozy plants. Cozy chairs. A mahogany desk, no doubt the price of an Audi. And behind the good doctor, his Wall of Hubris: I counted seven framed degrees, hung with care and pride and more than a little jackassedness. *Oh-ho, you don't believe I'm important, eh? Well then, how do you explain these?!?!?!*

Wilson stopped writing for a second. "Your family has a history of psychosis, I believe?"

Dad nodded. "My sister."

A few dramatic underlines later, Wilson closed my file and pulled out a new pad of paper. It was smaller and pink. "I'm going to prescribe Aripapilazone," he said. "Ten milligrams a day—that's one tablet daily."

Out of the corner of my eye, I saw Mom grab Dad's leg and squeeze. He shifted, pulled his leg away, said nothing.

"I'm sorry," said Mom. They were the first words she'd spoken since we'd arrived. "Is that really necessary? Dr. Makundi was of the opinion that medication, in Mim's case, was premature."

Wilson took off his glasses, met my father's eyes briefly, then ripped the prescription from his pad. "I'm afraid Dr. Makundi and I disagree on this matter. It is your choice, of course, but this is my . . . *professional* recommendation."

I was the only one who caught this dig at Makundi. Or the only one who cared, anyway. *Professional*. Insinuating Makundi's recommendation was *less than*. As far as I was concerned, Wilson and Dad and their dedication to medication were more absurd than all the stuffed grizzlies in the land.

"We read about a drug that was getting good results," said Dad, looking at the prescription. "What was it called, Evie? Ability-something . . . ?"

Mom crossed her arms and looked the other way. She had a fire in her eyes I hadn't seen before.

The doctor nodded. "That's this. Aripapilazone is commonly known as Abilitol."

A pall fell over the room. A black shroud of disease and deathbeds and all the worst things from all the worst places. This mutant word, a tragic portmanteau, the unnatural marriage of two roots as different as different could be. *And do you, Ability, take Vitriol to be your lawfully wedded suffix?* I wanted to scream objections to the unholy matrimony, but nothing came out. My mouth was clammy and dry, full of sand. Dr. Wilson smiled ever on, rambling about the benefits of Abilitol while my father nodded like a toy bobblehead immune to the deepening shadow in the room.

As they spoke, I caught my mother's eye. I could tell by her face she felt the deepening shadow, too.

Neither of us smiled.

Neither of us spoke.

We felt the shadow together.

... 5 ...

The Sixth Letter

I WAKE UP to the hum of cross-country travel, the late sun on my face, and Arlene's heavy head on my shoulder. (If it weren't for her snoring, I would swear the old gal was either dead or in a coma.) Wiping away the thin string of drool dangling from Arlene's mouth to my shoulder, I nudge her head in the opposite direction and pull my backpack into my lap.

Prone to unwieldy dreams, I've always found naps to be more exhausting than refreshing, and this one was no exception. I dreamed about a science project from fifth grade. We were given a map of the world and told to cut out each continent, then piece them back together as they were millions of years ago when there weren't seven separate continents, but rather one supercontinent known as Pangaea. In real life, I did just that. But unwieldy dreams care nothing for the wields of life, and instead of cutting out continents in the dream, I decided to cut out the small state of Mississippi. Before I could do so, the page became actual land, and I found myself staring at the entire state from an aerial view: its tall boxlike shape with those sharp angles; the jutting jaw; at the bottom, a small neck running right into the Gulf of Mexico. Suddenly, Mississippi crumbled before my very eyes and sank into the water. No sooner was it gone than a mighty army of mosquitos took its place. Millions and millions of them, buzzing aimlessly, digesting hot blood, suspended in midair over the salty water. For a moment, they stayed in the exact shape as Mississippi, so it looked as if the state was still there—only buzzing, flittering about.

And then the army, as one, turned toward me.

That was when I woke up.

Wiping sweat from my forehead, I try to find the breath I lost during the dream. The rolling timpani of the bus engine, the horn section of murmuring passengers, and the occasional rimshot of backfire somehow help. It's a symphony of transportation, a soothing reassurance that I am closer to my mom, farther from Mosquitoland.

I dab at the wet spot on my shoulder (courtesy of Arlene's sleep-drool), and unzip my bag. Something about being hunted by bloodsucking devils compels a girl to double-check her resources. Popping the lid off the Hills Bros. coffee can, I count by twenty to seven hundred. The bus ticket cost one-eighty, so I'm—

My heart flips over in my chest.

What. Is. That?

From the bottom of the can, I pull out a thin tube of papers wrapped in a rubber band. My epiglottis flutters out of pure fascination. What secrets might Kathy be keeping in her beloved coffee can?

Arlene grunts, opens one eye, scratches the peach fuzz on

her chin, then drops her head on my shoulder. I nudge it gently toward the aisle, where it lolls for a second before flopping right back where it was.

Damn. Old broad's persistent.

Tucking the cash and coffee can back in my bag, I stuff the papers in my pocket, hold Arlene's head up with one hand, twist around in my seat, and peer down at the cute couple behind us.

"Wotcha, chaps." For some reason people listen when you're British, something I've witnessed firsthand from my mother's undyingly cool accent. "I really must get to the loo pronto, yeah? Would you mind terribly if I climbed over into your seats? There's a sweet old lady asleep over here, and I'm finding it rather difficult to get by."

Only I say the word *rather* like *rotha*.

As their mouths curl into a smile, I decide to withdrawal the "cute couple" status, at least as it pertains to their teeth. Seriously. They could use a trip or seven to the orthodontist. And before the guy even speaks, something clicks in my brain.

"Where you from, mate?" asks His Ugly Teeth.

When your mother is British, you are keenly aware of fake accents in movies and on TV, which is part of the reason mine is so good. It's also the reason I can tell this guy is, for sure, British.

"Oxbridge," I say. *Damn, Mim*. London, Cambridge, Oxford, Liverpool, Dover—I've even *been* to London. Twice, actually, for family reunions. But no. Oxbridge. Ox-effing-bridge.

Her Ugly Teeth smiles at His Ugly Teeth. "Love, don't you have a mate who lives in Oxbridge?"

He's holding back a laugh now. "Oh, yeah, well, Nigel used to, love, but he moved down to Bumlickton remember?"

"Was it Bumlickton or Loncamdonfordbridgeton?"

Unfortunately for me, they know a real British accent when they hear one, too. Laughing their monarchical asses off, they shift out of their seats to let me climb over. What with the overhead compartments, it's a tight fit, but I manage. I make my way to the back of the bus (the jeers of the Brits still ringing in my ears), then slip into the closet-sized bathroom and slide the lock to OCCUPIED. A tiny mirror hangs above the sink, barely large enough to reflect my face, and for just a moment, I consider using the war paint. It's been a while, right? Okay, fine, I just used it last night, but after the *BREAKING NEWS*, who could blame me? I stick my hand in my pocket, twist the tube with the little silver ring in the middle, and—

Patience, Mary.

Taking a deep breath, I push the lipstick farther down in my pocket, pull out Kathy's covert papers, and sit on top of the plastic toilet lid. I pull off the rubber band, unroll the papers, and read. The first sheet is a disgusting love letter between Kathy and my dad, something I'd give a kidney to un-see. Half standing, I raise the seat and toss the letter into the toilet. The next six pages are letters, too, but far different from the first, and written in very familiar handwriting.

Kathy,

In response to your last letter, the answer is no.

Additionally, please don't pretend that I won't beat this. How are things at Mary's new school? Tell her father I asked.

—Eve

....

Kathy,

I don't have a television in my room, which doesn't seem right. Would you mind checking on that for me? No one around here listens. And yes, I understand that it will get harder before it gets better. I'm the one who's sick.

—Eve

....

Kathy,

These damn people won't listen. Did you call about the TV?

—E

....

Kathy,

Feeling better. Please talk to Barry about an exit strategy.

—E

....

Kathy,

Seriously. I'm going to die in here.

Please help.

—E

The sixth and final letter is a haphazard scrawl, without salutation or signature. I read it at least a dozen times.

THINK OF WHATS BEST FOR HER. PLEASE RECONSIDER.

Every ounce of Mim-blood rushes to my head, wraps its tiny little platelets around my brain, and squeezes. I can't breathe. I can't think.

I can't.

Mom has cancer. Of the breast, lung, liver, it doesn't matter. Or typhoid, maybe. Do people still get that? I'm not sure. She could easily have contracted some deadly bird flu. I mean, they're effing *birds*. They can get to anybody. But no, that's silly. Or maybe not silly, but newsworthy. I'd know about it at least. No, cancer is the most likely suspect. People get cancer all the time. But why ask *Kathy*, of all people, for help?

My right hand, almost without my knowledge, squeezes into a fist, crumpling the first five letters into a tight snowball. I stand and raise the plastic lid. The love letter has sunk to the bottom, a metaphor worth its weight in gold. I toss the epistolary snowball in after it and push the handle to flush. Turning to the mirror, I wipe away the grime and stare at my reflection. It's anemic. Like a stick figure.

Fucking Kathy.

Before Mom's line had been disconnected, I used to call once a day. Kathy said maybe that wasn't such a good idea. She said I should give my mother some space, like we were talking about a cute boy or something.

In my hand, the last letter feels like a bullet, and suddenly, a new idea occurs to me. *What if these aren't the only letters Kathy's been hiding?* Mom left three months ago; for the first two months plus, I received a letter a week. Then, three weeks ago, the letters stopped. But what if they didn't? Kathy had made it abundantly clear she didn't want me calling Mom, so why would she be okay with letters? Was there another hidden coffee can somewhere with three weeks' worth of correspondence from Mom?

I open my fist, reread the bullet.

Think of whats best for her. Please reconsider.

Mom is talking about me. And what's best for me is to be with her. But Kathy doesn't want me to call Mom. And she doesn't want me to write Mom. Of course she wouldn't want me to *see* Mom.

A new hate is stirring low, a chasmic, fiery loathing. I stuff the sixth letter in my pocket, pull out my war paint. Normally, this is a sacred process, requiring no small amount of finesse. But right now, my finesse level is hovering somewhere around "Velociraptor." I am finesse-less. I have no finesse.

Just before the lipstick meets the sallow skin of my cheek, the toilet behind me gives a low belch. Somewhere below my feet, there's a rumbling gurgle, and for the first time, I see the sign under the mirror.

USE TRASH CAN FOR PAPER TOWELS

AND FEMININE PRODUCTS

DO NOT FLUSH

Suck a duck.

The sound of rushing fluids comes from somewhere behind the toilet, and I know what's next.

First things first: *my shoes*. I tuck away the lipstick, and hop up onto the sink just as rusty-looking fluids begin to trickle over the plastic rim of the toilet. From my improbable nest, I watch in horror as the fluids spread across the floor. Having never given two thoughts to the inner workings of a bus's sewage system, I'm left to imagine some giant stomach-like tank in the bowels of the vehicle boiling to its fill, an impending eruption triggered by the crumpled letters. One thing's for sure: it's starting to stink like, *whoa*. I scan the tiny cabin for something to fix this, anything to put a stopper on the seeping toilet: an emergency anti-flood lever, or a hydraulic vacuum, or some sort of ejection button to catapult me from the bus. But there are no levers, vacuums, or ejection buttons.

There is only retreat.

From the safety of my sink-seat, I reach across the room and slide the lock to UNOCCUPIED. By swinging my legs side to side, I'm able to gain enough momentum to get a decent hop off the sink, through the doorway, and into the aisle. It's not a pretty landing, but my shoes remain unsoiled, and that's something. I throw on my best *who, me?* smile, close the door, and make my way back to my row.

"Everything come out all right, dearie?" asks Arlene.

I smile like, *who, me?*, slide across her legs, and drop into my seat. Less than thirty seconds later, a loud commotion emerges from the back of the bus. Peering over my seat back, I see people wrinkling noses and waving hands in front of faces. A few are laughing, but it's shock-and-awe laughter, not *ha-ha how funny* laughter.

Looking down, I see the Brits staring at me with their shirts pulled up over their noses. Gas mask–style.

So that's the way it's gonna be. I'm on a bus full of smart-asses.

I fall back into my seat, look out the window with my good eye, and can't help but smile a little. For the first time in a long time, I'm right where I belong.

YALOBUSHA COUNTY, MISSISSIPPI

(818 Miles to Go)

… 6 …

Sometimes You Need a Thing

September 1—late afternoon

Dear Isabel,

I am a collection of oddities, a circus of neurons and electrons: my heart is the ringmaster, my soul is the trapeze artist, and the world is my audience. It sounds strange because it is, and it is, because I am strange.

My misplaced epiglottis is Reason #3.

About a year ago, my mother took me to the hospital because I kept throwing up. After running a few tests, the pediatrician told us that my epiglottis was displaced, an uncommon issue, but certainly nothing to lose sleep over. The thing is, when he said *dis*placed, I thought he'd said *mis*-placed, which hit me right on the funny bone. I pictured an absentminded Creator, scratching his head and turning the universe upside down in search of Mim's misplaced epiglottis. The doctor prescribed something, but my infantile esophagus persisted with savage tenacity.

More often than not, I have no control over where and when I throw up, but on rare occasions, I've been able to force the issue. Twice since the move, Dad and Kathy have left me home alone. And both times, I've helped myself to their bedroom. I stood on that horrible Berber carpet and observed their desks bumped up next to each other: a PC for the aspiring political blogger, a Mac for the aspiring romance novelist. Two desk lamps. One unmade bed. Two nightstands, one on either side, both with books and tissues. Half of these things, I recognized, half were foreign. And yet, there they were, mixed together as one, the familiar with the unfamiliar—the family with the unfamily.

That was usually when I threw up. On Kathy's side of the bed. The amount of sanitizer she's gone through, you'd think she was cleaning a gorilla cage.

But as I stated at the beginning of this entry, I am a "collection of oddities," and one oddity doth not a collection make.

The Great Blinding Eclipse is Reason #4.

A couple years ago, there was a solar eclipse. All the teachers and parents were like, *Whatever you do, don't look directly at the eclipse!* I mean, really, they were just going ape over it. Well, me being the kind of girl I am, I half heard what they said, half thought about it, half processed the information, and half obeyed it. I closed one eye and looked directly at the eclipse with the other.

Now, I'm half blind.

After the initial freak-out, I did what any rational person would do upon discovering a mystery ailment: I went online.

Online gave my condition a name (solar retinopathy), a cause (what happens from looking directly into the sun for too long), and a time frame (usually, it doesn't last more than two months). As I mentioned before, this happened a couple of years ago, so I suppose I've made peace with the potential permanency of my condition. (I just realized this paragraph is riddled with parentheses. I suppose I'm just feeling parenthetically inclined right now.)

(Anyway.)

So why do I mention all this? Why are my medical mysteries Reasons? I'm glad you asked. I've developed a theory I like to call the Pain Principle. The gist of it is this: pain makes people who they are.

Look around, Iz. The Generics are everywhere: shiny people with shinier cars, driving fast, talking faster. They use big words to tell fabulous stories in exotic settings. Take this kid at my school, Dustin Somebody-or-other. He talks all the time about his family's "estate." Not house. Fucking estate. His mother hired a butler/chef named Jean-Claude, who, according to Dustin, gives the entire Somebody-or-other family jujitsu lessons every morning at sunrise. (Followed by pancakes. Dustin never forgets to mention the pancakes.) Now—it would be easy for me to look at Dustin and think, *God, what an interesting life! How I wish it were my own! Woe unto me!*

But there's a quality behind Dustin's eyes when he talks, a dimness, like the slow fade of a dying flashlight. Like someone forgot to replace the batteries in Dustin's face. This kind of emptiness can only be filled with heartache and struggle and I-don't-know-what . . . the enormity of things. The shit-stink of life. And neither enormity nor shit-stink can be found in a pancake breakfast. Pain is what matters. Not fast cars or big words or fabulous stories in exotic settings. And certainly not some French-toasted-sunrise-sensei-servant-motherfucker.

I guess what I'm saying is, I've learned to accept my pain as a friend, whatever form it takes. Because I know it's the only thing between me and the most pitiful of all species—the Generics.

One last thing about being half blind, because I'm starting to get on my own nerves about the whole mess: I've never told anyone.

Signing off,
Mary Iris Malone,
the Cycloptic Wonder

ARLENE, WITH HER wooden box and assorted bouquet of early-bird aromas, and I, with my thoughts bent on the motivations of evil stepmothers, sit by the side of I-55, watching the Greyhound shake. (Carl, after a hasty pull-over, directed us off the bus, then waded shin-deep into what must be a week's worth of sewage.)

I stick my journal in my backpack and dare a glance around. My fellow passengers aren't staring daggers at me, they're staring scimitars: a trendy family of four in matching polos; a painfully ugly blonde, standing at least six-six; two Japanese men in heated argument; Jabba the Gut, his face in a starry sci-fi; the juvenile Brits; a little kid who looks like a Tolkien character; Poncho Man; and dozens of others, jabbering on cell phones, murmuring under their breath, each of them pissed at me for interrupting their super-important journey to Wherever.

"Are you keeping a diary of your travels, dear?"

Sweet Arlene, the Queen Arete of my Odyssey, coils her veiny fingers around that wooden box in a death grip. Her purse, she left on the bus. But not the box.

"Forgive me," she says, blushing. "I noticed the journal, but I shouldn't pry."

"No, it's fine. It's a . . . letter, I guess."

She nods, and for a split second, I think maybe that's the end of it.

"To whom?" she asks.

I sigh and look up at the shaking bus. "You wouldn't believe me if I told you."

Arlene clears her throat in that way old people do where you can't tell if it's a laugh or a cough or a life-ending gurgle or what. "Would you like to hear where I'm headed?"

Happy for the change of subject, I nod.

"Independence."

"The land of autonomy," I whisper, smiling.

She sort of chuckles, but her heart's not in it. "It's a town in Kentucky. My nephew lives up there with his . . . with his boyfriend."

The way my head whips around, you'd think it was spring-loaded. Not that this is any big thing, but coming from Arlene . . . well, maybe she's not quite as Leave-it-to-Beaver as I thought.

She looks sideways at me now, one corner of her mouth curling up ever so slightly. "His name's Ahab."

"The boyfriend?" I ask, smile squarely in place.

"No. My nephew. I'm not sure what his . . . boyfriend's name is. I haven't met him yet. They opened a filling station, and it's doing quite well from what Ahab tells me. Though he was a champion swimmer in high school, so I'm not sure why a filling station. But I suppose a man has to make a living."

This conversation has taken a turn for the surreal. Arlene's gay nephew, a champion swimmer named Ahab, and his unnamed boyfriend, have opened a gas station in Independence, Kentucky, and it's doing quite well from what ole Arlene hears. I don't know what to say. To any of it. I finally land on, "Good for them."

Arlene looks down at the box, so when she speaks, it looks like she's talking to it. "A while back, my younger sister—that's Ahab's mother—stopped answering his calls. We lived together at the time, and I remember he'd call three, four times a day, but she never answered. When I asked why, she clammed up, started crying. So I called Ahab myself. Asked him what he'd done to make his own mother stop answering his calls. And do you know what he said?"

I shake my head.

"He said, 'Aunt Arlene, you wouldn't believe me if I told you.'" Arlene's tone changes. "You don't have to tell me about your letters, Mim. They may be private, and if that's the case, you tell me to mind my own business. But don't say I won't believe you. You'd be surprised what I believe these days."

I consider her story for a moment. "Why'd your sister stop answering Ahab's calls?"

Arlene never takes her eyes off the box. "You know, when I was younger, I thought if I lived long enough, I'd understand things better. But I'm an old woman now, Mim, and I swear, the longer I live, the less things make sense." She pauses, sets her jaw, continues. "My sister didn't approve. Of the boyfriend. She never said so out loud, but some things speak loud enough on their own."

For a full minute we sit in silence, watching the bus shake. It takes me that long to process the wisdom of Arlene. "I'll make you a deal," I say, pointing to the wooden box in her hands. "You tell me what's in there, I'll tell you who I'm writing to."

Arlene smiles from the box to the bus. "I'm afraid I'd rather not talk about this anymore."

I'm surprised how disappointed this makes me. And not just because I want to know what's in that box of hers but because I think, deep down, I was ready to tell her about Isabel.

"Yo, missy!" Above the rear tires, Carl's head is sticking out of a little window, his eyes fixed on me. That tuft is looking especially frizzy. "Come on in here," he says, disappearing back inside the bus.

Every scimitar turns in my direction. I sling my bag over my shoulder, grateful for Arlene's supportive smile, and climb into the belly of the rocking beast.

I've only known two other Carls in my lifetime—an insurgent moonshiner and a record store owner—both of whom taught me important (though very different) life lessons. In my book, Carls are a top-notch species. But easing down the aisle, listening to the grunts and gags of my third Carl, I'm beginning to wonder if the streak has ended. Girding my nostrils, my lungs, my everything else, I poke my head around the corner and gag. The stench isn't terrestrial. It's not even extraterrestrial.

This shit (so to speak) is *mega*terrestrial.

Propped in the corner, a sopping mop leaks unidentified juices into a bucket; Carl's gloves are covered, too, and even though the floor and toilet are pretty well cleaned up, I'd bet all the cash in Kathy's can that this stink isn't going anywhere. It has seeped its way into the very framework of the bus.

I clear my throat, announcing my presence.

Carl's tuft skims the ceiling as he removes his gloves, and tosses them into the mop bucket. "Just wanna make sure you ain't blind."

My epiglottis flutters. Carl is unaware of the Great Blinding Eclipse, unaware of my solar retinopathy, but . . .

He lights a cigarette, takes a drag, and points to the sign above the sink. "Read that for me, will you?"

Relieved, I read the sign aloud. "Use trash can for paper towels and feminine products. Do not flush."

"You notice those last three words?" He sticks the cigarette out the window, taps off the ashes, and takes another puff. "They big 'n' bold, ain't they? So. I'm forced to ask . . . you blind?"

In the movie of my life, I flick that cigarette out of his mouth and educate him on the effects of secondhand smoke. Also, how to be nice. Carl is played by Samuel L. Jackson, and I, of course, am portrayed by Madam Kate Winslet.

Okay, Zooey Deschanel, then.

Fine. A young Ellen Page.

"I'm not blind," I say.

He nods, takes one last drag, and tosses the stub out the window, thus confirming my suspicions: not all Carls are created equal.

After stuffing the mops into a pygmy closet, he leaves me alone in the bathroom.

I stare at my face in the tiny mirror and wish a thousand things. I wish we'd never left Ashland. I wish Mom wasn't sick. I wish we hadn't gone to Denny's that day. I wish Kathy would jump off a cliff. I wish I hadn't thrown away those letters. I wish I hadn't squandered my proof. I wish I still had a tangible I-don't-know-what . . . thing.

I wish wishing were enough, but it's not.

Sometimes you need a thing.

… 7 …
A Metamorphosis Begun

"MIND IF I sit here?"

A familiar smile shines down on me, sending my epiglottis into orbit. And like that, Poncho Man sits in Arlene's spot. *My* Arlene. He leans over, removes a pair of penny loafers—with actual pennies tucked in the front flaps—and slides them under his chair. (Next to *my* Arlene's purse.) Turning to me with jack-in-the-box enthusiasm, he offers a hand.

"I never properly introduced myself," he says. "I'm Joe."

Think quick, Malone. I point to my right ear and shake my head. "I'm deaf."

He drops his hand, but his smile goes nowhere. "We talked. In Jackson."

The old Malone stick-to-itiveness kicks in; I turn to look out the window, pretending not to have heard.

The rest of the passengers file into their seats, the engine rumbles to life, and the bus slowly gains momentum. Wherever Arlene ended up sitting, she'll be getting a purse delivery pronto. I might just camp out in the aisle next to her.

"I've been watching you," says Poncho Man.

If there are four creepier words in the English language, color me a monkey's uncle.

I watch the slowly passing trees out the window. *You can't hear him, Mary. You're deaf and you can't hear him.*

"Chitchatting with the old lady and the bus driver," he continues.

If there were sand, I would bury my head in it.

"I know you can hear me."

If there were wet concrete, I would bury *his* head in it.

"Antoine," I whisper, still looking out the window.

"What's that?"

"My name." I turn to look at him. I want to see that phony smile wiped off his face. "It's Antoine."

Poncho Man (I will not call him *Joe*) does not relinquish his grin. In fact, it's wider than ever. "Not a very good liar, are you?" he says.

"Better than you, I bet."

He sighs, sits back, and pulls a book out of his poncho. I didn't even know ponchos had pockets. "That's doubtful."

"Oh yeah, why's that?"

"Because I'm an attorney."

While I look for his off switch, he goes on and on about his practice in southern Louisiana, which he runs out of a small condo, one he shares with his ex-secretary, now wife, and blah, blah, blah, blah, shoot me now.

"You wanna hear about my latest case?"

I open my mouth into a wide, fake yawn, look directly at him, and blink slowly.

"A while back," he starts, "one of our biggest clients, you may have heard of them . . ."

I pretend to search for something in my backpack for a full minute.

". . . and not only that, they wanted to sue for—get this—fraudulent roofing! Hand to God, I can't make this stuff up. So anyway . . ."

I sigh as loud as humanly possible.

". . . here's the best part—it was the *mother's* company! Can you believe that?"

In the face of Poncho Man's unyielding torrent of absurd babble, I raise my hand.

"Yes?" he says, looking somewhat amused.

"I'm sorry, but you seem to have missed the indicators."

"Indicators?"

He's smiling again, just like under the canopy back in Mosquitoland. God, this guy's a creep. I can't quite place the why, but I know the what: there's something there, something more than just your run-of-the-mill obnoxious bozo. Either way, it's time to dole out a heavy-handed serving of honesty. Brutal and bold, Mim-style.

"Yeah, listen, I really don't have the energy to point out each of the ways you've shirked the social cues of . . . well, society, so I'm just gonna say this: *I don't care, man*. I've fake yawned, slow blinked, loud sighed, and pretend searched. I considered murdering you, as well as a variety of suicides. Now I'm going to put this in a way I know you'll understand: you stole my friend's seat, and I'd rather die than listen to you speak. My case, counselor, is airtight."

He's not smiling anymore. "And my sentence, *Your Honor*?" he asks.

I lean my head against the chilly window just in time to watch the sun finish its descent. "A conversational restraining order."

ARLENE IS, UNWITTINGLY, one hell of a saboteur. A few minutes after I issued Poncho Man's restraining order, the old gal stopped by to get her purse. Which would have been fine, except she used my name. About a dozen times. Mim this, Mim that, even a couple *How do you spell Mim agains*, which I was just like, *Really?* Needless to say, after she returned to her seat, my case for silence crumbled.

"You a big reader, Mim?" asks Poncho Man, flipping the page of his book. "Food for the brain and the soul."

The sun set a while ago; most passengers are asleep, but a few, like the idiot next to me, are reading with their overhead spotlights. It's raining again, even harder than before, which makes for an unnerving ride. The windshield wipers on a Greyhound are hypnotic, completely different from those on a car or a truck—like sandpaper on tile.

"So delusional," whispers Poncho Man. His voice trails off, hangs in the air like a feather. For the first time since my closing argument, I look in his direction. The book he's reading is thin, the binding strung with a loose red yarn, frayed at the top and bottom of the spine.

"What did you say?" I whisper, still staring at the book.

He flips the cover closed, and I see the title: *Individualism Old and New.*

"It's this philosopher," he says, "John Dewey. The guy is really chappin' my ass."

It's not the same book. It's not the same book. It's not the same book.

He holds the book toward me. "You interested? Happy to loan."

Ignoring his offer, I turn to the window and search for the blurred landscape—but it's nighttime now, too dark outside, too light inside. All I can see is my own face, the sharpened lines of my jutting features, my long dark hair. I am more opaque than ever.

I shut my eyes, and in the pure nothingness, Poncho Man's book scrapes a vague childhood memory from the inner rim of my brain. Traveling through synapses and neurotransmitters, the memory is whisked into a delectable roux, now ready to serve: My mother is sitting in her yellow Victorian reading Dickens. I am a tender age, seven, maybe eight, walking around with a milk crate, pretending to buy groceries from our living room. *"And how much for the generic pine nuts?"* I ask in a feminine voice. *"Those are on sale for eighty-two dollars,"* I answer myself gruffly. Dad, sitting at his rolltop, assuming I hear nothing because of my age, peers over his Truman biography and frowns. *"You're not worried, Evie?"* he asks. *"About what, Barry?"* says Mom. *"I mean, look at her,"* whispers Dad, closing his book. *"She's acting like a . . ."* His voice trails off, but Mom gets the gist. *"She has no siblings, Barry.*

What do you expect?" Dad again, his frown more pronounced, his whisper more intense: *"This is exactly how it started with Iz. Voices and whatnot. Just like this."* Mom closes her book now. *"Mary is nothing like Isabel."* My father opens his book again, buries his head in it. *"Your lips to God's ears."*

"Mim?" Poncho Man's voice pulls me back to the present.

"What?"

He raises an eyebrow and half smiles, apparently amused. "You sort of went all . . . catatonic on me. You okay?"

I nod.

"You sure? I could . . . I dunno, maybe there's a doctor on board, or something." He twists in his seat, as if a man with a stethoscope dangling from his neck might happen to be sitting behind us.

"I said I'm fine."

Poncho Man licks his thumb, leafs through his book. "Well good, because I was just getting to the good part. You're not going to believe what Dewey says next."

"I was just getting to the good part, Eve. Here, listen—'Thought echo, voices heard arguing, voices heard commenting on one's actions, delusions of control, thought withdrawal—'" My mother interrupts him. *"What are you reading?"* I hear the sound of Dad flipping to the front cover. *"I got it from the library. It's called* Clinical Psychopathology." I am fourteen now, pressing my ear against my parents' bedroom door. *"That thing is bloody ancient, Barry. Is that yarn? It's falling apart at the binding."* Dad breathes heavily through his nostrils. *"That doesn't make it any less* relevant, *Evie. This guy who wrote it, Kurt Schneider, he's brilliant. Could probably*

*think circles around Makundi. See, look, he's provided a way to differentiate between psychotic behavior and psycho*pathic *behavior."* I lower my head to peek under the crack of their door. Mom's ratty slippers shuffle across the room. *"Psychopathic behavior? Jesus, Barry."* Dad sighs. *"I'm just telling you what I saw this afternoon."* This afternoon, Erik-with-a-kay broke up with me at lunch. Later, when Dad picked me up, I noticed he was acting weird. *"What you saw was our daughter upset over a boy,"* says Mom. It's quiet for a moment. And then—*"Evie . . ."* Dad's voice is desperate, sad, soft. *"She was asking herself questions, then answering them. Just like Isabel used to."*

"Okay, now I'm worried," says Poncho Man.

My misplaced epiglottis flutters, then calms, then flutters again. I pull my travel-sized makeup remover from my bag and push past his knees.

I can wait no longer.

Walking down the center aisle, I hear the endless line of massive semis speeding by outside, kicking up giant bursts of rain. In the second to last row, Arlene is passed out on Jabba the Gut's shoulder. He's reading a Philip K. Dick novel, unfazed by his seatmate's baby head.

Inside the bathroom, I slide the latch to OCCUPIED. The light comes on automatically, flooding the tiny room with a sickly yellow tint, as if everything were suddenly jaundiced. In the grimy mirror, I watch as my dead eye closes. This still freaks me out, as my actual perception is unchanged. The only way I know my bad eye is closed is that my good one sees it shut in the mirror.

Mom used to say how pretty I was, but I knew better. Still do. My features, independent of one another, might be considered enviable: strong jaw, full lips, dark eyes and hair, olive-brown skin. The attractive pieces are all there, but jumbled somehow. As if each facial feature stopped just short of its proper destination. I act like I don't care, but I do. I always have. And my God, what wouldn't I give to put the pieces together?

But I'm a Picasso, not a Vermeer.

From my pocket, I pull out my mother's lipstick—my war paint. It's a black tube with a shiny silver ring around the middle. I try my best not to use it in public. Even with a heavy dose of makeup remover, a reddish hue is noticeable around the cheeks, like a manufactured blush. But hue or no, I need this now.

I start with the left cheek, always. This habit is king, and it must be exactly the same, line for line. The first stroke is a two-sided arrow, the point of which touches the bridge of my nose. Then, a broad horizontal line across the forehead. The third stroke is an arrow on my right cheek, mirroring the first one. Next, a thick line down the middle of my face, from the top of my forehead to the bottom of my chin. And lastly, a dot inside both arrows.

"Even Picasso used a little rouge," I whisper.

And then it happens . . .

… 8 …
Recall

TELL ME WHAT you see here, Mary. I stare at my reflection in the shaking mirror, clutching the sink for balance. I'm blind and wet, and my name is Mary, not Mim, and I've never been in a fight, never been on a boat, never quit a job, never been to Venice, never, never, never . . .

The bottom drops out, and I'm down, on my side, floating in a strange sudden weightlessness, as if in water or outer space. From far away—one, two, a thousand pleas for mercy, animal-like screams, rabid and seething for survival. A minute, an hour, a lifetime—there is no time, there are no Things. I have no more Things. I have only scraping metal, screaming voices, and death.

And suddenly, my symphony of travel crescendos, achieving its rumbling, mighty End.

The bus is still.

On. Off. On—off—on. The jaundiced lightbulb flashes at random intervals. I lie on my side, staring straight into the now-cracked mirror. Like a joke with some sick punch line, my right eyelid is closed. For a moment, I am content to lie immobile, a cyclops among a thousand shatterings. Breath races through my lungs, veins, limbs, spreading like a virus to every corner of my body. It gathers strength, then, at once, rushes to my head.

There is life in my life.

To my left, the door hangs loosely by a hinge. UNOCCUPIED. The opening is narrow, but I squeeze under it, into the main compartment of the bus. Despite the pain, I pull myself off the floor and look around.

The Greyhound is tipped.

It's a simmering stew of glass and blood and sewage and luggage, a cinematic devastation. Like the lights in the bathroom, the cabin lights flicker on and off in irregular intervals. Some people are moving, some are moaning, and some aren't doing either. Carl is bleeding in about six places, administering CPR to one of the Japanese guys. I see Poncho Man help Amazon Blonde to her feet, right where I'd been sitting. I stand and stare for I-don't-know-how-long, until an ax crashes through the left wall—formerly the roof of the bus. Firefighters crawl through the wreckage like ants, pulling limp bodies around their shoulders, administering first aid. Two EMTs—one with acne and scraggly red hair—approach the limp body of a woman. The redhead leans over, puts his ear to the woman's chest. Straightening, he looks at his partner, shakes his head. Together, they hoist her from her seat and that's when I see who it is: Arlene.

My Arlene.

I am Mary Iris Malone, and I am empty, cleaned the fuck out. All that's left is a fierce hunger for flight.

I have to get out of here.

I stumble forward, stepping on a yellow dash. Then another

and another. *I'm walking on the highway. From inside the bus.* The windows, once lining the sides of the Greyhound, are gone, replaced by wet blacktop. Seats are jutting out of the wall, row after row of them. I step over and around people, and it's impossible not to wonder which ones are dead and which ones are unconscious—the difference between stepping over a person and stepping over a body.

The dam of my epiglottis cracks, then crumbles; I vomit on the ground in front of me.

And I see it. Thing of Things, impossible, yet inevitable. Poking out from under a threadbare Philip K. Dick novel, the corner of Arlene's wooden box. Like a time capsule, it remains blissfully unaffected by the annihilation of the world around it. I pick it up, stagger the rest of the way through the bizarro bus. Through the jagged perforation of hacked metal, I step outside, transported from one dreamlike scene to another. The rain soaks through my hoodie in seconds, and at first, all I can think is *I never even heard the sirens.* I pull Arlene's box tight against my stomach and turn in a slow circle.

A surreal panorama: fire engines, ambulances, state troopers, and curious bystanders are gathered, rain or no rain, right in the middle of the highway. Behind us, the headlights of a thousand cars go on for miles in complete deadlock. Amazon Blonde is being loaded into an ambulance. Jabba the Gut is going with her, probably for about three hundred pounds' worth of reasons.

"Here," says an EMT, draping her arm around my shoulder. "Lemme help."

"I'm fine," I say, pushing her off.

She points to my knee, where a crimson stain has soaked through my jeans. "So that was there before then, was it?" She leads me into the back of an ambulance, out of the pouring rain, and treats my wound. Once done, she drapes a blanket across my shoulders, then jumps back into the wet wreckage without a word. People are rushing on and off the bus, some crying, some bleeding, some hugging, and I can't help but think that before all this happened, I probably would have gotten off in Cleveland in a day or so, and, other than Arlene, not given one thought to these people. But now they're really part of things, part of my life, written in the History of Me.

Arlene.

Choking back a flood of tears, I pull her box out from under my blanket. *What in the world am I going to do with you?*

"You okay, missy?" Carl is towering over me like I-don't-know-what . . . a Tower of Carl, I suppose.

"Yeah. Just a cut." I shiver and pull the blanket a little tighter, concealing Arlene's box. "What happened?"

"Tire blew," he mumbles. "I reported a recall back in Jackson, recommended we either change tires or take a different bus, but no one listened. No one ever listens."

A-freakin'-men.

"You were traveling alone, right?" he asks.

"Yeah," I say. "Already called my dad, let him know what was going on. He said as long as I'm not hurt, I may as well go on to Cleveland. How's that work, by the way?"

Carl lights a cigarette, takes a long draw. God, he looks like a badass smoking in the rain. "I'll make arrangements. Whoever wants to can stay in a motel tonight, then we'll take a new bus in the mornin'. Everything'll be paid for, of course . . ." He trails off and seems to be considering something. "Listen—"

"You the driver?" interrupts the redheaded EMT. He's shivering in the rain, holding a cell toward Carl. Before taking the call, Carl—like some muscly action hero—rips off a bottom section of his sopping wet T-shirt and hands it to me.

"You got something on your face, missy."

Oh my God.

My war paint.

Somehow, it seems beyond appropriate that I stumbled through the ravaged bus with my face painted red. Mim the Warrior Princess. Battle survivor with a bloody wound to prove it.

As Carl limps off to take his call, I wipe my face with his rainy T-shirt and study Arlene's box. Surprisingly heavy, it has one of those old-fashioned skeleton keyholes. The contents don't shake or rattle or anything, but they do shift as I move the box side to side. On the bottom, I find four letters carved deep in the wood: AHAB.

... 9 ...

A Metamorphosis Completed

September 1—late, yo

Dear Isabel,

MY GREYHOUND BUS

(After Tipping on the Side of the Highway and Causing an All-Around Shitstorm from Which I May Never Fully Recover)

Okay.

So I suck at drawing. But *that*? Just happened. To me.

Ahem.

SON OF A BITCH, IT WAS TOTALLY CATASTROPHIC.

Sorry.

Had to get that off my chest.

Now. It would be easy for me to wallow in self-defeat or self-pity or self-doubt or a hundred other selves, but I won't. I'm just going to write.

I'm going to write, and that way I'll be okay.

Let's start with a name. I'll write down this name, and it won't mean anything to you, but when you read it, know that it means something to me. The owner of the name died on that bus, and while I didn't know her all that well, she was a friend, and those don't come easy. Not for me, anyway. She smelled like cookies and wore funny shoes and used words like *pizzazz*. Here's the name.

Arlene.

. . .

. . .

. . .

Okay.

I'm okay.

I'm headed to a motel right now, in a van with about twelve other people. Our bus was full, but most of the passengers seemed uninterested in continuing their relationship with Greyhound.

Relationship. That's exactly what it is. *Hey, gurl, I know I almost crushed you to death, but it was a one-time thing, and I swear it'll never happen again.*

Greyhounds are pigs.

Unfortunately, I don't have many options. Anyway, it takes more than a life-before-your-eyes-kill-your-elderly-best-friend type of bus accident to keep me from Cleveland.

My Objective is a bulwark never failing.

Moving on.

My war paint is Reason #5.

Mom's favorite lipstick: the only article of makeup I've ever been interested in. Call it a cosmetic deficiency.

The idea that this was abnormal hit early, around third or fourth grade. (A girl knows when she's being talked about, am I right?) But I didn't care. I rolled with it. Abnormalities abound! That was my motto. Until it wasn't.

In eighth grade, I joined the Ashland Blackhawks street hockey team. The league was a fledgling operation run by a throng of kids, meatheads mostly, looking for an excuse to punch someone. I was the only girl ('twas always thus), so they only rarely punched me.

The team captain, who doubled as league referee, was this punk kid of about fifteen named Bubba Shapiro. While other teams were called for high-sticking, clipping, cross-checking, and all manner of unsportsmanlike conduct, our team got off scot-free. Bubba looked exactly as you'd expect. Big, beefy—he even had a full-fledged beard, which at his age commanded enormous respect. (Not from me so much, but, you know, the meatheads ate it up.)

One day, a kid named Chris York didn't show up for

practice, and Bubba made an announcement. "Okay, guys, Chris came out at school today, so we're gonna have to push on without him."

I raised my hand and asked where Chris had come out of.

The meatheads laughed.

Bubba asked if I was an idiot, then said, "He's a fudgepacker, Mim. Queer bait. Brokeback Mountaineer. He's gay."

Again, everyone laughed.

Again, I raised my hand.

"Sorry, but . . . what does that have to do with hockey?"

Bubba rolled his eyes and explained that gays didn't like sports.

Well, here's the thing: I never really liked sports, either. The only reason I joined the team was that Dad said I would need some extracurriculars on my college applications. (Malone males are notorious overachievers.)

This association between sports and sexual identity continued to nag at me, until one night, while Mom was doing her makeup, I asked how I would know if I were gay.

"Tell me," she said, putting the finishing touches on her mascara. "How do you feel about Jack Dawson?"

I blushed and smiled. My eyes, I'm sure, took on a twinkling, otherworldly property. My parents had always been sticklers for film ratings (though I suspected Dad was the driving force behind this), and since *Titanic* was PG-13, I'd had to wait until—you guessed it—my thirteenth birthday, at which point, Mom and I watched it exclusively and repetitively. We'd seen it twenty-nine times (exactly, not approximately).

While the story and special effects were achievements in their own right, it was no secret why we loved the movie. Leo DiCaprio as the noble Jack Dawson was just too yum for his own good. (I swear I'm not one of those girls who *oohs* and *aahs* over weekly celebrity crushes, Iz, but in the case of Leo, I simply cannot help myself. I'd be lying if I told you I don't think about that scene down by the furnaces, in that old car . . . Blimey, it's hot in this van.)

Smiling, Mom reached for the makeup tray on her vanity. She grabbed the black tube with the shiny silver ring in the middle—this was her favorite lipstick, the kind she wore only on special occasions. "Scoot in here, Mary. Let me show you a thing or two."

For the next twenty minutes, I received my first and last makeover. I have no moral objections to makeup, you understand, it's just . . . I know me. And makeup isn't me. This, in addition to my edgy, hard-nosed, take-no-prisoner attitude, and I think I could have made a pretty decent lesbian. Not to pigeonhole the demographic. I'm sure there are plenty of lesbian softies out there, gobbling up tubs of ice cream and sobbing at the end of early-nineties romcoms. But when it's all said and done, I am Madam Winslet in that old car with Leo, not the other way around. And as simple as it sounds, I think understanding who you are—and who you are *not*—is the most important thing of all Important Things.

So that's the setup.

The teardown is a topic of substance and despair if ever there was one. Or as Bubba Shapiro might say—

unsportsmanlike conduct. But you really only need to know two things: first, I've been carrying around my mother's lipstick for a while now, occasionally using it to paint my face like some war-crazed chieftess preparing for battle; and second, it is vital that the lipstick be returned to its rightful owner.

I have to go now, because we just pulled into the motel's parking lot.

More Reasons to follow.

Signing off,
Mary Iris DiCaprio

MOM HITCHHIKED THROUGH Europe when she was younger. I remember her talking about the hostels she stayed in, and how they were complete dumps but she didn't care. They had stories to tell, little pieces of the people who had stayed in them before—what they wore, what they ate, what they believed. Mom said she loved staying in a place where "anything might have happened even if nothing ever did." And she always ended her stories by saying, "Granted, they all smelled like a moth's shoe, yeah?"

God, I wish I could have known her back then, in her hitchhiking glory days. The Young Fun Now, twenty-four/seven.

I stuff the stick figure journal in my bag and hop out of the van.

"Alrighty," says Carl, limping from the front office of the

Motel 6. Dude is a superhero. Bandaged and bruised, and not one word of complaint. I suppose the streak continues. If this guy's not a true-blue Carl, then I don't know a thing. He passes out keys with dangling bottle caps. Mine has the number 7 scrawled on top.

"These are your room keys," he says. "Greyhound's gonna drop off a new bus overnight. I set up a six thirty wake-up call for everyone tomorrow mornin', so let's meet back here at seven thirty on the dot. You don't show up, I'll assume you got another ride. I ain't your mama. Got it?"

One of the Japanese guys raises his hand; I think it's the one Carl just CPR'd on the bus. "Excuse me, bus driver?" he asks, without a trace of an accent. "Where are we?"

Carl lights a cigarette, exhales out the side of his mouth. "Memphis. Just outside Graceland."

Everyone disperses, heading toward his or her respective rooms. I grab my bag with renewed spirit. *Graceland*. Home of my mother's all-time favorite artist. Undeniably, this is a good sign. Poncho Man (who apparently lost a shoe in the wreck, as he's currently wearing one penny loafer and one too-big sneaker) winks at me as he turns toward his room. "Sleep tight, Mim."

Go to hell, creep.

On the way to my room, I spot a pharmacy across the street. It's one of those real classy joints where the lightbulb in every other letter has gone dark; instead of PHARMACY, it reads, "P A M C ." Maybe it's the wreck, or the rush of blood from my leg wound, or the death of my friend, but I'm suddenly feeling impulsive and alive. I need change, and I need it now.

I cross the empty street and enter PAMC, surprised it's open this late. Between the elevator music and the sharp artificial lights, it feels like I just stepped onto a flying saucer. (Apparently, my aliens love the dude who sings "Never Gonna Give You Up." Because, you know, obviously.) An employee behind the check-out counter is filing her nails and humming along with the song.

"Hey," she says.

"Hey. Haircutting shears?"

"Aisle nine." She points a fiercely manicured fingernail.

I hustle down aisle nine and, as an afterthought, grab four packs of makeup remover. At the checkout counter, the girl blows her fingernails, rings me up.

"Makeover?" she says.

"Something like that."

Back across the street, I locate the room between 6 and 8. Hanging there with aplomb is a brass *L*. I twist the letter into the number 7, but it falls again. Too tired to care, I unlock the door with my bottle cap key and breathe in the sweet scent of a moth's shoe. I wonder—what might have happened in this room?

. . . Elvis wrote my mother's all-time favorite song, "Can't Help Falling in Love" . . .

. . . a rogue beekeeper, who insisted on the very freshest honey to go with his morning biscuits, snuck in a hive . . .

. . . a rabbi questioned his faith . . .

. . . a whore turned her trick . . .

. . . a somebody did their something . . .

In this room . . .

I toss my JanSport under a rickety AC unit and pull the

shears out of their plastic box. In the bathroom, I stare at my reflection in the mirror and visualize a new me: Mod Mim. Like Michelangelo with a block of stone, I see my lengthy mop of dark hair and know the end result before I begin. I snip with courage, purpose, urgency, styling my hair the way I've always wanted, but never had the stones to ask for—edgy, chic, short-short in the back, then angled down into longer sides, the bob cut of all bob cuts. And the bangs, my God, the bangs! I leave them long, just barely out of my eyes, sharp and straight enough to give Anna Wintour a run for her money. With only one good eye, I have to double- and triple-check all the lines to make sure they're even. Once done, I stare at myself in the fluorescent light and finally feel like the girl I am. The girl who gets called to the principal's office but hops a bus to Cleveland instead. The girl who survived a catastrophic accident. The girl who took matters into her own hands, figuratively, literally, fucking *finally*.

I feel more Mim than ever before.

... 10 ...
Inventory

7:42 LOOKS BLURRY.

7:43 is a little clearer.

7:44 . . .

Groggy, I will myself out of bed. I've never really been a morning person, but waking up in yesterday's clothes makes me reconsider being a person altogether. I stumble across the room, push back a curtain. Well. There's a bus. So that's good. Though I don't see anyone around it, which probably means everyone's still asleep, which probably means some lazy bones down in the front office forgot our wake-up calls. I grab the receiver, press 0, and wait. After exactly thirty-two rings (yes, I count, and yes, I wait that long, because really, once it passes ten rings it becomes a game of How Many Rings Can We Get to Before Someone Finally Picks Up the Gee-Dee Telephone), I hear the soft click of someone picking up on the other end. Except . . . no hello, or anything. Whoever it is, they don't say a word.

"Hello?" I say.

"Yez, hi." The guy has a thick accent of indeterminate origin. Gun-to-my-head, I would guess Estonian.

I carry the phone over to the dresser mirror and study my new haircut. "Hi."

"Yez, hi."

Well, this is weird. "Oh—hi, yes. I, umm, was with the group of about twelve or so that came in last night after our bus got demolished on fifty-five."

I am met with complete silence. This Estonian guy could use a lesson or two in telephone etiquette, though I suppose it should come from someone who speaks his native tongue. Thank God I was born with an unending supply of Malone stick-to-itiveness.

"Well, last night, Carl—that's our bus driver—he set up a six thirty wake-up call. And I never got one."

Silence.

"I'd hate for everyone to miss the bus, so to speak. Ha."

Silence.

I clear my throat.

Finally, on the other end: "Yez, hi. Okay."

Click.

Turning from the mirror, I hang up but let my hand rest on the phone for a second.

I should give Dad a ring. Just to let him know I'm okay. Out of curiosity, I unzip my backpack and pull out my cell phone. Fourteen missed calls from Kathy. Blimey, that's a lot of shit music. A pang of something, injury maybe, settles in my stomach, when I see that Dad only called once. I've been gone overnight now, and he's called *once*. And there's a voice mail.

I dial the code and listen:

"Mim, it's . . ." Throat clear. *"It's me. I mean, it's Dad."* Sigh. *"Mim, where are you? We're all sort of freaked here."* Short pause. *"Principal Schwartz says you've been skipping school. If you're worried we're mad, we're . . ."* Long pause. In the background, I hear Kathy say something. Dad responds. He must have covered the phone, because I can't make out any of it. *"Listen,"* he says, sighing again. *"About the other night. I hate the way that conversation ended. You have to understand, no matter what happened between me and your mom, I'll—"*

I snap the phone shut. If Dad wants to discuss the *BREAKING NEWS*, he's gonna have to find me first. Though I wouldn't put it past Kathy to call the cops, which could seriously complicate things. Maybe if I just let them know I'm okay, without telling them what I'm doing . . .

I think through the phrasing first, then open the Internet browser on my phone. The thing is ancient, and while Wi-Fi is possible, it certainly isn't cheap. Though right now, that only serves as extra incentive. After a few seconds, I'm connected. I open my Facebook profile and update my status:

"Not dead. Not abducted. (Though aliens are, as always, welcome.) You'll hear from me when you hear from me."

I reread the wording a few times, press Post, then chuck the phone in my bag. After a quick shower, I pull on a clean tee and underwear, cursing myself for not bringing another pair of pants. I slip on the same hoodie and bloodstained jeans, then take a closer look at Arlene's box. The brass lock, the reddish wood, all of it is in fine condition, wholly unaffected by the crash. I have no idea why I picked it up, except . . . leaving it there, in the middle of everything, just didn't seem right. It obviously meant a lot to Arlene, but it's not like I can get it to her nephew, the preposterous swimmer turned successful gas station operator Ahab. I don't even know the guy's last name. Or Arlene's, for that matter.

Pushing back the Arlene-shaped knot in my throat, I tuck the box away and pull out my bottle of Abilitol. Like a Siren, it tempts me with whispered promises of the ever-elusive Normal Life. If I were home right now, this would be Dad's shining moment, the one in which he eagerly explains the pill's function. He always used the same tone when he talked meds, a slick salesman-slash-drug-dealer-slash-nerdy-dad combo. *"It balances the serotonin levels, Mim. It'll adjust your brain chemicals. Dopamine and that sort of thing. It just evens everything out so you can live a normal life."* I always expected him to end those speeches with *"Everybody's doin' it, man!"* Peer pressure is one thing, but when your dad's the pusher, it's something else entirely.

The bottle stares up at me now as only a bottle of prescription meds can do, redefining the art of seduction. I stare right back . . .

Mary Malone—Aripapilazone
10MG—TAKE ONE TABLET BY MOUTH DAILY
Refills: No
Qty: 45
Dr. B. Wilson

And the memories tumble: Antoine knocks over ink splotches, knocks over Bach, knocks over *Tell me what you see here, Mary,* knocks over, knocks over, knocks over . . .

I tip a single pink pill into my palm and hold it up to my good eye. Small. Strong. Tempting. "One ring to rule them all," I whisper, immediately regretting it. Sometimes, things are more embarrassing when you're alone. I guess when no one's around to hear your stupidity, you're forced to bear the brunt of it.

I grab my new pair of shears from the dresser, and, in the spirit of Utopian mutiny, cut the pill in half. I'd expected the thing to shatter, but it doesn't. It's a clean cut, right down the middle. I grab my water bottle, swallow one half of the pill, and toss the other in the trash.

All packed up, I sit by the window and pull my mother's sixth letter from my pocket. Softened by sweat and rain, the ink is faded a bit, though not beyond recognition.

Think of whats best for her. Please reconsider.

Back on the bus, I'd been too worked up to notice the missing apostrophe. I picture Mom writing this, impetuous and angry. She'd have to be to make this kind of—

The phone rings.

I look at the receiver.

It rings again.

And again.

Surely not. I cross the room and pull the phone from its cradle, daring this to be the call I think it is. "Hello?"

"Yez, hi—dis ees your vake-up coll."

Click.

There are times when I absolutely, 110 percent, without a doubt, *have* to laugh at a thing. 'Cause if I don't, that same thing will make me go stark-raving bananas.

I hang up the phone and laugh until I cry.

… 11 …
Hyena vs. Gazelle

AFTER WE BOARD the new bus (much nicer than the old one), Carl hands everyone an envelope full of vouchers and coupons. Not only do I get a row to myself, I find one with an outlet just below the window. After plugging in my phone, I stow my JanSport in the overhead compartment and spend the next hour or so watching the kid across the aisle eat deli ham straight from a Ziploc. In and of itself, this isn't noteworthy, but as the kid looks dead-on like a young Frodo Baggins, it is, I believe, the worthiest of all notes. (*We shall go through the Mines of Moria! But first, let us replenish our energy with finely sliced deli meats. Eat, drink, be merry! Elves! Ham! Huzzah!*)

"Exactly why I don't have a boyfriend," I whisper, turning to the window.

Because you've referenced The Lord of the Rings *twice before lunch, or because you're talking to yourself?*

I have to admit, I've got me there.

A couple of hours later, we pull off for lunch at a remote exit; Carl gets on the mic and goes through his spiel about not leaving valuables on the bus, and how much time we have at this stop.

"If you ain't back in forty-five minutes, I'll assume you found yo'self a ride. We're an hour from Nashville, and *this* time, we'll be *on* time. I ain't your mama, and I *will* leave without you."

Attaboy, Carl.

Once off the bus, someone asks about the restaurant, to which Carl points at a sign over a nearby gas station door.

ED'S PLACE: CHICKEN-N-GAS

The image in my brain is unsettling to say the least: Ed, a disgruntled Vietnam vet, stands over a stove with two ashy cigarillos hanging from either side of his mouth; he's stirring a giant pot of his famous chicken-petroleum soup. It makes sense, too, because where I've had good luck with Carls, I've never met a single Ed I didn't want to ninja to death. They're scoundrels through and through. I enter Ed's Place not with an attitude of optimism but with an attitude of ninja-ism.

There are four tables, each with checkered paper tablecloths. I wait until Poncho Man sits, and then pick the table farthest from him. Unfortunately, they're all pretty close together.

"Mim!" he whispers. Pointing to my hair, he gives a thumbs-up. "Looks great!"

I throw on my most sarcastic smile, give him a thumbs-up, and slowly raise my middle finger. A bald man with a biker beard and apron hobbles over to Poncho Man's table and greets him by name. "Hey, Joe, want the regular?" Poncho Man smiles, nods, then carries on a short, albeit jovial-looking conversation with the guy.

He's been here before.

I don't have a chance to process this information fully before the Bald Biker Beard is at our table taking drink orders.

"What kind of coffee do you have?" I ask.

"What kind?" says the waiter, only he says it like, *Wit kand?*

"Yeah, I mean, Ethiopian, Kona—it's not Colombian, is it?"

Under his beard, the waiter's jaws are chomping something, presumably a piece of gum. After a few uncomfortable seconds of silence, I spot the name sewn on his shirt pocket: ED.

And all is right with the world.

"Never mind." I sigh. "I'll just have a chicken sandwich, please."

"Ain't got chicken sammich."

I choose a smile over a *judo* chop. "The subtitle of your establishment indicates otherwise."

He raises an eyebrow, chomps, says nothing.

"Okay, fine," I say. "Burger?"

"What'd you wanna drink?" he asks.

"Orange soda. Please."

"We got grape. We got Coke. We got milk."

"Milk? Really?" I hate this place. "Fine, I'll have . . . grape soda, I guess."

Ed goes around the table, takes everyone's order, then shuffles off. In order to avoid the uncomfortable nearness of strangers, I thumb through the thick envelope of vouchers from Greyhound. One coupon offers a half-price massage at some mall in Topeka. The next is for a free go-cart ride at a place called the Dayton 500. The only coupons of any real value are three free nights at a Holiday Inn, a fifteen-dollar gift card to Cracker Barrel, and a few Greyhound vouchers. Fair trade, I suppose, for almost murdering us.

After maybe ten minutes, a tray of food crashes into the middle of the table. Ed leans over my shoulder, his beard brushing my face, and tosses a plate at each person in turn, announcing the orders as he goes. "And last but not least," he looks down at me, not with a twinkle in his eye, but a twinkle in his voice. "A gourmet burger for the little lady. And a *milk* to warsh it down."

"I didn't ord—"

"Bone-appeteet!" he says, hobbling away with a maniacal laugh.

I poke at the burger, which could probably double as a hockey puck. Choking down half of it with the milk, I push my plate away. I'll eat in Nashville.

Carl announces a fifteen-minute warning; I grab my bag and follow a long hallway toward the back of Ed's Place. The restroom is a two-staller with a filthy sink, foggy mirror, and wallpaper of creative expletives. I deadbolt the door, hang my bag on a hook, and, careful not to touch *anything*, pee in record time. After washing my hands, I unzip my bag, and just as I'm about to add the vouchers to Kathy's coffee can, I hear it—a cough.

Just one. Quiet. Timid, almost. But definitely a cough.

Cash in hand, I peek underneath the stall divider. There, in the second stall—one penny loafer, one too-big sneaker.

What the hell . . . ?

Slowly, the shoes shift, and the door swings open. Poncho

Man smiles at me, briefly glancing at the cash in my hand. "Hello, Mim."

Still kneeling, I remain frozen, reduced to the role of Busty Blonde in my own slasher. "What are you doing in here?" I ask. His leg brushes my knee as he steps to the faucet and runs his hands under the water. Thinking back, I don't remember a flush.

"Oh, I find the ladies' room to be much more serene. You should see the men's room. Makes this dump look like the Ritz." He wipes his hands on his poncho, then turns toward me and tilts his head. "I meant what I said, Mim. Your haircut is beautiful. And also, sort of—inevitable? Is that the right word?"

Go, Mary. Now.

I regain motion, stuff everything back in my bag, and start for the door. "I'm leaving."

He steps in front of it, blocking me in. "Not yet."

Breathe, Mary. I push my bangs out of my eyes, push the panic down, push, push, push . . . "I'll scream," I say.

"I'll tell on you."

I flinch. "You'll what?"

"I overheard your little convo with Ed out there—you wouldn't drink Hills Brothers Original Blend if your life depended on it. Which means that coffee can I just saw"—he points to my backpack—"isn't yours. Ergo, what's *inside* probably isn't either."

His words are ice. They hit my gut first, then spread in all directions, filling my ears, elbows, knees, toes—the extremities of Mim, once a balmy ninety-eight point six, now a glacial effigy. Until this moment, the uncomfortable nearness of Poncho Man had been held at bay by other passengers and locks on doors.

Now, it's just us. There are no devices, no buffers. He stands there, taller than I remember, bulkier, blocking my way to the safety of my pack. I feel his eyes on me now, trailing from my hair, down my body, lingering in places they don't belong—and for the first time in a long time, I feel like a helpless girl.

He steps closer. "You are beautiful, you know."

I'm shivering now, my bones and blood on full alarm—it's a primordial instinct, Predator versus Prey, passed down from a thousand generations of women who, like me, feared the inevitable. We'd seen the footage of the hyena and the gazelle, and it always ended the same.

"So beautiful," he whispers.

I close my good eye. In my mind, the bathroom dissolves into a reddish hue, the corners dimming like the vignette of an old art house film. The metamorphosis begins at Poncho Man's feet, his mismatched shoes bursting open at the toe, revealing short, sharp claws. His pants bulge at the knees and thighs, every pulsing muscle defined beneath the cheap fabric. His poncho stiffens, hardens, ripples into a spotted fur coat; matted and dirty, the blacks and oranges and browns of his mangy hide reflect the red light of the room, and behold! The metamorphosis of Poncho Man is complete, with one last addition: Fangs. First one, then another, sprouting forth like two young oaks in fertile soil.

"Nothing will happen," he says, his voice thick. "Nothing you don't want."

And in that tone, I understand—I *know*—I'm not his first. "Fuck you. Move."

He reaches out, grips my arm just above the elbow. It's firm and painful. "Why would you say that to me?"

Scream, Mary.

"You're too good," he whispers, leaning his head closer. I can smell his breath, every ounce as ashy and deceitful as I'd imagined. "I know you."

A scream had been boiling in my stomach, and was about to take flight, until . . .

"I know your pain," he said.

My pain.

"I'd like to be friends, Mim."

I am Mary Iris Malone, and I am not okay.

"You want to be friends, don't you?"

I am a collection of oddities . . .

His grip is aggressive. "We could be more than friends, too."

A circus of neurons and electrons . . .

His breath is warm.

Ready . . .

His lips are cold against mine.

Set . . .

His tongue—

Go . . .

Reaching down deep, my misplaced epiglottis locates a certain milk-soaked hockey puck; it gathers every ounce of the semi-digested beef and dairy, then, with pure force and accuracy, launches a vomit for the ages directly into Poncho Man's mouth.

He chokes, gags, *growls . . .*

Spinning, I unlock the door and exit the bathroom, breathing in the freedom of the rarely savvy gazelle.

September 2—noon

Dear Isabel,

A quick note: I don't think a vivid imagination is all it's cracked up to be. I'm quite certain you have one, but if not, thank the gods of born-with gifts and move on. However, if you're cursed as I am with a love of storytelling and adventures in galaxies far, far away, and mythical creatures from fictional lands who are more real to you than actual people with blood and bones—which is to say, people who *exist*—well, let me be the first to pass on my condolences.

Because life is rarely what you imagined it would be.

Signing off,
Mary Iris Malone,
Storytelling Lackey

NASHVILLE, TENNESSEE

(526 Miles to Go)

··· 12 ···

Anomalies

IN SIXTH-GRADE ADVANCED English, my teacher presented a challenging assignment: find a single word to best describe you, then write a paper as to why. During the two weeks leading up to the paper's due date, I pored over the dictionary each night, searching for that one word which might perfectly define Mim Malone. In the end, I chose the word *anomaly*. (I had it down to that, or *cheeky*, and by my reckoning, it would be far easier to define my many moods with a word whose very definition was a person or thing that couldn't be defined by any one thing. This, I thought, was irrefutable logic at its finest.) I remember the last paragraph of that paper like it was yesterday.

> *"In summary, I am 110 percent Anomaly, plus maybe 33 percent Independent Spirit, and 7 percent Free-Thinking Genius. My sum total is 150 percent, but as a living, breathing Anomaly, this is to be expected. Boom."*

Back then, I closed all my papers with *Boom*. It added a certain profound punctuation—a little high class among the meandering bourgeois. If I remember correctly, I received a C minus.

But even today, inasmuch as an anomaly is a thing that deviates from what is standard, normal, or expected, I can think of no more appropriate word to describe myself.

I hate lakes but love the ocean.

I hate ketchup but love everything else a tomato makes.

I would like to read a book *and* go to a fucking party. (I want it all, baby.)

And, pulling into the Nashville Greyhound Station, I am reminded of how much I hate country music—but blimey, I just can't get enough Johnny Cash, the grandfather of that very genre. And, of course, Elvis, but I don't really count him as country. Those were Mom's two favorite musicians. We used to sit on her old College Couch in the garage, and listen straight through *Man in Black* or *Heartbreak Hotel*—vinyl of course, because there really is no other way to listen to music—just soaking in the scratched-up honesty of those two baritones, because damn it all, they'd lived life, and if anyone had a personal understanding of the pain of which they sang, it was Cash and Presley. At least, that's what Mom said. As I grew up, my tastes changed, but when I think about it, even the music I listen to now has a certain tragic honesty to it. Bon Iver, Elliott Smith, Arcade Fire—artists whose music demands not to be *liked* but to be *believed*.

And I do.

I believe them.

Carl pulls the bus into the station and grabs the mic. "Okay, folks, welcome to Nashville. If this is your final destination"—he smiles, and I wonder if those chipped teeth are courtesy of the accident—"well, you made it. If not, you done missed your connecting bus. Just go on up to the ticket desk, they'll set you up. And don't forget your vouchers. Lord knows you earned 'em." He clears his throat, continues. "As a Greyhound employee, I apologize for the incident outside Memphis and hope it don't discourage you from choosing Greyhound in the future. As a human being, I apologize for the incident outside Memphis and wouldn't blame you one damn bit if you never rode another Greyhound again. Now get the hell off my bus."

I make it a general rule not to clap for anyone. Seeing as how few concerts and sporting events I attend, it's never really been an issue. But after Carl's rousing oration, this bus is going wild, and I find myself slapping my palms together in spite of my rule.

I grab my backpack from the overhead bin and slide into the aisle, keeping my good eye on Poncho Man. After—let's call it the Incident of the Bile in the Restroom—I made two important decisions: number one, I would lay off *The X-Files* reruns, as my capacity for monstrous imaginings has had free reign for long enough; and number two, I would not turn him in. The *X-Files* thing, I decided in about three seconds. The not-turning-in-a-perverted-troll-of-a-loafer-strutting-poncho-wearing-motherfucker I thought about the rest of the way to Nashville. And while nothing would give me more pleasure than handing his ass over to the cops, getting to Cleveland is an absolute nonnegotiable. Period. I say something about the Incident of the Bile in the Restroom, and that's that. I'd be dragged back to Mosquitoland, a traitor among the bloodsucking scavengers. On top of my not being in Cleveland for Mom during her hour of need, Poncho Man knows about my Hills Bros. can. Kathy would press charges, I'd be arrested for theft, and instead of spending Labor Day with Mom, I'd spend it in juvie.

Bottom line: I can't be *certain* Poncho Man will strike again. But turn him in, and I can be certain my Objective is done for.

So yes. It sucks. But honestly, I can't figure a way around it.

Poncho Man is at the front of the line; I watch him nod to Carl, then step down off the bus. Now—I just need to get my ticket, get lost in a crowd, and pray that's the end of it. He goes one way, I go another, and ne'er the two shall meet.

Carl is sitting in the driver's seat, saying good-bye to everyone as they pass. Whatever questions I had at the beginning of my trip pertaining to this guy's true Carl nature have been answered and then some. He's about as Carl as they come. I smile at him, and even get ready to shake his hand (which requires serious preparation on my part), when he grabs me by the shoulder. He leans in, his eyes full of familiar mischief, and whispers, "Good luck, missy." Then, releasing his grip, he smiles and winks, and suddenly I know exactly who he reminds me of.

And it's not Samuel L. Jackson.

Once off the bus, I locate the nearest bench and pull out my journal.

September 2—afternoon

Dear Isabel,

Let's pull back another layer of the Giant Onion of my Reasoning, shall we? Reggie is Reason #6.

He always stood on the same corner back in Ashland: knee-high combat boots, frazzled hair, dirty face, winning smile. Mom said the reason Reggie stood on the same corner (Samaritan and Highway 511, if you want specifics) was that it was the closest traffic light to the downtown shelter.

I had soccer at the YMCA on Wednesdays after school (more unwanted extracurriculars). From Taft Elementary to the Y it was a straight shot down Claremont to East Main, a drive which should have taken no more than five minutes. But we never went that way. Instead, Mom, her eyes gleaming with the Young Fun Now, took Smith Road to Samaritan Avenue, then 511 up to East Main. It added an extra ten minutes, but she didn't care. Every Wednesday, without fail, Mom rolled down her window at the corner of Samaritan and 511, and exchanged three bucks for a smile and a God-bless from Reggie.

One Saturday, while shopping for a new something or other, Dad happened to be in the car with us when we came to that exact corner. Dad had never met Reggie before, and as far as I knew, he didn't know about my mom's generosity toward the homeless. As we pulled up, Mom reached for the *window down* button, but before she could press it, Dad started in on what a lazy bunch the homeless were, being the dregs of society and whatnot. "He could get a job," Dad said, casually throwing a thumb in Reggie's direction. "If he wasn't such a lazy drunk."

Mom looked right at Dad and didn't say a word—just calmly rolled down the window.

Reggie walked up. "Howdy, Eve. Mighty fine mornin'."

Still looking at Dad, my mom responded, "Indeed it is, Reggie. Here you go."

I was concerned about what Dad would say once that window was rolled back up. I guess Reggie could feel the tension, because after taking the cash, he looked right at me in the backseat and winked, his eyes full of a comforting sort of mischief. Then, looking back at my mom, he gave a two-fingered salute. This salute had always been accompanied by a *God bless.* But this time, Reggie said, "Good luck, Miss Evie."

My mom rolled the window up, never once taking her eyes off Dad. "Good luck to you," she said. (She could be stone-cold when she wanted to be.)

Later, just before bed, I asked her if Dad was mad that she gave three bucks to Reggie. She said no, but I knew better. I asked if Dad was right, if Reggie was nothing but a lazy drunk. Mom said some homeless folk were like that, but she didn't think Reggie was one of them. She said even if he were, she would still give him three bucks. She said it wasn't her job to pick which ones were genuinely starving and which ones were faking it.

"Help is help to anyone, Mary. Even if they don't know they're asking for it."

I said that made a whole lot of sense, because it did.

And it still does.

Here's the thing, Iz: my mom needs help right now. And I know it, even if she doesn't.

Signing off,
Mary Iris Malone,
Samaritan Avenue Vagabond

... 13 ...

Everything Sounds Better on Vinyl

"EXCUSE ME, DO you have the time?"

I look up from my journal and almost keel over. The stranger has a unibrow, a bushy mustache, severe acne, three-inch-thick glasses, and overly chapped lips.

So. Many. Things.

I vomit a little, force it back down. "Sorry, I'm just—" . . . *unsure which facial feature to avoid* . . . I blink, then gulp, then use my words. "Yes," I say, pulling my cell phone out of my bag. "Almost one."

He stomps off, leaving me to stare at my phone. Twenty-eight missed calls. Twenty-six from Kathy. Two from Dad.

Attaboy.

A waste bin sits by my bench, beckoning. I could just throw the stupid thing away, be rid of Stevie Wonder and His Sonic Detritus once and for all. Reluctantly, I stuff the phone in my bag, along with my stick figure journal, then march over to the ticket counter and hand the lady my voucher.

"You traveling alone?" she whines, chomping on gum.

I'm ready this time, armed with a new strategy. "Yes, ma'am. My dad is sending me up to Cleveland to live with my mom, see. They got divorced earlier this year, a tragedy of Shakespearean proportions, and it pretty much devastated me to the point of murdering myself, but really, how does one go about it?"

The lady continues chewing, wholly unimpressed.

"I know, I know," I say, nodding, smiling, "and before you say it, yes, I thought about sleeping pills, but how many do you take? My luck, I'd take just enough to do some serious damage, but not quite enough to do the trick, you know? Doomed to roam the streets of Cleveland, some tragic kid with a half brain, everyone whispering as I pass, *There's the girl who failed at living* and *dying*. So yeah, I'll pass on pills, but the car in the garage thing, that sounds promising, don't you think?"

She pops a bubble the size of a grapefruit, takes my voucher, hands me my ticket. "Number sixteen seventy-seven to Cleveland," she says, "departs at one thirty-two. You got thirty minutes, kid."

"Thanks," I say, taking the ticket. "You're a real treat."

Outside, the downtown area is abuzz with traffic and music; tourists young and old swarm into boot parlors, record stores, and vintage guitar shops, trying to get a jump on Labor Day deals. Live bands are set up in a dozen storefront windows like mannequins, advertising twang instead of tweed. And the honky-tonks, my God, the honky-tonks! Until now, I'd assumed a honky-tonk was a quiet bar full of strange people I would never want to talk to. In reality, they're obnoxiously loud bars full of strange people I would never want to talk to. I pass one with a band blaring something about a bedonkey-donk, which I can only assume is the Official Honky-Tonk National Anthem. I'm already jealous of myself five minutes ago. Because you can't un-know a honky-tonk.

Across the street, a life-sized statue of Elvis beckons, and suddenly, nothing else matters. I grip my backpack and hustle over for a closer look. It's sort of sad, actually, though not altogether unrealistic. The hair looks about right, anyway. From his later days. That's when it occurs to me—*Mom would love this.* However imperfect this trip has been thus far, I've now stopped in both Graceland and Nashville, two cities synonymous with Cash and the King.

This is a good sign.

I take another look around and hook my thumbs in my pockets. I whistle, I smile, I throw on my idiot face. Give me your hats, your honky-tonks, your boots, your bedonkey-donks. I am Mary Iris Malone, tourist extraordinaire.

Behind the statue is a store called Hat Shoppe. Summoning every ounce of Malone stick-to-itiveness, I walk inside. The floors are wooden, the people are loud, the music is I-don't-know-what . . . The first hat in reach has black and white spots. I pick it up, and, just out of curiosity, inspect the tag on the inside: MADE WITH AUTHENTIC COW HIDE. Well that's good and gross.

I take a deep breath.

I put it on.

I look at myself in the mirror.

I set it down.

I walk out.

As far as I'm concerned, it never happened.

I spend the next ninety seconds in the adjacent Boot Shoppe, then over ten minutes in a record shop. (S-H-O-P. For real. It's not hard. Actually, it's two letters easier.) Pre-loved vinyl is a weakness I inherited from my mother, one I'm quite proud of. I had a record player long before my classmates decided it was cool. And when they finally came around, I didn't rub this in. Everything sounds better on vinyl. It's not a trend. It's a fact.

I almost purchase a near mint copy of *Remain in Light* by the Talking Heads but talk myself out of it. There's no telling what sort of expenses I might encounter between here and Cleveland. Speaking of which . . .

What little sustenance may have been garnered from a hockey pucked–burger, I'd put to far greater use during the Incident of the Bile in the Restroom. Which is to say, I'm starving. At a nearby taco stand, I order three *carnitas* with extra cilantro, then wolf them down on the walk back to the Greyhound station. Once there, I keep my head down (on the off chance Poncho Man is still around) and step in line for the sixteen seventy-seven at Gate B. After a few minutes, the line inches forward. I stick my hands in my jeans pocket and grip Mom's lipstick.

Shit.

I should've bought that Talking Heads record.

She would have loved it.

September 2—1:32 p.m.

Dear Isabel,

My mother was the greatest alarm clock of all time. Every morning, without fail, she threw back the curtains to let the sun in, and always, she said the same thing.

"Have a vision, Mary, unclouded by fear."

Just like that. It was so wonderful. (Of course, this idea of unclouded vision would come to mean another thing entirely after the Great Blinding Eclipse, but that's neither here nor there.) The quote was an old Cherokee proverb, one that her mom told her, and hers before that, and so on and so forth, all the way back to the original Cherokee woman who coined the phrase. (Mom's father was British, but her mother was part Cherokee, which is, I think, a perfect example of history getting the last laugh.) I was so proud of this heritage, Iz, do you know what I did? I started lying about the degree of Cherokee blood in my veins. I was something like one-sixteenth, but honestly, who wasn't, right? So I claimed one quarter. It just sounded more legit. I was young, still in middle school, so I went with it the way kids that age do. The more admiration this garnered from teachers and friends, the closer I felt to my ancient ancestry, my kinswomen, my *tribe*. But the truth will out, as they say. In my case, this outing took on the sound of my mother's unending laughter in the face of my principal, when he told her the school was going to present me with a plaque of merit at the next pep rally: the Native American Achievement Award.

Needless to say, I never received the award. But even today, there are times—most notably when I wear my war paint—when I really feel that Cherokee blood coursing through my veins, no matter its percentage of purity. So from whatever minutia of my heart that pumps authentic Cherokee blood, I pass this phrase along to you: have a vision, unclouded by fear.

Not sure what made me think of all this Cherokee stuff. Maybe it's the plethora of cowboy hats and boots I've seen today. Politically correct? Probably not. BUT I'M ONE-SIXTEENTH CHEROKEE, SO SUCK IT.

Anyway, I just remembered there's a bag of chips in my backpack, so I'm gonna put the kibosh on this note with another one of my mother's Cherokee proverbs.

When you were born, you cried while the world rejoiced. Live your life so that when you die, the world cries while you rejoice.

Funny, as a child, I never knew whether to laugh or cry when Mom said that. But now I know the truth. You can laugh *and* cry, Iz. Because they're basically the same thing.

Signing off,
Chieftess Iris Malone

I SHUT MY journal and slide the lock to UNOCCUPIED.

This new bus is far from packed, which means I get my

own row again. Considering the rare collection of individuals on board, the having-my-own-row thing could not be of greater import. It's a freak show, really. Reminiscent of my time in the Deep South. Mosquitoland: the thorn in my side, the rock in my shoe, the poison in my wine. Unfortunately, it appears the thorn, the rock, and the poison have followed my path north.

29B is breast-feeding.

26A has fallen asleep while snacking on a box of Cheez-Its.

24B is playing Battleship with 24A, complete with warlike sound effects.

21D is wearing Bugs Bunny slippers and a T-shirt that says NO ONE CARES ABOUT YOUR BLOG.

19A and B must be mother and daughter, a beautiful Hispanic duo. They're asleep on each other, and it's actually kind of adorable. So okay, they're fine.

And . . . *blimey*, 17C is good-looking. How did I not notice him before? I pass him on my left, careful not to stare. He looks like that guy in *Across the Universe*. (Gah, what is his name?) Suddenly, my beloved Goodwill shoes and favorite red hoodie seem an odd choice. Certainly, they aren't my most flattering articles of clothing. My jeans are fine I suppose, albeit a little bloody at the knee. But yeah, the hoodie—hmm. I should've put on Mom's old Zeppelin tee this morning, tight in all the right places. At the very least, I could've—

What the hell?

Having reached my seat, I remain standing, frozen to the spot. A paper bag—brown, thin, square—is propped next to my backpack. I sit down, pick up the bag, and immediately know what's inside. I've purchased enough vinyl to know a record when I'm holding one.

Talking Heads' *Remain in Light*.

Near mint condition.

Every ounce of blood rushes to my face as this sets in. I raise my head just enough to peer over the top of the seat in front of me.

And there he is.

The perverted-troll-of-a-loafer-strutting-poncho-wearing-motherfucker himself, six rows up, smiling like a hyena.

In the movie of my life, I crack the record in two, open the window, and toss the pieces to the side of the highway. But as the Greyhound windows don't open, I have to settle for the first part. It's a shame, because Mom loves all things David Byrne, but I won't have any piece of Poncho Man sully our time together. I pull the vinyl from the sleeve and crack it in two.

The hyena isn't smiling now.

Collapsing in my seat, I breathe, think, adjust. It's possible he's not following me. We probably just have similar routes. So what, then, I avoid going to the bathroom? Spend the rest of the ride looking over my shoulder? It's not too late to turn him in, though I would still be sacrificing my Objective.

Think, Malone.

I toss the remains of the record in the seat next to me. Outside, the afternoon sky passes in a blur. I stare at it with my good eye and wonder . . . I have money. I have brains. I have a fount of intuition.

So intuit, already.

I pull out the itinerary that came with my ticket. Next official stop: Cincinnati.

Options.

I could get a cab. Or . . . hitchhike.

Boom.

Yes. What better way to get to Mom, she of the European hitchhiker's guild?

Ditch the bus.

I pull the bag of chips from my backpack. They're warm and crisp, and by the time I open the bag, I've made up my mind.

I want out. Of all of it: the random stops, the strange smells, the uncomfortable nearness of Poncho Man. I'll ditch the bus in Cincinnati. At least I'll be in the right state. Really, there's no downside, except . . .

Munching, I twist in my seat and peer around the edge.

Crunch.

17C is three rows behind me, across the aisle, pressing a digital camera against his window.

Crunch.

He's older than me, probably early twenties, so it's not completely out of the question—us getting married and traveling the world over, I mean. Right now, a five-year difference might seem like a lot, but once he's fifty-four and I'm forty-nine, well shoot, that's nothing.

Crunch.

There's a quality about him, something like a movie star, but not quite. Like he *could* be Hollywood if it weren't for his humanitarian efforts, or his volunteer work, or his clean conscience, no doubt filled to the brim with truth, integrity, and a heart for the homeless.

Crunch.

He has longish brown hair and beautiful dark green eyes. His stubbly beard isn't preteen-ish, it's I-don't-know-what . . . rugged, yes, but not only. It's the stuff of hunters and builders. And carpenters. It suggests outdoorsy intelligence. It's desert-fucking-island stubble, is what it is.

Crunch.

A navy zip-up Patagonia fits perfectly, wrapped around his upper torso like a . . . well, like something. His shoulders aren't broad nor are they narrow; his jeans aren't skinny nor are they loose; his boots aren't clean nor are they dirty.

17C is just the right amount of himself.

He is my perfect anomaly.

Crunch.

Apparently done taking pictures, he dismantles his camera, stows it under his seat, and pulls out a book. Between the hair, boots, jacket, and camera, he's really working the Pacific Northwest, pre-hipster, post-grunge thing, which I have to say, I just love. Squinting, I try to see what book he's reading, though I don't suppose it would really—

Shit.

I jerk back in my seat. Did he see me? I think he saw me.

Crunch.

I need to keep my head in the game anyway . . .

Crunch. (Those eyes.)

. . . if I'm going to see this new plan through.

Crunch. (That hair.)

We'll be in Cincinnati before you know it.

Crunch. Crunch. Crunch.

I tip the bag of crumbs, aiming for my mouth but hitting my hair and face instead. Thank God for the high seat backs.

INDEPENDENCE, KENTUCKY

(278 Miles to Go)

... 14 ...
Grammatical Shenanigans

"HOW MANY SCOOPS do you want?"

I stare through the glass at the dozen or so tubs of ice cream. "How many can I have?"

"Umm. As many as you *want*."

"Ha, right, okay. Well, here's the thing"—I look at her name tag—"Glenda. How many scoops I *want* might kill me. Like, actually, kill me dead. Plus, I don't really feel like breaking records in this category. So . . . what's the current scoop record again?"

Glenda sighs. "Seven."

Jackpot.

Even though Cincinnati is something like twenty minutes away, our driver (whose name I've already forgotten, but I assure you is the very opposite of Carl) insisted on stopping for pie. That's right. Pie. Over the microphone, he'd announced that Jane's Diner had the best pie this side of the Mighty Mississippi, and that he'd be a monkey's uncle if he was gonna pass right by without helping himself to a slice, and that if we knew what was good for us, we'd help ourselves to a slice, too, and that we'd surely be thanking him later.

Naturally, I decided never to eat pie again. As luck would have it, across the street from Jane's was this little place called—I kid you not—Aces Dairy Dip Mart Stop Plus. I could not resist. (And really, why would I want to?)

Glenda scoops, I pay, and a few minutes later, I carry my double-chocolate-espresso-chip-raspberry-mint-caramel-lemon waffle cone across the street, the happiest girl this side of the mighty effing Pacific.

A patrol car is flashing lights in the parking lot of Jane's Diner. There doesn't seem to be any commotion, but a cop is giving someone a stern talking-to in the back seat.

I lean against the bus and watch my fellow passengers through the window of Jane's Diner. It's one of those trailers without wheels, which I never really understood.

Removing a vehicle's wheels in order to make it a stationary venue makes about as much sense as buying a bed, then using the wood to make a chair. But this isn't what bugs me most about Jane's Diner. What bugs me most is the sign on the front door.

"COME ON IN," WE'RE OPEN

I chuckle mid-lick. People just can't help themselves when it comes to quotation marks. As if they're completely paralyzed by this particular punctuation. I guess it's really not that big of a deal, but it does seem to be a widespread brand of easily avoidable buffoonery.

Through the window, I scan the crowd for Poncho Man, but

I don't see him anywhere. No matter. In less than an hour, it's adios anyway.

"I done knowed that, Purje. You ain't listenin'."

A couple wearing matching cowboy hats exits Jane's Diner, their voices covering serious ground.

"I am too, darlin', but iffin' you cain't getter done here in Independence, you cain't getter done nowheres."

I choke on a tart lick of lemon.

"Ahhhhh, sheetfahr, Purje, jus' shut up and listen fer a sec."

"Excuse me," I interrupt. "Did you say Independence?"

They look at me as if they'd just as soon shoot me. A wad of tobacco comes flying out of the man's mouth, landing inches from my precious high-tops.

Enchanté, Purje.

"So what'f we did?"

Oh my God, they did. I'm here. Home of Ahab, Arlene's nephew, the champion swimmer turned gas station tycoon. Across the overpass, there're at least four gas stations—it could be any one of them.

"Listen," says the one called Purje, "this here's one o'th'great frontier towns in all 'merica. I'll kiss a monkey's ass 'for I'll listen to ya denigratin' Independence."

I take a second to appreciate the fact that this man can't pronounce *America* but knows the word *denigrate*. The woman sticks her right hand in her vest pocket, and for a minute, I'm legitimately afraid she's packing heat. Instead of a gun, she pulls out a flask, takes a long swig, passes it to Purje.

"Of course not, sir. I would never. Independence seems like a charming little town. I just . . ."

The land of autonomy.

"You jus'?" says Purje, eyeballing me.

From the relative comfort of my bus seat, the decision to ditch the Greyhound had been a fairly easy one, the prospect of hitchhiking to Cleveland sounded downright adventurous. But gazing around rural Kentucky, the realities of my plan settle in my stomach like a brick.

"Th' hell's wrong with her, Purje?" whispers the woman.

Purje shakes his head.

I toss the rest of my ice-cream cone on the ground and start toward the bus door. "Thanks, guys. Keep it classy."

Hopping up the steps, I picture Arlene—a grande dame from the old school, mistress of geriatric panache, and my friend—clutching that wooden box for dear life. And a dear life it was. Now I have the opportunity to deliver that box, to finish what she started, to honor her dear life.

I have the chance to complete Arlene's Objective.

And I'll be damned if I'm not gonna take it.

I grab my backpack from the overhead compartment and start back down the aisle, when a voice stops me on a dime.

"You skipping out?"

At the top of the stairs, I turn and see 17C (heart be still) propped on his knees in a seat toward the back of the otherwise empty bus. He's holding his camera next to the window; it's obvious I've interrupted some kind of photo shoot.

"What?" I whisper, suddenly wondering what the hell I'd been thinking, cutting my own hair.

"I asked if you were skipping out," he said.

I step into the aisle, pushing my bangs out of my eyes. It's a simple question requiring a simple answer, but for the moment, my tongue seems vacuum-sealed to the roof of my mouth. I'm pretty certain I need a nose job, and my armpits itch, which—what the hell?

Pull it together, Malone.

I nod and smile, and he nods and sort of half smiles, and oh God, if that's only half the smile, I can't imagine the whole one. He has a black eye, which I hadn't noticed before. Even with the shiner though, the eyes are a warm green—bright, stunning, unforgettable. His eyebrows are thick. Not bushy, just thick, as if they were drawn using the broad side of a marker.

"Well, good luck," he says.

Outside, the cop car is in his direct line of vision. He follows my eyes, then blushes and puts the cap back on the lens.

"Yeah," I mutter. "Good luck to you, too."

He leans back in his chair, closes his eyes and whispers, "Thanks." Then, almost in a breath, "I'm gonna need it."

In the movie of my life, I have scenes and dialogue, rather than experiences and discussions. Instead of friends, a cast; instead of places, a setting. At this moment—a definite movie moment—I blink in slow motion. The camera zooms in on my eyes as I drink in the enigmatic 17C. The audience sits in silent wonder, a combination of hope, sadness, and wistful longing for romance stirring in their bellies. Alas, the girl is leaving, and the boy is staying, and 'twas always thus. The likelihood of their stories intertwining again doesn't make for a very believable plot. Though I suppose that depends on a person's definition of believable.

From a thousand metaphorical miles away, a sweet voice rings in my ears. *You'd be surprised what I believe these days.*

Channeling the faith of Arlene—and with her precious wooden box strapped to my back—I step off the bus. More than anything, I want to be with Mom right now. Whatever her sickness is, she needs me desperately, and I know this. But all my favorite movies have one thing in common: a singular moment in which you can feel the director telling his character's story as well as his own. It is beautiful, poignant, and appallingly rare.

I don't know what's in this box, but I am part of its story, as it is part of mine.

Making my way back across the street, I consider the role of 17C in my movie. It's a hard sell, our characters meeting again. But I won't count it out just yet. Because there's nothing I hate more than a predictable ending.

… 15 …

Effing Attitude

"GOING FOR NUMBER eight?"

I smile, but it fools no one. "Good one, Glenda. Seriously though, how have you been?" *How have you been?* My problem is, I never know what to say to people. I clear my throat and press on. "I was wondering if you could tell me where I might find a gas station owned by a guy named Ahab."

Glenda leans behind the counter, reappears with a spoon.

"I know it's a strange question," I say, "but it's important."

Dipping her spoon into a vat of cookie dough ice cream, she comes up with a generous scoop. I give her a second, thinking she's thinking. She's not, as it turns out. What she is doing is eating the ice cream with orgasmic vigor.

I know I shouldn't, but I can't help myself. "S'pretty good, yeah?"

Glenda smacks her lips. "I don't know anyone by that name. Unless you're talking about *Moby-Dick*."

I imagine myself scrambling over the vat of cookie dough, grabbing her by those split ends, and shoving her face in the tub of ice cream. It could be my thing, what I'm known for: a

Mim-swirly. Staring at Glenda's self-satisfied expression, I choose to murder her with kindness instead. I raise both hands and put air quotes around my next three words. "Thank you, Glenda."

Aces Dairy Dip Mart Stop Plus is within walking distance of all four gas stations. They're in a little cluster on the other side of the overpass—my best bet at finding Ahab. I grip my backpack and walk across the bridge. Every time a car zooms underneath, the whole thing wobbles a few inches, and here are the things I imagine: the road crumbling under my feet; the bridge caving in as I fall to the highway below; a chunk of cement crushing my head; a monstrous cloud of debris like the videos from nine-eleven . . .

WTF, Malone.

I need to cheer the hell up. I should do whatever happy people do when they're being happy.

I try whistling.

Nick Drake.

Impossible, as it turns out. I might as well be tap dancing to the theme from *Jaws*. Come to think of it, maybe that's why I've always thought Nick and I would have gotten along so well. I bet he had zero patience for the kind of thing where someone just oozed their good mood all over the place. (RIP, Nick. RIP.) For the rest of the walk, I strike the perfect balance between happy and miserable, which is, surprisingly, a narrow margin.

The nearest gas station has a sign out front that's so faded, I can't tell if it's a BP or a Shell or a Marathon or what. Probably something preposterous like Ed's Place. God, I bet that's exactly what this is. Like a Saharan cactus, a dusty pay phone stands forgotten in the corner of the parking lot, which reminds me of my cell phone, which reminds me of Stevie Wonder, which reminds me of Kathy, which reminds me of Dad. They're probably worried. They're probably sort of freaking out by now.

Eff 'em.

The door jangles as I push it open.

"Afternoon!" says Man Behind the Counter.

I almost drop my backpack when I see his name tag: HI, I'M "ED," AND I'M HERE TO HELP YOU. My brain explodes into a thousand pieces of incredulity.

It's an Ed. In quotes. Congratulations, Universe. You win.

I turn on my heels and walk out of the gas station; I don't even care if that was Ahab's boyfriend or not. Henceforth, I have a new policy, and it is unflinchingly rigid: no Eds, no mo'.

The next gas station is owned by a guy named Morris, who is pretty frowny and tragic. Luckily, he answers my questions in short *yep*s and *nah*s, and I don't have to spend any more time with him than is absolutely necessary. The third gas station is owned by some-guy-who's-not-Ahab. The last station is an actual Shell, and the young girl behind the counter blows a giant bubble with her gum and offers me free cigarettes. (Sometimes I think Shell might be taking over the world, and I just can't believe everyone is okay with this. I mean, pretty soon we're going to have gum-blowing girls offering free cigarettes to underage kids on every street corner in 'merica, and I would like to state for the record, I am not okay with this.) Somehow, I end up under the very bridge I'd envisaged collapsing, watching my Greyhound speed by, northbound sans Mim.

I raise a hand as it passes, not in farewell, but in good riddance.

And that, as they say, is that.

Alone in Independence.

How terribly fitting.

I pull out Mom's lipstick, twirl it in my fingers, and try to think what to do next. Maybe it's the unseasonably warm weather, or the sinking realization that I just waved good-bye to 17C forever and ever, or the residue of Glenda's third-rate spirit, or the shortage of sound sleep I got at last night's motel, but I'm feeling decidedly insurgent and exhausted. All these Eds and Morrises and Guys Who Aren't Ahab, and Young Girls Who Blow Gum and Offer Free Cigarettes, and unending disappointments, disenchantments, and a hundred other disses have just drained me.

So eff it.

I'm going to sit. Right here, and only for a minute.

I pull my knees up, rest my forehead between them, and stare at the ground. The cracks on the pavement come together in the shape of a rabbit. The twitchy nose, the long feet, the fluffy tail, it's all there.

How strange.

... 16 ...

White Rabbit

"MIM, WHY DON'T you have a seat?"

"Why don't you drop dead?"

"Mary, sit. Your mothe—Kathy and I have something to tell you."

"Oh my shit, Dad. Really?"

"God, Mim, language."

"That woman is not my mother. And I'm not Mary, not to you."

"We have news, would you like to hear it, or not?"

"Hey, hey, I'm Walt."

I jolt awake.

The rabbit is still there, but a different shade. I rub my eyes as a blurry pair of green Converse comes into focus.

"Hey, hey, I'm Walt."

On either side of the highway, the shadows of the trees are longer; traffic is heavier, slower. Rush hour. I curse, stand up, and brush the street off my jeans. My bandaged leg is throbbing from the awkward position of my impromptu nap.

"Hey, hey, I'm Walt."

The owner of the Chucks is about my height, my age, and

for all I know, he's been standing here introducing himself all afternoon. His hair, poking out beneath an old Chicago Cubs baseball cap, isn't so much long as it is scraggly and stringy, like a stray mutt's. He's holding a Rubik's Cube in one hand and an almost-empty twenty-ounce Mountain Dew in the other. Before I can introduce myself, he throws his head back and chugs the last of the soda. With authority.

My smile takes on a life of its own. "Hey, Walt. I'm Mim."

Nodding, he holds out a dewy hand. I shake it—and suddenly, space and time shift. It's the summer before third grade. A new family has just moved in across the street. They have a boy, Ricky, about my age. We have the same bike, a kick-ass neon Schwinn—qualification enough to become fast friends. His speech is slurred and his mind slow, but he walks fast. Every step is intentional, quick-footed, as if he's always late for something. We hang out that whole summer. And things are good. And then school starts. Ty Zarnstorff, in front of everyone on the playground, says, *"Hey, Mim, if you love Ricky the Retard so much, why don't you marry him?"* Everyone laughs. I'm not sure why, but I know enough to know it's not nice. So I punch Ty, breaking his nose and earning a one-day suspension. That night at dinner, I ask Mom what retarded means, and if Ricky is a retard. She says, *"Retard is a mean word used by mean people. Ricky has what is called Down syndrome, and all it means is that he's a little slower than most."* A few minutes later, Dad goes to the bathroom. Mom takes a bite, clears her throat. *"There are worse fates than being slow-witted,"* she says. *"You broke that other kid's nose, right?*

The one who made fun of Ricky?" I say, *"Yes ma'am, I did." "Good,"* she says, taking another bite.

"Hey, hey, you okay?"

I am pulled back to reality by a kid currently stuffing the pocket of his jeans with an empty Mountain Dew bottle. Exactly the sort of thing Ricky might do.

"You do the Dew, Walt?"

He laughs a laugh for the ages, and my young heart damn near melts all over the side of the road.

"What are you doing?" he asks, shifting focus to his Rubik's Cube.

"What do you mean?"

"I mean—what. Are. You. *Doing*?"

I might just never stop smiling. "Well, I'm . . . taking an accidental nap under a highway overpass, I guess."

"No," he says, hell-bent on solving the cube. "I mean as a part of big things."

Walt's statement is vague at best, gibberish at worst. But here's the thing: I understand exactly what he means.

"I'm trying to get to Cleveland," I say. It's not a lie, but it certainly doesn't answer the spirit of the question. "By Labor Day, if possible."

"Why?"

Traffic is pretty much at a standstill under this bridge. If I'm gonna do this, now's the time. I begin sizing up drivers for the best prospective ride, by which I mean, someone who doesn't look like an ax murderer.

"Reasons are hard, man."

"Why?" he asks again.

I hate leaving this kid by the side of the road, but surely he has someone with him. "Walt, are you with a friend, or . . . your mom, or something?"

"No. She's with the white pillows. In the casket."

I turn toward him. He looks serious enough.

"Hey, look," he says, holding up his Rubik's Cube, now complete. "All done. Done good. Good and done."

"Walt—where do you live?"

He throws his head back, messes up the cube, as if he doesn't trust himself not to peek. "New Chicago," he says. "Do you like shiny things? I have lots of shiny there. And a pool." He looks me up and down. "You're a pretty dirty person right now. You could use a pool. Also, there's ham."

I am Mary Iris Malone, and I am 100 percent intrigued.

"You wanna come with me?" asks Walt.

I push my bangs out of my eyes and slide my backpack on. Mere feet away, traffic inches along, luring me with a steady hum of engines. "I don't think I can, buddy. I'd like to, but—"

Without a word, the kid tears up, turns, and walks away.

Watching him go, I can't explain the why, but I know the what—I feel like a sack of shit.

A Subaru (with a plastic bubble attached to the top like a giant fanny pack) rolls to a stop in the traffic; its passenger-side window rolls down.

"You need a ride?"

Inside, a nice-looking woman checks her rearview mirror,

then smiles at me. Her son, presumably, sits in the back seat, engrossed in some handheld video game.

"Traffic's starting to move, hon," she says. "In or out."

I open the passenger door and hop in. "Thanks."

"No problem." She lets her foot off the brake, and creeps slowly through the heavy traffic.

We pass a derelict white building on the right. Off-white, really. The offest white there ever was.

"You traveling for Labor Day?" she asks.

I set my JanSport between my feet. "Something like that."

"You and everybody else." She points through the windshield. "Long weekends, people really come out of the woodwork, you know?"

I nod politely. From the back seat, her kid grunts, mutters something about how dying is lame. I'll assume he means a video-game death.

"So," she says, "where're you from?"

"Cleveland," I answer, wondering how many questions this ride is going to cost. I reach into my pocket for the comfort of my war paint.

"Nice town. We love Cleveland, don't we, Charles?" She continues talking, but I'm no longer listening.

I am no longer anything at all.

The lipstick is gone.

". . . to an Indians game for his father's birthday. Didn't you, Charles?"

I reach down, unzip my bag—the box, the coffee can, a water bottle, shirts and socks . . . no lipstick. "Pull over," I mutter.

"I'm sorry?"

Where did I see it last? I definitely had it when I left the bus. I had it when that stupid girl offered me cigarettes. I had it . . . in my hands when I fell asleep. "Can you pull over, please? I have to get out."

"Are you sure?"

Let it be under the bridge. "Yes, I'm sure. Pull over."

The woman, forever nameless, pulls the Subaru to the side of the highway. I grab my bag, give a halfhearted "Thanks," and hoof it back to the bridge.

Please let it be there.

Due to the crawling traffic, we'd only gone about a hundred yards or so. I arrive under the bridge breathless and search every square inch near the spot where I'd fallen asleep. To make up for my lack of vision, I quadruple-check, but it's no use. The lipstick isn't here. I stare at the ground, unable to move, unable to think, just . . . thoroughly not able. And just as this reality sets in—of arriving at my mother's sickbed without one of my primary Reasons—I see it.

Not the lipstick.

Kneeling, I rub the cracks in the pavement: the nose, the tail, the feet . . . such a specific shape, my Pavement Rabbit.

Do you like shiny things? I have lots of shiny there.

I see an image on the horizon: every step is intentional, quick-footed, as if it's late for something.

I put my head down and sprint.

"DO YOU LIKE the Cubs?" asks Walt.

All inquiries related to the lost lipstick have been stonewalled with questions like this. Do I like the color yellow? Do I like sausage? Do I like dinosaurs? It's a preference marathon, and I'm slowly wearing down.

"I don't know, Walt. Sure."

Sports is a thing, and I recognize that—but it is not *my* thing. Football, basketball, soccer, and yes, hockey, all seem beyond pointless. Baseball, however, I get. Or at least, I don't *not* get. Back before the *BREAKING NEWS*, it was one of the few things Mom and Dad and I all enjoyed. Something about the narrative of the sport, I think, is what we found appealing: the unique personality of each player and team; the intricate strategies based on who's at bat, who's on base, and who's pitching; the minutiae, the inches, the history. Plus, it's relaxing. Three hours a day on a well-manicured field—I guess my family idealized that kind of idle recreation, as we rarely encountered anything like it within our own home. I never had a favorite team, but I know enough about baseball to know that the Cubs have pretty much the worst luck of any team in all of professional sports. Like, in the history of History, no team has ever been as unlucky as the Chicago Cubs.

"You wanna go to a game?" asks Walt, a look of pure excitement on his face. "We should eat first, but then we could go to a game. If we can get tickets." He raises his index finger in the air like he's had a profound idea. "We have to have tickets, though. Tickets."

As the hour passes, traffic thins to an occasional car or semi careening into the sinking sun. We follow in kind, on the margins of the highway, the oddest of couples.

"So, Walt—I wouldn't be mad or anything, you know? If you took the lipstick. I just need it back. It's really important."

"The shiny lipstick?" he says.

I glance sideways at him, wondering if he knows he just gave himself away. "Yeah, Walt. It's got some shiny on it."

He nods. "No, I don't have it."

Just as I wonder what it would take to physically search the kid, he hops over the nearby guardrail and disappears into the adjacent woods. "This way, Mim!"

Back under the bridge, for just a moment, the option to continue my trip sans war paint had been just that—an option. But no longer. The thought of moving on without it, when I know *exactly* where it is . . .

Ahead, the pink sun becomes a dingy crimson, and soon, it will fade entirely. I sigh and turn back toward the shadowy woods. "Curiouser and curiouser," I whisper. And with the daring temperament of Alice herself, I climb the guardrail and follow my white rabbit into the trees.

… 17 …
Firework Thoughts

A DIALOGUE OF dead leaves underfoot; our social cues, like twiggy trees kaput. This conversation of a wood at night; so different from a highway during light.

Stop thinking in fucking iambic pentameter, Malone.

I follow Walt, the peculiar wayfarer, uphill. After twenty minutes or so, the ground begins to level a bit. Five minutes later, the trees diminish, and I suddenly understand a lot more about the kid's situation.

In the middle of a circular clearing, a ragged blue tent stands like an emphysema patient; its withering canvas is bent, torn, faded, and ripped. Beside a dead campfire, a cornucopia of pots and pans pours out of an overturned milk crate. Wet T-shirts dangle from bony branches around the edges of the clearing advertising roofing companies, church soccer leagues, and obscure rock bands.

A shallow pit full of feces permeates the clearing from ten yards away. I don't know whether I'm relieved or terrified by the box of toilet paper next to it.

Never, I think, raising my shirt collar up over my nose. *Not in a million years. Literally, one million. I would hold it for a million years.*

"It's my land, New Chicago," says Walt, disappearing inside his tent.

Putting some distance between the shit pit and myself, I climb atop a boulder the size of a Smart Car. What with my depth perception, it takes a few tries, but I manage eventually. Far below, the occasional flickering headlight is the only sign of human life. It certainly feels isolated up here, like some post-apocalyptic zombie movie. Through the thinning fall trees, I squint my good eye until the headlights blur into luminous stars, cosmic proof of the outside world; it spins and spins, ignorant of more than just this kid's mountaintop campsite—it's ignorant of the kid himself. I know this is true, because the Subaru lady didn't stop for Walt. She stopped for me.

"Ready to swim?"

Walt looks up at me with wide-eyed enthusiasm. He's shirtless now, holding a flashlight and sporting a pair of cutoff daisy dukes. The Cubs hat and the green Chucks he's still wearing, as well as that infectious smile that sets my heart aflame. It's the same smile my dad and I used when we made waffles, only Walt's is magnified somehow, like I-don't-know-what . . . the *Belgian* waffle version or something.

"Here," he says, offering a wad of denim. "My backup pair."

Hopping down from the boulder, I take the shorts and hold them out in front of me. They're a little wide in the waist, and far shorter than any shorts I've ever worn.

Walt throws his finger in the air, spins on his heels. "This way to my pool!"

He stomps through the woods, bare-chested, peach-fuzzed, and pale-thighed, laughing his ass off, throwing that index finger in the air, and I have to give it to him—this kid has absolutely nothing in the world to call his own, and look how happy he is. No family? No friends? No home? No sweat. Hey, hey, he's Walt, and he's alive, and that's enough. In light of his situation, my problems suddenly seem brazenly adolescent. Like a spoiled child crossing her arms and demanding some expensive new toy.

I follow him to the other side of the shit pit, where a murky lake awaits. Walt props the flashlight against a rock, then throws his arms open, as if—*ta-da!*—presenting a vaudeville show. The water is beyond brown. It reminds me of the rusty-shat fluids that poured from my old Greyhound like a hose. Dysenteric concerns aside, I wonder who actually owns this land. If some deadly Amazonian bacterial disease doesn't get me, a bullet courtesy of the land's proper owner might.

I open my mouth to say, *Sorry, buddy, you're on your own.* Yet somehow, the words that come out are "Gimme a minute."

I step behind a tree and quickly pull off my hoodie, shoes, socks, and jeans. *WT-fucking-F, Malone.* This is nuts, and I know that, but for some reason, I can't stop laughing. I don't know what it is, but slipping on the hoochie-mama shorts, I almost fall over due to uncontrollable laughter. I step out from behind the tree to find Walt in the middle of the lake, splashing himself in the face, acting like a goofball.

"What happened to your leg?" he asks, suddenly looking very concerned.

"I was in a bus accident," I say, still giggling. "But I'm okay."

"The bus had an accident?" he asks, climbing up onto the opposite bank.

"It flipped on the highway. But I'm fine, really. Just a scratch."

Walt, apparently satisfied, backs up a few paces and throws his finger in the air. "This is how you do it, okay, Mim? Like this, watch." He charges the lake with the ferocity of a Civil War captain leading his men into combat. But also—and if possible, *more* so—like a lanky five-year-old who just discovered what his arms and legs are for. It's awkward, fumbly, and beyond beautiful. A few yards from the water's edge, he trips over his own feet and rolls haphazardly into the lake. His head pops up out of the water like an apple. "Ha-ha! Did you see that, Mim? That was pretty good, huh? Okay. Your turn."

I take a few steps back—wondering if there's anything I wouldn't do for this kid right now, even if he did steal my war paint—and hurl myself into the murky depths. The water is surprisingly refreshing, inside and out; after all that smiling and laughing, my mouth hurts, but I don't care, because I'm here with Walt, enjoying the Young Fun Now.

Mom would love this kid.

After a brief splash-fight with Walt (because duh), I float on my back, letting the lake seep between my fingers and toes. The moon is young, but bright, and for a moment, I stare at it with my good eye.

"You're going to help your mom," Walt whispers. It's not a question. He's floating about ten feet away, looking right at me through the dusky light—it's not creepy or anything, just intense. Ricky used to do the same thing.

"How do you know that, Walt?"

He dips his head under the water, leaving me in complete suspense. After resurfacing, he wipes his eyes and smiles at me. "I heard you. While you were asleep. Under the bridge."

Great.

"What else did I say?"

"Something something fireworks," he says softly. "Then other somethings. I don't know. I have firework thoughts, too."

Now it's my turn to go under. Dipping my choppy hair back, I push my sopping bangs out of my eyes and turn my head from Walt. So the kid heard my Big Things after all.

"I understand," he whispers. "Your mom needs you. And you need her."

There are times when talking just pushes out the tears. So I float in silence, watching the final touches of this perfect moonrise, and in a moment of heavenly revelation, it occurs to me that detours are not without purpose. They provide safe passage to a destination, avoiding pitfalls in the process. Floating in this lake with Walt is most certainly a detour. And maybe I'll never know the pitfalls I've avoided, but I can say this with certainty: a sincere soul is damn near impossible to find, and if Walt is my detour, I'll take it. In fact, I wouldn't be one bit surprised to hear him use the word *pizzazz* in a sentence.

I close my good eye and see myself as I might look from above, as I might look to a mosquito hovering over a hot lake. I see Mim: her face, pallid and feeble; her skin, pale and glistening; her bones, brittle and twiggy; an army of trees surrounding her. She floats next to a boy she met only hours ago, missing her mother, missing her old life, missing the way things used to be. Now she is crying because even after all that laughter, she can't shake that feeling, one of the worst in the world . . .

I am tired of being alone.

"You need help?" Walt's quiet voice brings me back to the now, the real, the detour.

I, Mary Iris Malone, smile at the bright new moon. Wiping away my tears, I wonder if things are finally changing. "Yeah, Walt. I might."

… 18 …

Caleb

WHEN IT COMES to my war paint, my circle of trust is sparse. Nonexistent, really. There is no circle. Up until the bus accident, it had been a complete secret. And maybe it still is. Between the weight of imminent death, followed by the rush of having succeeded where others had failed—and there really is no kind of success like survival—it's possible the passengers had issues more pressing than that of Mim Malone walking among the wreckage, wearing lipstick on her face like Athena, goddess of war. I sure hope so. Because the idea of Poncho Man witnessing that side of me is enough to make me rip my bangs out by the root.

"Who are we fighting?"

"No one, Walt. Hold still."

In the light of a crackling campfire, I cup Walt's face in my hands and induct him into my über-exclusive club. Though without the lipstick (which *must* be in that blue tent of his), I'm forced to use mud. Luckily, there's no shortage.

"There," I say, topping off his two-sided arrow with a dot in the middle. "Done."

He smiles, laughs, and does a little jig around the campfire. "You want me to do you now, Mim?"

"No thanks, buddy. I can manage."

I dip my finger in the soft mud and with the precision of a surgeon, apply the makeshift war paint. It's my first time without a mirror, but as it turns out, I have superior muscle memory. Once done, I grab another tin of ham and sprawl in front of the fire, feeling more Mim than ever before. The two of us sit with mud-painted faces, eating like the King and Queen of I-don't-know-what . . . Hamelot, I suppose. Walt belches, then covers his mouth and laughs uncontrollably, and I'm wondering who I need to see about protecting that laugh as the Eighth Wonder of the World. Its echo finally subsides as he pulls out his Rubik's Cube.

"I like our mosquito makeup," he says softly.

I imagine the state of Mississippi crumbling, then sinking into the Gulf, just like in my dream, leaving naught but an army of vengeful mosquitos. "What?"

Happily working on his cube, Walt points to his face and says, "It's a mosquito."

And he's right. These lines I've spent hours perfecting—vertically from forehead to chin, the two-sided arrows on either cheek, then, a horizontal one just above the eyebrows—could easily be the outline of a mosquito. An anemic stick figure mosquito, but a mosquito nonetheless.

"Do you like the ham?" he asks between clicks.

Still processing the fact that I've been drawing a mosquito this whole time, I don't answer.

"I bought it with my father-money," he says.

"Your what?" I ask in a fog.

"My father-money. He gave it to me before sending me to Charlotte. It's in a secret hiding spot, with my shiny things."

I don't know which part of his story to *WTF.*

Wait. Yes I do.

"Walt—your father sent you to Charlotte?"

Head down, he works silently on his Rubik's Cube. In no time flat, the red cubes are aligned.

"Walt, where's your dad?"

He looks up at the sky for a moment, lost in thought.

"Walt?"

"Chicago," he says, turning back to his cube. The green ones are lined up. "Hey, hey, green are good."

As direct as possible, I try again. "Why aren't you living with your dad, Walt?"

He's twisting and clicking and all-out ignoring me. I consider what he said earlier, about his mother being in a casket. If his father was left alone to take care of a kid with Down syndrome—God, surely he didn't just hand money to his kid and send him packing. Walt can't be more than fifteen, sixteen tops.

"The Cubs are in Chicago," he says, white squares intact. "They're good. They're my favorite."

Poor kid. I don't have the heart to tell him, on top of everything else, his favorite baseball team is the absolute worst. "Yeah, Walt. Those Cubbies are something else."

"Yeah, man," he says, shaking his head. "Those Cubbies are something else. We should go to a game sometime. But we have to get tickets first." He throws his finger in the air. "Tickets."

"What are you guys talking about?"

The shadow behind Walt could have been there five seconds or an hour. It's creepy, but creepier still—Walt isn't fazed. He doesn't jump, doesn't look up from his Rubik's Cube, isn't startled in the slightest. The owner of this new voice steps from the trees like a cautious predator. He's tall. Freakishly so. And wearing a red hoodie like mine.

"Cubbies, Caleb," says Walt. "We're talking about the Cubs."

The kid called Caleb grabs a tin of ham and plops down next to Walt. Sticking the edge of the can between his teeth, he pops it open. "Walt, what have I told you about the Cubs?"

Walt frowns, finishing off the blue squares. "The Cubs suck balls."

Caleb nods and takes a giant bite. "Right on. The Cubs suck balls, dude. Always have, always will, you follow?"

I am suddenly aware of my lack of clothing. For some reason, I hadn't minded the daisy dukes in front of Walt, but with this new kid . . . well, I'm not about to stand up and walk around in these short cutoffs and a soaking wet T-shirt. I pull the blankets up around my legs, covering as much as I can.

"Whaddaya guys got on your face?" says Caleb, staring at me from across the fire.

Suck a duck. I forgot about the war paint. My circle of trust, it seems, is ever-expanding.

"Nothing," I say, trying to think up an excuse. "We were just—nothing."

Caleb nods and smiles, his teeth full of processed ham.

There's something about his voice, smile, smell, clothes, hair, hook nose, and shifty eyes that makes me about as uncomfortable as a nun in a whorehouse, as my mom used to say. He's sitting right here in front of me, a physical being, but hand-to-God, Caleb feels more like a shadow than a person. He pulls a pack of cigarettes from his pocket, sticks one in his mouth—along with the canned ham—and lights up.

"You were just nothing, huh?" Now he's talking, on top of chewing and smoking. "Real eloquent there, sweetheart."

"My name's Mim, jackass." I pull the blanket up close to my chin, and imagine myself in a small room alone with Caleb. He's tied down, and I have one pair *nunchucks*, one pair *katanas*, one pair *sais*, and one *bo* staff. I am Mim the lost Turtle in a Half Shell.

He tosses a half-eaten canned ham into the woods and gets up to grab a new one. "Okay, then, *Mim Jackass.* Sounded like you guys were having a real nice discussion about moms and dads and roses and rainbows and shit. Now *my* old man—he was a real creative son of a bitch. Used to beat the hell outta me with household appliances, you follow? Irons, pots, pans, toasters, and the like. For no good reason, too. He wasn't a drunk, which I guess would have been *a* reason. Thing is, he didn't need a drink to be hateful, you follow? He was just fine at it sober. But one day, I was all growed-up, see. So you know what I did? Pulled the fire extinguisher out of his garage and beat the shit out of him."

Caleb howls, tossing his second can into the woods. I'm beginning to wonder if he isn't my exact opposite: a violent, smoking moron who throws tin cans into nature. His laugh morphs into a hacking cough, reminiscent of old Arlene's respiratory issues. The main difference being, she was ancient, and he can't be more than eighteen.

"So the state sent me to live with foster parents," Caleb continues, having pulled it together. "Second night I'm there, my foster dad, a guy named . . ." He taps his chin with his finger, but I can tell it's an act. He knows the guy's name, or else he's making it up. "Raymond, that's it. Raymond raises a fist, but I'd had enough of that, see. Out of the frying pan, as they say." Caleb puts down his spoon, then peers across the fire at me, eyes ablaze. "I stabbed that son of a bitch right there in his kitchen."

I swear it's a shadow. A talking, eating, smoking, cursing shadow.

Walt stands up, fidgets with his spoon, puts it in his pocket, then walks toward the tent. "I'll get blankets."

For a moment, Caleb and I are alone. I avoid eye contact by studying the dirt.

Don't look up.

The sound of Walt rustling around in the tent mixes with the fire's crackling, which mixes with my heart pounding, which mixes with my blood pumping, which mixes with, mixes with, mixes with . . .

I look up.

Through the dying flames, Caleb is staring at me, and I'm reminded of the familiar nothingness of an old television set. Growing up, my dad refused to buy a new TV. The colors in the corners of the screen were beginning to fade, a promise that before long, every movie would be black-and-white. But here's what I remember most: That old television, when turned off, produced a little click just as the screen went blank. And within that click, the stories and characters of my shows were swept away, as if they'd never existed at all.

In Caleb's eyes, I see that old television.

Turned off.

Like the shows never existed.

September 2—late at night

Dear Isabel,

Topics of substance and despair abound! They're sprouting up all over the place, in fact. To wit, I just met someone who scares the shit out of me. As I write this, he's sleeping (I think-hope-pray) on the other side of a campfire, so I need to be quiet and quick.

Here's the thing: this person reminds me of a terrible feeling I once had, and it's one of those terrible feelings that might not be as bad as I remember it. So I need to write it down, because sometimes writing a thing down is a good way to work something out. So here goes.

Three straight birthdays, I snuck out of the house with my friend Henry Timoney to the Retro Movie Plex. Henry and I first became friends in the school library, where we each noticed the other reading a Crichton Collection copy of *Jurassic Park*. Our relationship gained traction when Henry berated the movie for allowing Mr. Hammond to escape Isla Nublar alive. I, being a rationally minded literary purist, agreed. However, I voiced my opinion that what the film lacked in the way of subtle nuances and erudite accuracy, it more than made up for in special effects, cinematography, and Jeff Goldblum goodness. Henry, being a rationally minded cinematic purist, agreed. (My parents, film-rating sticklers that they were, had no idea I'd taped over their *Carol Burnett* marathon when *Jurassic Park* was aired during a free trial of HBO. I'd been watching it in secret for years.)

"You sure know a lot about *Jurassic Park*," said Henry. "For a girl."

"I know a lot about a lot of things," I said. "For anybody."

Henry nodded and straightened his glasses, and we quickly became what we'd always be: friends by default.

Now, as fate would have it, Retro Movie Plex, a theater that only aired older movies, happened to be showing *Jurassic Park* that very weekend—the weekend of my eleventh birthday. But as the film was rated PG-13, there was no way my parents would allow me to go.

So Henry and I developed a foolproof plan.

It began with my sneaking out the front door after dinner while my parents watched the nightly news. Henry's big brother, a meathead named Steve, had a friend who worked at the theater and had agreed to sell us tickets even though we were underage. Steve would be our ride to and from the theater. I was sexually attracted to Steve insomuch as I was an indiscriminate, preadolescent girl. Was he good-looking?

Sure. Very. Extremely. But no amount of hotness could make up for his constant misuse of the word *literally,* overuse of the word *bra,* and downright baffling pronunciation of the word *library.* As in, *Check it, bra, I literally died yesterday in the libary, when . . .* Alas, I was eleven, and he was devastatingly male—my hands were tied.

Lack of subtle nuances and erudite inaccuracies notwithstanding, *Jurassic Park* was ten times better on the big screen, and by the time it was over, Henry and I vowed never to criticize the film again. On the way home, I sat in the backseat of Steve's Jetta, and while he navigated the snowy streets of downtown Ashland, I navigated the ripple of muscle at the base of his neck. (Yeah, okay, that's weird, but I'm being honest here—before I ever knew about sex, it knew about me.) As the car rounded into my driveway, I saw the light in the den turn on, and in that instant, I knew I was in trouble. Steve and Henry wished me luck as I walked inside. My parents were waiting on the couch, cross-legged and tongue-tied. Mom got up and clicked the TV off. No need for conversational details. I had walked right into the thick air of punishment.

Grounded. One week.

On my twelfth birthday, my theatric insubordination paid dividends to the tune of *Highlander II: The Quickening.* (I have to say, my parents could have saved their punishment on this one, as the movie was punishment enough. Blimey.) Afterward, Sexy Steve drove us home, and as I was a year older, new images sprang to mind: less boxing-ring-chest-pounding, more bedroom-floor-topless-romping. And, upon pulling into my icy driveway, I was not at all surprised to find the den light on. Steve and Henry wished me luck. I went inside, and—another week grounded.

For my thirteenth birthday, we chose *The Shining,* which messed me up for weeks. Afterward, Steve drove us home, and as I was now thirteen, I saw through the bullshit. Sexually speaking, Steve was dead to me.

As he made the turn onto my street, I geared myself up for a grounding. Sneaking out to a bad movie, having goofy fun with Henry, riding home with Steve, then getting caught—at the time, I wouldn't have admitted this, but the getting caught was just as much a part of my birthday tradition as anything else.

But on this night, the den lights were off. Climbing out of the Jetta, both Steve and Henry congratulated me on finally getting away with it. I nodded in a daze and walked inside.

The TV was on in the empty den, but muted.

No one was awake.

No one was mad.

No one cared.

My God, Iz . . . I hope you don't know what that feels like.

Signing off,

Mary Iris Malone,

Friend by Default

P.S.—I wish I hadn't written this down.

... 19 ...

The Talismans of Disappointment

I WAKE UP in cutoffs, mud caked to my face, and a roaring stomachache. The moan—which started in my toes, then wriggled its way through my veins and arteries, organs and muscles, all the way to my lungs—almost escapes. But the kinetic power of a moan is nothing compared to the willpower of a Mim.

It's the kind of middle-of-the-night you feel in your bones. I don't know what time it is, but my bones tell me it's somewhere between two and four a.m.

As I sit up, the journal topples off my chest. I stick it back in my bag, slip on my high-tops, and creep off toward the shit pit. (Congrats again, Universe. Yours is a suspiciously acute sense of humor.) Circling the dying embers of the campfire, I notice Caleb's empty bedding, but in the slipstream of such indigestion, it seems almost trivial. In fact, nothing means much of anything right now, other than the immediacy of my bellowing bowels and a permanent embargo on canned ham.

After the silencing of the bellows—well, things begin to mean things again. And Caleb's empty bedding is a definite something. Before I have a chance to guess what, I hear a noise just outside the clearing.

I freeze . . . quiet . . . listening.

At some point during my time in New Chicago, my ears acclimated to the echoing cacophony of birds chirping, leaves cracking, twigs snapping—the natural sounds of autumnal nature. I shut my good eye and sift through these noises like a forty-niner panning for gold.

Yes, there—right there—definite whispers.

I creep toward the edge of the clearing. Spidery trees and wispy branches, dead leaves crackling like old parchment, and a moonlight subdued—middle-of-the-night-forest is one creepy-ass place. I follow the soft speech toward an oak. At its base, a single shadow, tall and wiry, turned sideways, talking animatedly to someone just out of sight. I squat down on my hands and knees, sinking my knuckles into the soft dirt, willing the sound of my breath away. There are two distinct voices.

". . . it, that's the plan. Get the whole stash, though. None of this half-ass horseshit."

"What about the girl?" asks Caleb. After our little campfire story time, I'd recognize his voice anywhere.

"Sweetheart's a liability, ain't she?"

They're talking about me.

"She's kinda cute," says Caleb. "Even with the mud."

The moon is just bright enough to see Caleb's outline, but from this angle, I can't make out the second person.

"Keep your eyes on the prize, Caleb. That girl gets in our way, we'll just have to take care of her. You can do that, right?"

A brief pause. This second voice has a strange guttural quality, as if the person is eating cake while talking. *"Caleb?"*

"What?"

The second person makes a noise like he's spitting or something, then says, "If the girl gets in our way, I need to know you will take care of her."

My heart is at an Olympic pace.

"Yes," whispers Caleb. "I will."

"Good. We're close now, you feel it?"

Holding my breath, I inch closer and picture what I must look like—lurking in the dark woods wearing these ridiculous cutoffs, my hair matted in clumps from the murky lake, and to top it off, my muddy war paint, acting as true camouflage.

"Yeah. Four hundred more should do the trick."

"Well shit, the kid's gotta have that and then some stashed away. Now remember, last time we tried, he had the cash tucked down in the bottom of his sleeping bag. So we'll check there, plus the suitcase."

I'm closing in now, circling around through leaves and brush. It's slow-going, but any faster, and I'd lose the stealth factor. I need the stealth factor. The stealth factor is crucial.

"You and I have had enough trouble out here to last two lifetimes, see. What we need is a fresh start. Beaches and girls and, who knows, might even get us a job in the movies. Shit, our story is prob'ly worth millions."

"Prob'ly billions," says Caleb.

"You're an idiot sometimes, you know that? Nothin's worth *billions*. Anyway, millions is plenty."

Fingertips to forehead, I am caked in sweat. I crouch as low as possible, move quickly, quietly, efficiently, dart around the final tree, then duck and roll behind a prickly fern. I can already tell my stealthy instincts have not led me astray; I'm in prime vantage point, the perfect position to see who Caleb is talking to. Still holding my breath, I peer around the fern.

"I could be a writer," he says. "I've always wanted to write."

My skin crawls as Caleb contorts his face, answers himself.

"Yeah, we'll write it ourselves. More money that way."

Now back to his original face and voice.

"Sure, more money. But it might open other doors, see. For other projects."

I close my eyes, willing this to be a dream. In some miraculous sonic anomaly, I hear the voice of my father, miles and miles away, whispering in my ear: *Here we have a rare first-hand account of the Schneiderian First-Rank Symptoms of schizophrenia. Thought echo, voices heard arguing, voices heard commenting on one's actions, delusions of control, thought withdrawal, thought insertion, thought broadcasting, and delusional perception* . . . Suddenly, I'm in the living room back in Ashland, playing bank teller, doing the voices of both the teller and the customer. *"Something's wrong with her, Evie."*

Eyes still closed, I grip the fern for balance. It pierces my palm. A shriek pulls me from the memory.

"Who's there?" says Caleb.

The shriek was my own.

Now it's Mom's turn to whisper in my ear . . .

Run, Mary.

Turning, I Goodwill myself through the woods, darting past

trees, hurdling limbs and branches. I am Arrow Iris Malone, Olympic Record Holder in the Wooded Sprint, running straight and true, striking at the heart of my prey, the clearing. I burst through the line of trees, dive into my bedding, pull the blanket up to my chin, and close my eyes.

Caleb approaches, crashing his way through the woods, his lanky gait wrecking the pureness of the soundscape. And I am struck, now more than ever, at what an unnatural person he is. His footsteps crunch and crackle, closer, closer. He can't be more than a few feet away now. They stop, just by my head. Eyes closed, heart pounding, I am a statue.

Minutes pass.

He's standing there, I know it, waiting for me to make the first move.

Fake-sleeping in front of a psychopath in the middle of the woods is, believe it or not, harder than it sounds.

I pray that my right eye is actually closed, and will my breath to slow; my hand, which landed on my chest when I dove into bed, is rising and falling with each breath.

The external sounds of the forest dissipate.

The internal sounds of my body swell.

He's there.

I know it.

Don't move, Mary.

I used to lie in bed with my hand on my heart, just like I am now, and listen to my parents fight. That's when I discovered something: with extreme concentration, I could hear my own insides over the sound of Mom and Dad's yells. Blood coursing through veins, muscles stretching and creaking; sometimes, I could even hear my hair growing. It was bizarre, no doubt. But the worst, by far, was the amplification of my heartbeat. I would hear that sucker pounding and pounding, and consider all the things I hadn't done, and all the things I didn't even know about not doing, and all the heartbreaks I would never experience, the ones that led to love and everything else, and what if right there—what if right *here*—right now—I actually hear my heart stop beating?

beating . . .

beating . . .

beating . . .

Caleb hasn't budged. His uncomfortable nearness is palpable.

Each breath, in and out, rising, falling.

I think of those days long ago, lying in bed, terrified not of the yelling but of what the yelling meant. And here's what I learned: it's impossible to wonder *when* your heart will stop beating, without wondering if that time is now.

NO COFFEE.

This is my first thought upon waking.

I am alive.

A close second.

I rub the fall air from my eyes, willing my brain to get its wheels out of the mud.

"Mornin', honey."

Across the campfire, Caleb sits in all his shadowy glory, a cigarette hanging from one side of his mouth, a spoon of ham from the other. He pulls a tin from the box and offers it to me. I vomit in my mouth, swallow, shake my head.

"More for me," he mutters.

Shivering, I sit up and pull the blankets around my shoulders. I must have fallen asleep while I was pretending to be asleep. Pretty damn effective, I'd say.

"How'd you sleep?" The corners of Caleb's mouth curl into a faint smile.

"Like a log," I lie. "You?"

"Same."

I scan the clearing quickly, avoiding Caleb's shifty eyes. "Where's Walt?"

"Shit pit," he mumbles, chews, puffs. I see him glance toward the tent, and wonder if he's already made a pass at Walt's money. I'm guessing not, or he wouldn't be here.

He's trying to figure out what to do with me.

I grab my backpack and rummage around for the makeup-remover pads, eager to be rid of last night's war paint. Mud or not, the pads should do the trick. Unfortunately, they're at the bottom of the bag, forcing me to acknowledge my many talismans of disappointment: one wooden box (wherefore art thou, Ahab?); one cell phone (thirty-nine missed calls); one bottle of Abilitol (if habit is king, I'm the joker); one terse letter (*Think of whats best for her. Please reconsider.*); and last, but certainly not least, one Hills

Bros. coffee can (behold! the Mistress of Burgling). A morning of harsh disappointments tends to slide down the gullet a little easier with some fresh java behind it. But as New Chicago seems to be heavy on the tainted meats and light on the gourmet beans, I'm forced to swallow my disappointments as they come.

I locate the makeup remover and begin wiping the caked mud off my face.

"You know. . . " says Caleb. His cigarette is now a stump. Sucking down the last of its juices, he flicks it into the ashes of last night's campfire and looks up. His turned-off eyes stir a strange combination inside me, of both fight and flight. As if waiting for his sentence to finish itself, Caleb sits with his mouth open, the accusation there in spirit, but not word. Not yet. The thing is, it doesn't have to be spoken. I can feign ignorance till I'm blue in the face, but I was there. I know the deep end of his soul's pool. I know Caleb's dark secret: not *who* he is, but *what*. A shadow. A creepy-ass-*Gollum-Gollum*-schizo-effing shadow.

"Hey, hey, Mim!" Walt yells, bounding out of the woods, buttoning his pants. His face is still covered in dried mud. When he sees my clean face he stops. "Is the war over?"

Lord bless and keep the House of Walt for all of eternity!

"Sure is, Walt. Come here, let me clean you up."

Caleb tosses his bedding into the tent, his accusations dangling on the tip of his tongue. "Well." He yawns. "I'm gonna take a shit in the pit and a wash in the lake. Walt, I got something I wanna talk to you about when I get back."

"Okay, Caleb."

Then, looking at me, he winks. "You too, sweetie." He retreats into the woods before I have a chance to give him my *eat shit* squint. (It's a dynamite squint, too, one I save for the purest of assholes.)

After cleaning Walt's face, I stick the pack of makeup remover back in my bag. My good eye lands on my bottle of Abilitol, and for a split second, I imagine the shape of a great grizzly charging me head-on. I see its sharp claws, its glassy eyes, its lolling tongue—I catch my breath and stuff the bottle down in the bag.

Fuck it. I can miss a day.

"Hey, Walt," I say, a plan beginning to take shape. He's eating ham—like it's his first, last, and only—watching a bluebird tug a worm from the ground.

"Yo, Walt," I whisper.

The bird seems desperate for its early, earthy breakfast. Walt is enthralled. "Hey, hey," he says, still staring at the bird.

"You ever been to Cleveland?"

His head turns from the carnivorous bird to me. In my ear, I hear my mother again. *Have a vision, Mary, unclouded by fear.*

I have limited experience, but I know this: moments of connection with another human being are patently rare. But rarer still are those who can recognize such a connection when they see one.

The camera zooms in on Walt's piercing eyes.

It cuts to a close-up of my own.

The connection is there, wriggling below the surface, just like that worm. And what's more, we both feel it.

In the distance, Caleb is splashing around, making a ridiculous racket.

Walt looks toward the lake, then whispers, "He won't like it."

May the House of Walt live forever and ever, Amen!

"No he won't, Walt."

... 20 ...

Run, Run, Run

IT FEELS NICE to be out of those cutoffs and into some real clothes again. Downright delightful, actually. Pulling my repacked JanSport tight, I wrap one of Walt's extra blankets between the straps and my chest. The kid has spent the last few minutes packing one of those hard, fifties-style suitcases full of canned hams, blankets, and God knows what else from that decrepit blue tent.

"Okay." I put my hands on his shoulders. "We just need to get back to the overpass. We can get a ride from there, okay? Just stick close and—"

Suddenly, Walt raises an arm. In his hand, he's holding my mother's lipstick like a champion's torch. "I found your shiny," he says, avoiding eye contact.

I reach for it, but can't stop looking at Walt—the kid is about to cry.

"Thank you, Walt," I say, taking the lipstick in my hands.

Without another word, he reaches his arms around my waist in a gentle hug. I'm surprised how natural it feels, as if a team of scientists designed his arms to fit the precise specifications of a heartfelt embrace. In his hug, I feel the things he tries to say but can't. I feel his pain and childlike innocence, his unencumbered joy and I-don't-know-what . . . life, I suppose. All the good things from the very best of places.

"We need to get going," I whisper, slipping the lipstick in my pocket. Caleb has gone quiet, conjuring all manner of nerve-racking scenarios in my head.

Walt straightens his Cubs cap, grabs his suitcase in one hand, his Rubik's Cube in the other, and leads the way down the hill.

In an all-out sprint.

The shrubbery is dense but doesn't slow him one bit; he's weaving in and out of bushes and trees with surprising agility. By contrast, I follow behind like an errant sled, haphazard and zigzagged.

A minute later, I hear it—behind us—a third set of scurrying leaves. Walt must hear it, too, because he picks up the pace considerably.

"Where y'all running off to?" Caleb's voice comes in rasps.

Ten paces ahead, Walt is absolutely hoofing it. "Mim?" he yells over his shoulder.

"I'm here, buddy! Keep going!"

Behind me, Caleb gasps like he wants to say something, but can't. Clearly, the cigarettes have taken their toll; his lungs are absolutely screaming for air. Unfortunately, he's not the only one wearing down. Either the aftereffects of last night's woeful sleep have kicked in or my youthful stamina is wavering. At the bottom of the hill, we hurdle the metal guardrail. It's early morning on a holiday weekend, so highway traffic is scarce. Right now, I would give all the cash in Kathy's can for a passing car, truck, van, just . . . *someone*. My head droops, my backpack sags, my shoes lag, the *slap-slap* of their worn soles on asphalt growing slower with each passing step. Under the bridge, we sprint past the very spot where I met Walt. It was only yesterday, but God, it feels like a month ago. On the other side, Walt races around a miniature hill, through a line of shrubs and bushes, and into the gravel parking lot of the same derelict building I'd seen from the window of the Subaru. Off-white. The offest white there ever was. A single pump in the middle of the lot has a handwritten sign taped over the handle: 87 OR BUST.

It's a gas station.

Like a track star, Walt digs in on the homestretch. Even with that hard suitcase slamming his knees, he reaches the front door at least twenty paces ahead of us. I watch him pull a set of keys from behind an ice machine, open the door, and step inside. Caleb is only feet behind me now. I will my burning legs through the entrance, hear Walt slam and lock the door behind me just as Caleb flings himself against the double-paned glass. And like that, the cool and collected Caleb is gone, replaced by some zombie-eyed maniac pounding his fists against the door, gasping for breath, raging-bull mad.

I turn in a circle, trying to catch my own breath. The gas station is dark and empty, still closed for the day. "Walt, what are we doing here?"

"Obeying," says Walt, bouncing on the heels of his feet. "He said run. Run and let him know. When there's trouble, I have to let him know."

I take a second to catch my breath, letting Walt's bizarre statement sink in. "Who?"

Walt bends at the waist, setting his suitcase and Rubik's Cube on the tile floor. He turns toward the refrigerated section, pulls out a Mountain Dew, pops the cap, takes a long swig, then wipes his mouth with the back of his sleeve.

"The karate kid," he says.

… 21 …
Rooftop Revelations

BLIMEY, THIS KID'S full of surprises.

"The what?" Only it's more like, *the-hell-you-say???*

He looks at me with a blank expression, tilts his head like a dog.

"Walt?"

Nothing. At all. And then—everything at once. He tosses the empty twenty-ouncer into a trash can, throws his suitcase over the checkout counter, hops over after it, and disappears around a back corner.

Like I said . . . *surprises.*

I throw my bag over the counter and jump it myself. These last couple days have been tough on my poor leg. At this rate, that cut will probably heal into some horrible disfigurement. Just add it to my list of medical oddities.

Around the corner, I spot Walt's green Chucks on the top rung of a ladder, now disappearing through a trapdoor in the ceiling.

"Wait up, Walt!"

Caleb has stopped banging on the front door, which is

unsettling, to say the least. I picture him crawling like a snake through the ductwork—hissing, spitting, eagerly calculating an alternate point of entry.

After scurrying up the ladder, I emerge through the same trapdoor and climb out onto the roof. It's still morning, but the sun is out in full force, beating down on the gravel and cement. Broad pipes, ventilation fans, and all manner of rusty eyesores sprout up like weeds every five feet or so. Planted right in the middle of the gas station roof is a massive tank; it's circular, like an aboveground pool, only taller. Standing at least eight feet high, it takes up more than half the surface area of the roof.

"Where is he, Al?"

I follow Walt's voice around the side of the tank and find him standing next to a 340-pound whale of a man in aviator sunglasses. The guy is lounging shirtless in a folding chair, sipping an umbrella drink. He's frightfully pale, a condition magnified by dark oil stains smeared across his face. Layer after folding layer, his stomach hangs down over his swimming trunks.

"Walt"—I point toward the fat guy—"you see him, too, right?"

The man's blubber shakes as he laughs. He sips his daiquiri through a crazy straw, looks from Walt to me. "Nah, I'm just a figment of your imagination, kid. What, you were expecting a hookah-smoking caterpillar?"

Walt, ignoring us both, bounces up and down on the heels of his feet. "Where is he, Al, where is he?"

I cross the roof, joining them in the partial shade of a fake palm tree, doing my best not to throw up on the Pale Whale's third circle of blubber. "Walt, we gotta get off this roof, man. We're sitting ducks up here."

"Who the hell are you?" asks the Pale Whale.

An image, from the most vivid quarters of my imagination: a car changing this man's oil. "Mim," I say. All I can muster.

"Ma'am?!" he blurts. "What kind of name is that?"

I find it hard to believe this man could criticize anybody's anything. "You find the bottom of that daiquiri yet? What is it, eight a.m.?" I turn to Walt. "Listen. We don't have time for this. Caleb's insane. It's only a matter of time—"

"That's just bad manners, see."

Spinning, I see Caleb round the circular tank, holding a sizeable hunting knife. A trickle of blood drips from his hands onto the gravel roof. He coughs, then pulls a cigarette from his back pocket and lights it. "Sorry, Al—had to bust a double-paned window to get in." Inhaling, his eyes dart around. "Where's your boyfriend?"

Gas station plus boyfriend.

"Karate class in Union," says the Pale Whale, smacking his lips around the straw.

An odd smile spreads across Caleb's face. He steps closer, the sharp end of the hunting blade shimmering in the light of the morning sun. "Like a fuckin' six-year-old," he mumbles.

Al pinches one nostril, blows snot out the other—just like a whale's blowhole. Sliding his meaty hands behind his head, he sighs, and for a moment it's quiet, as if none of us are entirely sure whose turn it is to talk. Then, with the subtlety befitting a man of his stature, Albert breaks the silence. "You're a freak show, you know that, Caleb?" The folding chair squeaks under his weight. "Seriously, you should sell tickets. People would come from miles around to see you talk to yourself. Speaking of which—when you do that, is it a natural, everyday sort of thing, like putting on socks?"

Caleb's eyes twitch, but he doesn't answer.

"I shouldn't make fun," continues Albert, rubbing his aviators on the bottom of his shorts. "I suppose that's a brand of bat-shit crazy you just can't help."

Caleb stands frozen, blood still dripping from the cut on his hand.

Al raises his daiquiri to his lips. A stubborn slice of strawberry gets stuck in the straw. He sucks harder, squeezing it like Augustus through the glass tube in *Charlie and the Chocolate Factory*. He swallows it down, tilts his head at Caleb. Like an old-fashioned pistol duel, it's not about who draws first, but who draws quickest.

"Get the hell off my roof," says Albert, each of his stomachs rising, falling.

Caleb pulls back his shoulders, and once again, I notice his red hoodie. The same as my own. I picture my Abilitol in the bottom of my bag, shrouded in the darkness of its canvas tomb, screaming a promise of normalcy.

"I'm not crazy," whispers Caleb, twirling the knife in his hands.

And suddenly, from months ago, my father's voice: *"Here, Mim."* I take the bottle and roll my eyes. *"Don't look at me like that,"* says Dad. *"I'm trying to help. Just get in the habit of taking one with breakfast every day. Habit is king."* I glance at the label on the bottle, wondering how it got this far. *"Dad. I don't need them."* He pulls orange juice out of the refrigerator, pours a glass. *"I need you to trust me on this, Mim. You don't want to end up like Aunt Isabel, do you?"* That's when I know he's scraping the bottom of the barrel, searching for anything to get me to cooperate. Taking the glass from his hand, I pop a pill in my mouth and drown it down with the rest of his juice. Every last drop. I wipe my lips with the back of my hand, stare him dead in the face. *"I'm not crazy."*

"Sure you're not crazy, Caleb," says the Pale Whale. "You just keep living your little fantasy life, son. Lord knows, I've been there." He slaps his belly. "But damn it all, I wouldn't trade these rolls for your level of crazy, not for all the rotisserie chickens in Kentucky. You know why? 'Cause at the end of the day, when my fat ass tumbles into its king-sized waterbed, I sleep like a baby. I know who I am."

"Oh yeah?" Caleb twirls the knife again, arching one eyebrow unnaturally high. "And who are you?"

Albert the Pale Whale sips his daiquiri, smacks his lips together, then leans back and sighs. "I'm Albert, motherfucker. Who are you?"

As Caleb steps toward Albert, I grip the war paint in my pocket and picture the long blade piercing those layers of blubber. Gallons of fluid would gush from the wound like a fire hydrant; hidden arteries, having spent the last two decades being stretched and filled to their fullest capacity, would now be exposed, severed, freed from the heaviest of loads. The wailing, whaling mess would pool around his bloated ankles, gather under the folding chair, then rise up and up, lifting the leviathan carcass off the roof, spinning him like a top, and tossing him off the edge of his own broke-ass, off-white gas station. We'd be swept up in the Blood Flood, too, Walt and I, carried away like Noah's Ark, or rather, like the animals of afterthought, left to fend for themselves in the apocalyptic precursor to the rainbow.

This is what I imagine.

But it never happens.

Just as Caleb reaches Albert's chair, a blurred figure plummets on top of him, knocking him to the ground. Within seconds, Caleb is back on his feet, wielding the hunting knife at this new adversary. At first glance, the man seems too ridiculous to be real. He's wearing a black strip of cloth around his forehead like a ninja, goggles, a long gold chain around his neck, a flowery wifebeater, and a pair of shockingly familiar cutoff jeans. Dripping wet from head to toe, he's smiling like he's having a ball.

Next to me, Walt claps, while Albert chuckles and sips his drink. "Fuck him up, Ahab."

Never mind my epiglottis—my entire body flutters at this.

It's him.

It's them.

The fight doesn't last more than a minute. In a roundhouse kick that would have made Jet Li proud, Arlene's legendary nephew sends Caleb's hunting knife sailing over the edge of the roof. With him disarmed, it's hardly a fight at all. A couple of hook-kick combos and graceful strikes to the chest, arms, and head, and Ahab has a whimpering Caleb trapped in a half nelson on the gravel roof.

"Walt," says Ahab, dripping wet, smiling from ear to ear. "Go downstairs, call the Independence police station. Ask for Randy, tell him to get his ass over here."

Walt giggles, runs around to the trapdoor.

"You okay, honey?" Ahab looks up at Albert, leaving me to wonder at the sheer physics of their relationship.

"I'm all right," grunts the Pale Whale. "Thanks to my knight in shimmering armor."

"Shining," I whisper, still gripping my war paint and trying to piece together the sequence of the last few minutes.

Ahab notices me, seemingly for the first time. "Who're you?"

"That's Ma'am," says Albert, slurping the last of his daiquiri, then pulling a brand-new one out from under his chair.

I clear my throat. "It's Mim," I say, rapping my knuckles against the side of the tank. "What's this?"

"We call it the Pequod," says Ahab. "Perfect place for a little sun and relaxation."

I raise my eyebrows. "What—inside?"

The Pale Whale chuckles and sips.

Ahab tightens his grip on Caleb. "It's a pool, kid."

Looking from Ahab to the tank, I can't help but wonder what kind of people drink daiquiris and go swimming on top of a gas stations at eight a.m. on chilly fall mornings. But I'll thank the gods of, you know, whatever, that they do. Because I'd be dead right now without these two.

Walt comes running around the tank. Pool. Whatever.

"Randy's on his way," he says.

"Good." Ahab hoists Caleb to his feet. "You guys can hang downstairs till he gets here. He's a dick of a dick, so he'll probably wanna take you down to the station for questioning out of sheer boredom. Don't say anything about the pool, okay? He'd find some city bylaw and have it removed."

Walt gives him a thumbs-up, scurries down the rungs. I stand still for a moment, wondering if this is the right time. Certainly, it's not how I pictured it happening.

"What's up, Ma'am?"

I take a knee, unzip my JanSport, and produce Arlene's wooden box.

For a second, no one says anything. Finally, Ahab says, "Where did you get that?"

His question is quiet, not accusatory.

"Arlene," I whisper. "Your aunt—I was on the bus with her. The one that crashed."

Albert sits up in his chair and takes off his aviators. There's something in his eyes, some deep well of empathy.

"What's wrong with everybody?" grunts Caleb, still in Ahab's clenches. "It's just a box."

Without thinking twice, Ahab lifts Caleb up by his hoodie, and punches him once, twice, three times in the face. Blood splatters across the gravel roof, as well as a single tooth. The look in Ahab's eyes isn't murderous. It's the look of a man who did what had to be done. Caleb drops to the ground unconscious. Considering the solemnity of the moment he interrupted, I'm thinking he got off pretty easy.

Ahab is in front of me now, looking at the box, then at me,

and I suddenly can't stop crying. It's crazy, because Arlene was his aunt, not mine. I didn't know her all that well, not really. I didn't know her favorite color or movie, or what kind of music she liked, or if she preferred lakes to oceans. I didn't even know her last name. But maybe those aren't the things that channel love. Maybe the true conduit is more elusive than that. Maybe. And I think Ahab understands, because now his hand is on my shoulder, and he's crying, too, and he doesn't ask any questions, which I'm beyond grateful for. Handing the box over, I search for something memorable and eloquent to mark the occasion. Arlene was one of a kind, a true friend when I needed one, a grande dame from the old school. She was the sweetest of old ladies, and I will miss her dearly. All of these things are true, but the words I choose are far more profound.

"She smelled like cookies," I whisper through tears.

Ahab laughs and so do I, and it occurs to me again how often laughter accompanies tears. Now Albert has joined us, and when I look up at him, the sun hits me squarely in the face. He slides his aviators into my hands, then pats me on the back.

"Finder's fee," he says.

Ahab lifts the gold chain off his neck. Dangling from the end, an old-fashioned skeleton key fits the lock perfectly. He turns his wrist, opening the box with a click.

This is his, not mine.

I pick up my backpack and walk halfway around the tank when his voice stops me. "You wanna know what's inside?"

Maybe it's the sun, or the emotion of reuniting Ahab with some piece of his dear dead aunt, but whatever the reason—

in this moment, on the rooftop of this gas station—I miss my mother terribly.

I turn, take one last look at Ahab, dripping wet in his ridiculous clothes, holding his precious wooden box; behind him, his whale of a boyfriend is back in his chair, lounging in the shade, sipping a daiquiri like he's on the beaches of Aruba.

"You could tell me," I say, rounding the tank. Then, slipping on Albert's aviators, I throw open the trapdoor. "But I probably wouldn't believe you."

... 22 ...

The Mistress of Moxie

September 3—midmorning

Dear Isabel,

Dim the lights.

Raise the curtains.

Cue the amped-up, percussive spy music. (Film noir, not Bond.)

Standing in the shadows of trees, rooftop pools, and fat, drunken slobs, Our Heroine comes face-to-face with a different kind of shadow: her arch nemesis, Shadow Kid (duhn-duhn-duuuuh!!!!). Shadow Kid tests Our Heroine's theory that heroes are not without blemish, villains not without virtue. *If Shadow Kid holds a single ounce of virtue in his heart,* thinks Our Heroine, *it is kept well hidden.* It isn't the first time her theory has been put to test, and it won't be the last.

With more than a little help from her sidekicks, Our Heroine escapes the clutches of Shadow Kid unscathed, unfettered, and unmurdered. Much to her chagrin, however, she now must deal with the inept Constable Randy, and though Our Heroine has done nothing wrong . . .

Okay, cut, cut, cut.

Sorry, Iz—I had every intention of keeping up the cloak-and-dagger-Bogart-forties-black-and-white bullshit, but honestly, I just don't have it in me. I'm too hungry. And pissed. I'm hungry and pissed, and I'm sure you understand.

So.

Northern Kentucky seems to be experiencing a substance and despair monsoon.

How do I know this?

Well, right now I'm sitting in an interrogation room at the Independence police station. I'm not under arrest or anything, but apparently little things like constitutional rights don't matter here in Independence. (I know. The irony. I just . . . I can't.)

Anyway, it appears I have some time on my hands, so let's talk Reasons.

Reason #7 ends with a pill, and begins with a grizzly bear.

GRIZZLY BEAR

(Feared, Murdered, Stuffed, Admired)

Ferocious? Yep.

Out of place? Bingo.

Key ingredient to the world's most awesome doctor's office waiting room? You bet your sweet ass.

I still remember my first visit to Dr. Makundi's office like it was yesterday. The waiting room had toys for the kids and magazines for the parents, but it also had *that* life-sized, stuffed grizzly. For everyone.

On the first of what would turn out to be just under a hundred visits to Dr. Makundi's office, I walked right up to that giant brown grizzly and touched its claw. I was eleven at the time, and it was a bear, so really, I had no choice. (I mean. It was a bear. A *bear*.) So I stood there, cowering in its ever-still shadow, staring into those great glassy eyes, positive the thing would come alive at any moment and swallow me whole. I recalled one of my favorite childhood stories, *Pierre* by Maurice Sendak, about a lion who swallowed a naughty boy named Pierre. (Have you read this book? My God, it is deliciously macabre!) Anyway, as I was quite a naughty child, I was sure the bear would turn out to be just like that lion, which is to say, I was sure he would swallow me whole.

But he did not.

"Mim," said my father, waving me over.

Clearly, Dad had no respect for murdered/stuffed bears. Reluctantly, I pulled myself away from the terrifying taxidermy and sat in the chair between Mom and Dad.

"You're okay with being here, right?" said Dad.

I nodded. There was, after all, a bear.

Mom put her arm around me. "If you're uncomfortable with any of Dr. Makundi's questions, just say the word, okay? We can leave whenever you want."

Dad, thinking I couldn't see him, rolled his eyes. (This eye roll, combined with a textbook nostril flare, would become his trademark, a look that would haunt me well into my teen years.) "It might be tough sometimes," he said. "But *you're* tough, right? My tough girl. You'll answer whatever the doctor asks, won't you tough girl?"

I nodded, because whatever, there was a fucking *bear* right *there.*

Anyway, I'll cut to the chase here, Iz, as a slew of doctor visits doesn't exactly make for stimulating reading. Dr. Makundi, as it turned out, was more than a decent doctor. He was a decent man. He was short and round and always wore a bow tie. He was the only East Indian I've ever encountered who had red hair. Like, *Weasley* red. In fact, he used to joke that he was Irish-in-hiding. (*"My name is even camouflaged . . . MAC-oondi,"* he'd say. And then laugh, effing *heartily.*) He let me talk when I needed to talk, and he talked when I needed to listen. He even played Elvis in the background without my having to ask. Over the next four years, Makundi and I took our time "getting to the root," as he called it. His methods went like this: wait, talk, think, watch, listen. Sitting with him required patience and a certain bold individuality. I had plenty of both, so it worked. Makundi had his own practice, which I know doesn't really say much these days, but he really did it up old-school. He wasn't tied down to any one notion of popular treatment, or pulled hither and thither by powerful drug companies. He played games and told stories because as he put it, "Life is more fictional than fiction." He did things his way. And that was good enough for me. And that was good enough for Mom.

Dad was unconvinced.

It started with a smart man named Schneider who wrote a smart book, which helped a lot of people. Dad read this book and joined the ranks. Now, joining the ranks can be a good thing. (Take NATO, for example. Or cage-free eggs.) But joining the ranks can also be a not-so-good thing. (Take the Nazi Party for example. Or the rise of the McNugget.) Dad bought into the notion that there was One Right Way to solve a problem. Or rather, to solve *my* problem. And guess who wasn't solving my problem correctly? (Hint: he owned a bear.)

At the beginning of what turned out to be our final session—before Dr. Makundi even had a chance to get to the branch, much less the root—Dad stepped in. "We need to talk," he said. And just like some angsty, one-sided breakup, my father explained to affable Dr. Makundi all the ways the good doctor had let us down.

. . . Schneider this and Schneider that . . .

. . . Makundi's methods, while commendable, simply weren't relevant in this day and age . . .

"What day and age is that, Mr. Malone?" asked Makundi.

"The day and age of new discoveries in the world of medicine," answered my father.

Dr. Makundi sat on the other side of his rickety wooden desk, peering over the top of his glasses, listening to my father expound secondhand thoughts. I remember watching his face as Dad talked, thinking, in a way, the man was a product of his own theories, more fictional than fiction. Countless hours of sessions we'd spent focusing on the facts, trying to reconcile reality with whatever unreality was in my own head. But if Dr. Makundi, the Irish-Indian-bow-tie-wearing-grizzly-loving doctor himself had taught me anything, it was that our world could be astoundingly unrealistic.

The good doctor removed his glasses and spoke quietly. "*Symptoms* of psychosis, Mr. Malone, are not themselves psychoses. As I'm sure Schneider himself would agree, were he here today. Alas, he is not. Most of his work, as I'm sure you know, was published in the twenties." He winked at me, looked back at my dad. "The day and age of new discoveries in the world of medicine, was it not?"

Two weeks later, I walked into a new doctor's office, one whose methods better fell in line with those of my father. One whose life had no fiction, no bow ties, no Elvis.

He didn't even have a bear.

(If I were writing a book, Iz, this would be my chapter break. I mean, right? *He didn't even have a bear.* Boom, muthafuckas.)

So . . . I'm sick. Supposedly. And Dad is worried. Obviously. I think he's afraid of history repeating itself in the worst way.

The reason I'm bringing all this up now is because I just spent the better part of the morning staring down the business end of a foot-long hunting knife, which in and of itself is terrifying. Only here's the thing—if I'm honest with myself, the knife wasn't what I was afraid of. I was afraid of the person holding the knife. Shadow Kid.

I don't know if you read comics, but if you do, you'll notice there usually isn't much that separates the villain from the hero. Lonely outcasts, masked identities, troubled childhoods, misunderstood by all—very often, there's a pivotal scene toward the end (usually during a massive thunderstorm) wherein the villain tries to convince the hero that they're the same.

This morning, Shadow Kid had me cornered, and all I could see were the great glassy eyes of a grizzly bear. Before long, the bear's eyes were my own, and I was convinced we were the same. There wasn't a cloud in the sky, but it sure felt like those thunderstorms from the comics.

But then something happened—standing there on that roof, I remembered once, years ago, when Dad took me mini-golfing. During a few of the earlier holes, I'd noticed a last-second flick of the wrist, or a fleeting smirk, which led me to believe he was putting forth less than his best effort. We were on the back half of the miniature course: the token "giant windmill" green. I don't remember who was winning at the time, but it was close. Closer than it should have been.

"Dad," I said. "*Try* this time."

Picking up his quarter, he raised an eyebrow. "*This time*? I've been trying every time, Mim. You're a pro."

I was standing behind him when he teed off. His ball

rolled down the turf aisle, a straight shot through the tiny tunnel, narrowly missing a windmill blade, and through to the other side. From where we were standing, the six-foot windmill blocked our view of the hole, making it impossible to see where Dad's ball had landed.

"Pretty sure I shanked it," said Dad. "I'll go check."

He rested his putter on his shoulder and strolled around the windmill, out of sight. While he was gone, I noticed the green ahead of us had one of those fold-out circus mirrors. Its position made it look as though there were six or seven holes, effectively camouflaging the true hole. A young couple kept hitting their golf balls into the mirror, cursing, then smiling like they didn't care. For a second, I tried to figure out which of the holes was the real one. And then I saw it. One side of the mirror was angled toward the hole on our green. In its reflection, I saw Dad pull his ball out of our hole, then set it down by the edge of the walkway, a good ten feet away. He threw on a smile, then rounded the windmill back on my side.

"Yup," he said, shrugging. "Shanked it."

Dad, for all his faults, was still Dad. He didn't just will himself to lose that game so that I might win—he rigged it so that there was no other way.

I had people. Who loved me. People who cheated to lose. There's really something to this, Iz, something that separates me from Shadow Kid. And I think this is what makes the storm pass.

People say I'm sick. Dad sure believes it. At his insistence, I've been on meds for the past year or so.

Shit.

Constable Randy returns.

Long story short, I'm not going to take the medication anymore, because I don't need it. Mom never thought so, and neither did Makundi.

Abilitol is its name.

And it is Reason #7.

Signing off,
Mary Iris Malone,
Grizzly Whoa-man!

"ARE YOU DONE?"

I nod, stuff my journal away, and give the officer my sarcastic-undivided-attention look. (It's a good one.) We aren't suspects—a fact I pointed out *twice* before he dropped us in this room—but this hasn't kept Independence's Finest from treating Walt and me like bottom-feeders.

"Okay, then," says Officer Randy, plopping his awkward frame across the table. "What do you think a man in my position should do?"

I want to ask him what position he thinks he's in. Survey says: *bowling ball on a straw.* Seriously, in all my years I've never seen a noodle like his, like someone grabbed him by both feet and blew air into his toes. This man is one hard sneeze away from scoliosis.

"I don't understand the problem," I say. "We already told you what happened on the roof. You can't keep us here, we've done nothing wrong."

Randy shuffles his papers around. Blimey, looking at his giant head almost makes me wish I'd stared at that dumb eclipse with both eyes wide open.

"You know what I did yesterday?" he asks. "Arrested an accused child molester. So you'll have to excuse me if I'm less than cordial."

The words of Officer Randy take me there. *(I'd like to be friends, Mim. You want to be friends, don't you?)* The clicking of Walt's cube brings me back.

It's quiet for a moment; Officer Randy sighs, says, "Okay, look. Bottom line. I've got two minors involved in a possible murder attempt."

"Dude. We were the murderees, not the murderers."

"I know that. And under normal circumstances, I'd call your parents, explain the situation, tell you to expect calls from an attorney, and send you on your merry way. But these aren't normal circumstances, it would seem. These are very odd circumstances."

Constable, you have no idea . . .

"Because when I ask you a simple question—what's your name, where're you from, where're your folks—you clam up. Ahab vouches for both of you, says you're heading to Iowa, or something, but he's a moron. Either way, that's not enough to—"

"Cleveland," says Walt.

Randy frowns at him. "What?"

"Cleveland, not Iowa." Walt has his head down, completely enthralled with his cube.

Think fast, Malone. I lean in across the desk and lower my voice. "Okay, fine. Officer, my name is Betty, and this is my brother, Rufus, and we're from Cleveland. A few years back, I was self-diagnosed with abandonment issues and—"

"Self-diagnosed?" Randy interrupts.

"What did I say?"

"You said self-diagnosed."

"That's right."

Next to me, Walt is nodding emphatically.

"So anyway," I continue, "after our parents died, my brother here was put under my guardianship."

"How old are you, Betty?" Officer Randy asks, scribbling away in a notebook.

"Eighteen," I answer, barely able to keep a straight face. "So I took Rufus here under my wing. Well, I've had a few abandonment episodes recently, real ugly shit, you understand? So we're headed to Boise to live with our Aunt Gerty. I've got a job lined up with Pringles, and Auntie Gee has agreed to let us live in her bonus room above the garage."

Randy's pen stops abruptly. "Boise's in Idaho," he whispers, a *gotcha* smile spreading across his huge face. "Ahab said *Iowa*."

I clear my throat and cross my arms. "Yeah, well, like you said, Officer. Ahab's a moron."

Officer Randy furrows his bulging brow. *Dear God, please let him buy this story*. There's no telling what sort of chain reaction a curious cop in northern Kentucky might set off. I could kiss my Objective good-bye, that's for sure.

"You guys wait here," he says. "I'm gonna get on the horn with the captain and see what I can do about getting you to Boise."

The human bobblehead wobbles from the room. I hop up, poke my head out the door, and watch him disappear around the corner.

"Okay, Walt, listen up." I turn, expecting him to be in la-la land with his cube. Instead, he's standing right behind me, smiling, suitcase in hand. God bless him. "We're not arrested, but it looks like we're gonna have to break out of jail. You with me?"

"Hey, hey, yeah," he says, bouncing on his heels.

Closing my good eye, I will every ounce of stealth, speed, and moxie into the toes of my Goodwill shoes. Mom—the flame of my fuse, the wind in my sail, the tick-tick-ticking clock in my ear—is sick. Labor Day is two days away. Forty-eight hours. I breathe in, out, in, in, out. I am energized. I am galvanized. I am mobilized, oxidized, and fully realized.

I am Mary Iris Malone, the Mistress of Moxie.

Stepping lightly into the hallway, my trusty high-tops lead us onward (ever onward!) through the small-town bustlings of the Independence police station. We fly past the bulletproof window protecting the captured dregs of society; past the closet-sized kitchen, with its engine-oil coffee and floppy box of day-old donuts. With buoyed spirits, surging stealth, and the white-water rapids of adrenaline, we follow my Velcro-laden friends into the foyer of the station: past the old lady in hysterics over her lost cat; past the debauched he-she in cowboy (cowgirl?) chaps; past the gorgeous guy with a black eye—

I stop on a dime. Walt runs into my back, giggling.

The guy with the black eye. It's *him*—17C, from the Greyhound.

"Come on," says Walt, still chuckling under his breath. "We're breaking out of jail." He grabs my sleeve, and pulls every part of me—save my heart—out the front door.

... 23 ...

The Many Perfections of Beck Van Buren

"SORRY, LITTLE LADY. C'aint sell it to you without you got a valid driver's license."

The guy pulls an apple out of I-don't-know-where, then plants it in his Moses beard. I can only assume there's a mouth in there somewhere.

After our prison break, I was all set to hitchhike, when Walt spotted a FOR SALE sign in the window of a blue pickup in this guy's yard. The problem is this: for certain, shall we say, *cycloptic* reasons, I've avoided taking the driver's test like the plague.

I pull my permit—which the great state of Ohio only requires a written exam to obtain—from my backpack, and flash the card in Moses's face. "I have this. Same thing, basically."

He cracks a bite of his apple (damn thing is crisp), chews, says nothing.

Walt unlatches his old suitcase, pulls out his Rubik's Cube, and gets to work. Moses raises his eyebrows; I can actually see his patience waning.

"Okay, fine," I say, pulling out a wad of cash. "How about

three hundred dollars? That's fifty bucks more than you're asking, cash in hand."

Walt clicks the red squares into place, claps me on the shoulder, and does a little jig right there on the front porch.

"What's wrong with him?" asks Moses, still eyeballing Walt.

"He's Walt, man. What's your excuse?"

Moses stops chewing momentarily, then backs up to shut the door.

"Okay-no-wait-wait-look, I'm sorry. My friend and I just walked from the police station, so we're—"

"You see Randy down there?" he asks, cracking another bite.

"I . . . what?"

"Officer Randy. You see him?"

"Yeah, but—"

"How is that ole sonuvabitch? Still a rat bastard?"

I am Mary Iris Malone, a baffled bag of bones. "Are you gonna sell me your truck or not?"

"Not," he says with a mouthful.

I twist my mom's lipstick in my pocket. "Okay, I think we got off on the wrong foot."

"Kid, I got stuff to do. Without a license, I c'aint sell her to you. Now you and your . . . friend, here, need to clear off my porch."

"I have a license," says a voice behind us.

I turn to find 17C scrolling through pictures on his camera, standing in the front yard like a deep-rooted tree, like he's been there for years. Somehow, that black eye only makes him more desirable.

"And you are . . . ?" asks Moses.

A) Perfect

B) The god of Devastating Attractiveness

C) A flawless specimen, created in a lab by mad scientists in an effort to toy with the heart of Mary Iris Malone

D) All of the above

I circle *D*. Final effing answer.

He sticks his camera in a duffel bag and straps it around his chest. "I'm Beck," he says, stepping up onto the porch and throwing an arm around my shoulder. "Her disapproving big brother." He turns sideways, mere inches from my face. "I thought I told you to wait for me in the parking lot, sis."

Pushing my bangs out of my eyes, I'd pay literally, probably, I don't know, maybe four hundred dollars for five minutes of prep time in a mirror right now.

"Oh, right," I say. "Sorry . . . bro. Forgot." My usual witty vocabulary seems to have regressed into mushy, fragmented infant-speak.

Beck sighs, leans in toward Moses. "She'd lose her arm if it wasn't attached."

"Head," I mutter.

"What?"

"I'd lose my *head* if it wasn't attached." I roll my eyes, praying it looks sisterly.

"What did I say?" asks Beck.

"You said arm."

He gives a *psshh*. "I don't think so."

"Walt?" I say.

Without looking up from his cube, Walt corroborates. "The new boy said 'arm.'"

Beck shrugs and turns back toward a bewildered Moses. I can almost hear the rusty wheels churning in his head, processing our little production. From somewhere behind him, he pulls out another apple and cracks a bite.

"You said cash, right?"

WALT TOSSES HIS old suitcase in the bed of the truck; we pile in and pull out of Moses the Apple Eater's front yard. Beck mentions food, to which Walt and I hastily agree. On top of being insanely hungry, I'm not relishing the idea of exchanging stories with Beck. I'd love to know who he is and where he's going (not to mention how he got from the Greyhound bus yesterday to the Independence police station today), but I'm sure he's wondering the same about me. We'll catch up, but we'll do so with full stomachs.

At Walt's prodding, Beck pulls into a line of cars at a fast-food place called Medieval Burger. When this trip is over, I'm going to have to look into one of those trendy full-body cleanses, something to detox all this processed meat out of my system.

"Did they even have burgers in the Middle Ages?" I wonder aloud.

"Oh, sure," says Beck. "Nothing more refreshing after a long day of crusading and pillaging and walking through the mud and what have you."

Oh God, he's *witty*. "The Middle Ages were quite damp, weren't they?"

"And dreary."

Walt flips on the vintage turn-dial radio of the old truck and scans the waves. Landing on a Reds versus Cubs baseball game, he claps his hands and leans in to listen.

The line inches forward, stops.

"So?" says Beck.

I turn to find him looking at me, arms crossed.

"So what?"

"How about a name, for starters?"

"How about *your* name?"

"I already told you. It's Beck."

"I just figured that was, you know, an alias or something."

Before he can respond, his cell phone rings. Pulling it from his jacket, he checks the caller ID and answers. "Yeah, hey." Pause. "No." Longer pause. "Claire, listen . . ."

I become inexplicably interested in the analogue clock in the dashboard. It appears to be broken, as neither hand is moving. Interesting. Inexplicably so.

"It'll just take a few minutes," he says. "I know." Pause. "Okay, Claire." Short pause. "Thanks." He hangs up.

Color me intrigued.

"So." He glances sideways. "What about that name?"

I'm ready this time. "What, you mean—for the truck? Fabulous idea." I twist around, look through the cab window, and tap my chin. "I'd say he looks like a Phil."

Beck smiles. "I have an uncle named Phil."

"No shit." I pat the dashboard. "Uncle Phil it is."

We pull up to the speaker, and I wonder if Beck is as grateful for the interruption as I am. One of us is gonna have to break eventually.

We give our orders and drive up to the window.

"Here," I say, taking a twenty from Kathy's can. "I got this."

Beck doesn't even put up a fight, which is both mildly curious and annoying. We pull into an empty parking spot while he divvies out Walt's burger and fries, then his own. "So," he says, folding up the bag.

"Umm, my food is still in there."

"Oh, I know. And you'll get it—but it's gonna cost you."

"You mean more than the twenty bucks I already dished out?"

Beck unwraps his burger, takes a bite, and nods. "S'good, too," he says, his mouth full. "Real . . . medievally."

I smile, wondering whether I'd rather punch him or jump him. "And what exactly does medieval taste like?"

He holds up the bag with my food in it. "Care to find out?"

I've never been part of a conversation like this, where my heart is jelly and my brain is in my shoes. I should be pissed at his boyish antics, but right now *should* is miles away.

On the radio, the broadcasters discuss an impending rain delay. Blissfully engaged, Walt digs into his fries; Beck is already halfway done with his burger. I roll my eyes, sigh in my most overly dramatic tone, and offer my hand across Walt's back. "Fine, I'll go first." Beck takes a bite while shaking it, and if I thought his look was stunning, his touch is downright majestic.

"I'm Mary Iris Malone . . . but only my mother gets to call me Mary."

I'm in deep before I know it. With a few carefully omitted details (the *BREAKING NEWS*, my war paint, my solar retinopathy—God, freak show, anyone?), I proceed to unload on Beck. I tell him about the divorce and the move and the conversation I overheard in the principal's office. I tell him about Mom's mystery disease in Cleveland and the series of letters I flushed down the bus toilet, my only proof of Kathy's awfulness. I tell him about the bus accident and Arlene and Walt and Caleb and our perilous rooftop episode, which landed us at the police station. It's that scene in the movie where the nervous girl just keeps talking and talking, but unlike the douchebags in those movies, Beck actually seems interested in what I'm saying. And I hate admitting this—probably because I don't like being the most predictable character in my own film—but I'd be lying if I said I wasn't wearing my cute face the entire time. (I know my cute face when I feel it.)

Once done, I come up for air. "Wait, where're we going?"

"North," says Beck, merging onto the highway. "You said Cleveland, right?"

I vaguely recall him starting up the engine during my soliloquy. "What, you're gonna drive us?"

"How else you plan on getting there?" He hands over my food. "And here. I officially lift the embargo."

I'm not above eating fries while being indignant. If anything, indignation is bolstered by fries. "Umm, these are amazing. And—lest you forget, Uncle Phil *belongs* to me. I bought him with my cash-monies. That's how we plan on getting to Cleveland."

"Umm, yes they are. And lest *you* forget, I'm the one with the license."

"Just because I don't have a license—God, seriously, how good were these when they were warm? Never mind, I don't wanna know. Anyway, I know how to drive."

"I'm sure you do. But really, it's no problem. I'm sort of passing through, anyway."

"You're passing through Cleveland. On your way to what, Lake Erie?"

He gives another one of those half smiles. "Canada, actually. Or—Vermont."

Before I have a chance to point out that Cleveland really isn't on the way to Canada or Vermont, the skies open up. It's a heavy rain, each drop bursting like a water balloon on the windshield. After a few minutes of squinting and leaning over the steering wheel, Beck gives up, and pulls to the side of the highway to wait it out. In the new stillness of the truck, the warbled radio mixes with the pounding rain to create an odd sort of half silence. Broadcasters are going through stats now, filling time during the rain delay. Walt has his hat pulled down over his face, but other than that, he hasn't budged.

"So you're from Cleveland, then?" says Beck, sipping his soda.

I shake my head and unwrap the burger. "After things went to shit, Mom sort of relocated there. It's where she always wanted to be anyway. I grew up in Ashland, about an hour outside Cleveland."

"And she's in the hospital for this . . . disease, right? Your mom, I mean."

Reaching between my feet, I unzip my backpack and hand over the envelope with my mom's PO Box address. "For two months, I received a letter a week. Then three weeks ago, they stopped. This was the last one I got, and the only one since the move."

"You think your stepmom, Cassie—"

"Kathy."

"Right, Kathy." He hands back the envelope. "You think she's been hiding letters from you?"

"She always gets to the mailbox first. She tried to get me to quit calling so much. It's obvious she doesn't want us to communicate. Plus"—I pull out Kathy's sixth letter—"here—this is the letter from Mom to Kathy, the only one I didn't flush. I'm pretty sure Mom asked if I could visit, to which Kathy said no, to which Mom replied . . ."

"Think of what's best for her," says Beck.

"Bingo."

Beck holds it for a minute, slurps his drink. "It's got an error."

"I know."

"Think of *whats* best for her." He holds up the note as if I haven't read it a hundred times. "She forgot the apostrophe."

"I *know*."

He looks down at it again. "Hmm."

"What now, a dangling modifier?"

He smiles, hands back the crumpled letter. "It's probably nothing."

"Well, if it's probably nothing, then it might be something. What is it?"

"Nothing."

"Well you can't just say *hmm*, and then say it's nothing. A *hmm* is something. You have to tell me."

He chews his straw in I-don't-know-what . . . knee-wobbling sensuality. "So. You just gonna go camp out at this PO Box and hope your mom stumbles in from the hospital to check her mail?"

I smile-slash-glare at him, and—bloody hell, there's my cute face again. Strangely, I'm not as frustrated as I *want* to be. What I *want* to be is Beck's straw for two minutes. I swallow my last bite of burger (hoping he doesn't notice it took all of twenty seconds to inhale), then say, "I have a plan, and it is this. Step one, get to Cleveland. Step two, figure shit out. This is my plan."

"Flawless, if I may say so."

"You may."

Walt interrupts with a colossal snore. It tapers off a little, but still, how he fell asleep in that position is beyond me.

"What's his story?" asks Beck.

I give him a brief rundown of what little I know of Walt: dead mom, likes "the shiny," New Chicago, et cetera. Honestly, I'm stalling a little, buying time to consider Beck's offer to drive us the rest of the way. It's attractive for a few reasons, the main one being—well, I've never driven on the highway. I haven't driven much at all, for that matter. With only one good eye, it makes for quite the Evel-Knievel-motocross-ass-grabbing-death-defying experience. The stuff of YouTube legends, really.

Beck clears his throat. "So there's probably something you should know."

Here we go. Without meaning to, I reposition myself in the seat. My curiosity about Beck is suffocating, and it's just—I want so badly for him to be real, to be good, to be a person of major fucking substance and despair.

He looks me directly in the eye, leans in, and says, "Uncle Phil is a perv."

At this, my brain splits into two very distinct factions: the first encourages me to gasp, to throw my hand over my mouth, to say *No, not Uncle Phil! Beck, darling, say it ain't so!*; the second sits in silence, unmoving, thoroughly disappointed.

"Total degenerate," he continues. "At the last family reunion, he told everyone his bald spot was a solar panel for his sex machine."

I sit in silence. Unmoving. Thoroughly disappointed. (The second faction appears to be winning out.)

"What?" he says, noticing my less-than-enthusiastic response. "I'm kidding. I mean, I'm not, Uncle Phil *is* a perv, but—"

"Beck." I sigh, and it's heavy, because even though I don't know anything about this guy, I'd bet all the cash in the can he's on Team Pizzazz. So what then? What's holding me back from going with my gut?

Walt's Rubik's Cube falls from his lap. I pick it up and reach to turn off the radio.

". . . and year out, the Cubs seem to get these great young prospects,

only to watch them fizzle out, or never really reach their potential."

I pull my hand back, leaving the radio on.

In my entire life, I've never once felt anything akin to a maternal instinct. On the baby fever scale, I check in from the tundra. Pretty typical for a sixteen-year-old, probably. But something about Walt has stirred me up, brought out a protective side I never knew existed. More wolfish than motherly perhaps, but still. Something. The same something that's holding me back from going with my gut. And while I don't think Beck would harm us, or even hinder us . . .

"You okay?" says Beck, watching me work things out.

I look at the Rubik's Cube in my hands and wonder when *me* became *us*. "We don't need you to get us anywhere," I say.

Beck doesn't respond, and for just a moment, I am reminded of my odyssey's opening scene—Mim of the Past, alone on an empty Greyhound, marveling at the madness of the world, listening to the rain stampede across the metal roof like a herd of buffalo. Opening scenes are funny, because you never know which elements will change over time and which will stay the same. The world was, and is, mad. The rain was, and is, pouring. Looking at Walt, and yes, even Beck, I know one of my elements has definitely changed.

I've gone from me to us.

"I'm a junior at LSU." Beck leans his head against the back of the seat. "Or—I would've been."

How old is a college junior? This is immediately followed by *Holy hell, what's wrong with me?* I suppose the first faction of my brain won't go down without a fight.

"Long story or short?" he says, closing his eyes.

"Long."

And he begins, never once raising his head, never once opening his eyes. Walt's snoring, the radio, the rain—all of it fades while Beck talks.

Three years into a poli-sci major, he realized a) he hated poli-sci and b) he hated college. After a summer course in photography (here, I choked down a gag reflex), he discovered his "true passion" (another gag). His parents, divorced, did not approve. He took what little savings he had and purchased a one-way Greyhound ticket from Baton Rouge to Burlington, Vermont. It was to be "a photography pilgrimage." (And once more.)

"My parents think I'm at school," he says. "Big state school like that, it'll be another week, probably, before anyone realizes." Lifting his head, he smiles, but his heart isn't in it. He unzips his duffel bag, pulls out the camera. We sit in silence for a few seconds while Beck takes pictures of the rain against the windshield.

"And what about the shiner?" I point to his black eye. This, being a milder version of what I'd like to ask—*how did you end up in the Independence police station, hmmmmm?*

He trains the camera on a bug trapped between the windshield and the wiper blade. "I punched a guy. Twice, actually. He got me once in between."

"Jane's Diner," I whisper.

He nods, and begins a new story. And as soon as he starts, I know exactly how it will end.

... 24 ...

The Coming Together of Ways

THE DOOR TO the men's room was locked.

Beck stood, waiting in the hallway, when a young Hispanic girl exited the ladies' room next to him. *(19A and B must be mother and daughter, a beautiful Hispanic duo . . .)* "Her eyes," said Beck, "were puffy and red, and I thought it was odd, but she was probably thirteen, and with girls that age, you just never know." Seconds later, Beck saw a grown man come out of the same ladies' room. "His eyes were strange, like glazed over or something . . ." *(I notice his eyes are wet and shiny, but it's not from crying or the rain.)* The man shrugged, pointed to the locked men's room, said, "It couldn't wait." Minutes later, Beck entered the men's room, did his business, and, while washing his hands, peered into the mirror. Behind him was a single stall. He frowned, and stepped back into the hallway. When he knocked on the ladies' room, there was no answer. He poked his head inside, gave a faint, "Hello?" Still, nothing. Confident no one was inside, Beck entered the ladies' room, letting the door close behind him. "It just felt odd, you know?" said Beck, his camera dangling from his neck. "Like—dim, or something." *(The bathroom dissolves into a reddish hue, the corners dimming like the vignette of an old art house film.)* Beck looked around, noted the single stall—*one stall.* He remembered the look on the face of the girl only minutes ago, puffy and red from crying, and he felt the blood rush from his face to his gut. *(His words are ice. They hit my gut first, then spread in all directions . . .)* Turning, Beck exited the ladies' room, walked down the hall, and into the main dining area. "I saw the girl first thing," said Beck. "She was sitting in a booth with her mom and another couple. Her mom was chitchatting across the table, but the little girl—that girl wasn't saying a word. She looked shell-shocked." *(We'd seen the footage of the hyena and the gazelle, and it always ended the same.)*

When Beck scanned the room, he found the man sitting on a barstool, eating pie, "as if nothing had happened." *("Nothing will happen," he says, his voice thick. "Nothing you don't want.")*

Beck walked calmly to the bar.

Tapped the man on the shoulder.

"AND I PUNCHED him. Twice. In front of a cop."

"What?"

Beck adjusts the focus of his camera, goes back to taking pictures while he talks. "It actually ended up turning out okay. The cop was this gung-ho idiot starved for action."

"Randy. With the huge head?"

"Yeah, you know him?"

"Sort of. No, not really. It doesn't matter, go on."

Beck raises an eyebrow and scans through the photos he just shot. He hasn't met my eyes for a while now, and I wonder if there's something he's not telling me. There are only so many angles a person can get of rain on a windshield.

"Officer Randy interrogated us," he says, "and pretty much sorted it out. I got a lifetime ban from Greyhound for fighting, and spent my last few dollars at a Red Roof Inn in Union last night. They called me in this morning for some follow-up questions, then turned me loose."

"And what about Poncho Man?"

Beck stops taking pictures, but doesn't look at me. "How'd you know he was wearing a poncho?"

I hear my mother's voice in my ear. *Tell him.* "I just—I remember him. I remember a creepy-looking guy, is all. In a poncho."

Beck takes a second before he answers my question. "He's in jail."

"They arrested him?"

"Had to. The little girl spoke up."

I look out at the rain and think back to the flashing blue lights in the parking lot of Jane's Diner. I *knew* I wasn't his first. And if I'm honest with myself, I knew I wouldn't be his last.

But I could've been.

I could have said something. I could have saved that little girl myself, made it so it never happened. But my Objective had come first. And now—because of *me*—some little girl will never be the same.

I slip on Albert's aviators and let the tears come, hard and heavy. Life can be a real son of a bitch sometimes, bringing things back around long after you've said good-bye. Not only am I selfish, I'm a coward. That little girl spoke up. She did what I couldn't do.

She did what you wouldn't *do, Mary.*

"We should go," says Walt out of nowhere.

Honestly, I'd forgotten he was even here. I look at him—he's wide-awake, smiling like a kid on Christmas morning—and fight the urge to throw my arms around his neck, just kiss his cheeks for all of eternity.

Beck looks at me quizzically, then back at Walt. "Go where, buddy?"

"To the game," Walt says, turning up the radio.

". . . and now that the rain has finally stopped, I can't imagine a more perfect day at the ballpark. So once again, if any listeners are interested, we still have seven innings of baseball to play, and I'm being told there are plenty of tickets available."

At that moment, the rain stops.

Walt looks up and points through the windshield. The entire city of Cincinnati is spread before us in a breathtaking panorama. I take in this new clearness of the day with my good eye, in absolute awe of the sudden and wonderful metamorphosis. It's a landscape worthy of documentation.

"Beck," I whisper.

"On it," he says, raising his camera, snapping away.

How strange—only minutes ago, Beck was aiming in the same direction, documenting something else altogether. The city, in all its grandeur, had been there the whole time, hidden by the storm.

Walt claps his hands, squeals, bounces in his seat. Before I have a chance to settle him down, Beck turns his camera from the Cincinnati skyline to Walt, and for just a moment, the scene eases into slow motion. Beck's smile is intense and sincere, a smile with, not a smile at. Mom used to say you could tell a lot by the way a person treats the innocent, and Walt is nothing if not innocence personified. Ricky was, too. I think about Ty Zarnstorff and all his little bully clones, united in their mutual disdain for kids who strayed from the pack. No matter that the stray was harmless, gullible, weak. No matter that Ricky eventually gave up trying to make friends and settled into a pathetic desire to be left alone. No matter that I was a friend to Ricky that one summer, then, God save me, ignored him on the playground, and in class, and in the cafeteria, and in the gym. Son of a bitch, I can't believe I did that. And my instincts are no better off now. Rather than join in the laughter, the unadulterated joy, as Beck did, my knee-jerk reaction to Walt's excitement was to calm him down. Minimize his embarrassment. Minimize my own.

I turn to look out the window, smiling my own smile, more timid than I'd like. And I cry. I cry thinking about the Rickys and Walts of the world, smiling in the face of all those Ty Zarnstorffs. I cry because I've never smiled like that, not once in my life.

I cry because I love. For some reason, I always have.

… 25 …
Our Only Color

September 3—late afternoonish

Dear Isabel,

"Your mother and I are getting divorced."

Seven words. All it took to wash away the millions that came before. I'd heard them in movies, on TV, read them in books. I'd heard them probably dozens of times in my life, yet somehow, never . . . *in my life*, you know? Mom said a few words about "taking care of herself." Dad nodded during that part. Ironically, this was the most evident display of unity I'd seen from them in years. After Mom's bit, Dad gave a little speech about doing what was right for our family, no matter how difficult, and they hadn't worked out all the specifics yet, but it didn't change how much they loved me, and blah, blah, blah. It was the kind of speech where the first line was the only one that mattered. *Your mother and I are getting divorced.* Done. Ball game. That *is* the speech.

The night they told me, I barely slept. And when I did, it

was uneasy. (This letter contains no Reasons, so if you'd like to skip it, Iz, go right ahead. Honestly, I'm not even sure who these words are for: you or me.)

In a dream, I sat on the edge of my parents' bed, alone in their room. My stomach burned. And my throat, too, like lava. I could feel my tongue forming words, and while I sensed their urgency, I couldn't hear them. Something fell from my hands, landed on the carpet with a dull thud. I looked down and noticed my bare feet—*how had they grown so old?* I wondered.

Rising from the bed, I saw those old feet sink into the carpet. I kept a close eye on them, because they weren't mine, and you just can't trust someone else's feet.

Like a rusty freighter on the Atlantic, I drifted across the room. It took hours, days, years even. By the time my hip nudged the edge of my mother's vanity, I'd come to terms with my old age. Raising my head by inches, I saw the red wood of the vanity's curved legs, the cabinets with those shiny brass handles, and resting on top, my mother's makeup tray. Normally, the tray was full of her favorite perfumes, blushes, eyeliners, and concealers. But just then, it held only one item: her lipstick. The very lipstick she'd used on my one and only makeover.

In the dream, I could feel the vanity's tall mirror looming. *I must look up*, I thought. *I've spent a lifetime, crossed an ocean to look up.*

I looked up.

I laughed, cried, laughed.

I am not me, I said to the ocean, to the old feet, to the face in the mirror. And it was true. In the dream, the reflection staring back was not my own.

It was my mother's.

I raised my chin, my eyebrows and hands. I watched the chin, eyebrows, and hands of my mother in the mirror. I opened my mouth. Her mouth opened. I winked. She winked back. I spoke, she spoke.

Mary can't possibly understand what I'm trying to say, we said.

Fine, we replied. *She'll understand this* . . .

We picked up the lipstick. Calmly, we removed the cap and drew on our face. A Ferris wheel. Fireworks. A diamond ring, a bottle, a record. As soon as we finished each one, the drawings disappeared. We drew faster, a thousand things, each one more indistinct than the last.

The final drawing was more methodical.

In the mirror, our hands and face came together to paint the sky. Left cheek first, one decisive stroke. We drew the two-sided arrow, brought it to a point at the bridge of our nose—then the line across our forehead. The third brushstroke mirrored the first: an arrow on the right cheek. We drew a thick line from forehead to chin, and finally, a dot inside both arrows.

It disappeared, so we drew it again. And again, and again, like some sad automaton, doomed to an existence of unvaried motion.

Finally, it stuck.

We dropped the lipstick to the floor, where it splashed between our old feet. Our face was old, too, all the blood drained away.

The war paint is our only color, we said.

The next morning, I woke up in a sweat.

From my bedroom, I could hear Dad down the hall, talking in low tones. I got up, and without even bothering to put on pants, crept toward my parents' bedroom. Their door was cracked open just enough to see inside. Dad sat on the edge of his bed, talking on the phone. His voice sounded tired, and even from my limited vantage point, I could see the outlines of dark rings under his eyes. I could see that he was wearing the same clothes as yesterday. He said good-bye, then hung up and sat there for a second. I pushed open the door.

"Hi, honey," he said, turning sideways. "I didn't know you were awake."

"Dad," I said simply. It was enough.

He began talking, using words that made no sense at all. "She had to leave." I stood in the door, half-naked, holding my breath, rearranging what truths I thought I knew. "It'll only be for a while, until she figures things out." His words were oblong, misshapen. They fit into none of my known boxes, so I was forced to create a new one. In red pen, it was labeled GROW UP. "She wanted to say good-bye, but this was for the best." As he talked, I stepped inside this new box, pulled the lid shut over my head, hugged my knees to my chest, screamed my guts out, surrendered myself to all the worst things from all the worst places.

"Mim? You okay?"

My box melted. "Am I *okay*?" I stared at him for a second, unable to buy . . . any of it. Across the room, I saw Mom's vanity—the tall mirror, the red wood, the curved legs. My heart sank when I saw the makeup tray. I swept across the room, careful not to look at my feet. The dream was still too close.

"Mim, put on some clothes, let's talk about this."

The makeup tray—usually full of her perfumes, blushes, eyeliners, concealers—was empty. All of it gone, save one item: the lipstick. It sat on the tray like unwanted leftovers.

"Mim," said Dad.

I grabbed the lipstick off the tray and turned for the door.

"Mim."

But I was gone.

Back in my room, I stood in front of my own rarely used mirror, recalled the war paint from my dream, and began.

And it felt good.

I do not know why.

For the next two months, we stayed in that house, during which time a number of things happened, including but not limited to (1) I found the words *ten easy steps to a ten-day divorce* left in the Google search bar of the family computer, and (2) my parents were divorced twelve days later, compelling me to wonder which of the "easy steps" my father had botched, and (3) Kathy, who had once waited on us at Denny's, started coming around the house, and (4) I received no less than one hollow-sounding letter a week from my mother, assuring me that all was well, that I would be seeing her soon, etc., etc., which led me to (5) beg Dad if I could live with Mom in Cleveland, to which he responded (6) Out of the question, to which I responded (7) What the hell is going on, to which he (8) married Kathy and moved us way the hell away from Mom, bringing us to (9) when Mom's letters stopped, her phone was disconnected, and I was left 110 percent alone in this world, an island unto myself, a sad, lost little person living in one mosquito-ridden sweat storm of an ass-backwards state.

My whole fucking world had fallen apart, Isabel, that's the long and short of it. And no matter where I turned, I got no answers. For a while, I was pissed at my mom. Honestly, I could have survived all of it, even the *BREAKING NEWS*, if I could've counted on that *one* letter—hollow-sounding or not—per week. Just one.

But I'm beginning to suspect something, and it's almost too awful for words. Among the reasons behind Dad's recent actions (and there are *many*), what if one of them—God, what if one of them is her disease?

What if Dad got rid of my mom *because* she's sick?

Signing off,
Mary Iris Malone,
An Island Unto Myself

CINCINNATI, OHIO

(249 Miles to Go)

... 26 ...

Remember the Rendezvouski!

A FLOCK OF teenage girls stands in front of us in line, each one carrying identical shopping bags. The bags depict a group of ripped, shirtless dudes on a pier. Plastered across the top in bold marquee lettering it says LIVE YOUR LIFE.

It's an odd feeling, being chagrinned by your own generation. Long ago, I traded my pie-in-the-sky idealism—as it relates to what people are like and what they are interested in—for a more realistic worldview. It all starts in middle school. Friends with interesting quirks, like double-jointed thumbs, or overactive gastrointestinal reactions to Cheez Whiz, suddenly strive to hide the very things that make them interesting. Before you know it, you're in high school, wondering if you're the only one who actually read *Brave New World*, rather than its summary on Wikipedia. Or you're sitting in the cafeteria, pondering the complexities of the latest Christopher Nolan film while the nearest table of cheerleaders discusses whatever reality TV show is popular that week, then argues over who gives the most efficient blow job. I used to remind myself that it was only high school.

Surely, the real world would be different. But I'm beginning to wonder if the whole damn planet hasn't been Wikipedia'd.

This shopping bag, with its profound LIVE YOUR LIFE, is a great example of this. Short of discouraging death, it means absolutely nothing. Some suit in some high-rise thought it sounded cool, and now it's on a bag. In my face. Making me want to not live mine.

Walt, Beck, and I stand in the ticket window line. Beck is texting someone while Walt is holding a butterfly by the wings, inspecting its undercarriage.

"Y'all need tickets?"

A stranger sidles up next to us. He's wearing an army jacket, a turtleneck, mittens, earmuffs, and a scarf. Dude is either deathly afraid of a sudden cold front or in love with winter accessories. Actually, stick a pipe in his mouth, and he could pass as a snowman.

"No thanks," says Beck, tucking his phone away.

Snowman leans in. "I got primo tickets, man. Lap of luxury. Third base side, six rows back. Just above the dugout. Absolute fucking lap of luxury."

Beck looks at the long line, then at me.

"How much?" I ask.

Snowman shrugs. "You guys seem like nice people. I'll give you four for five hundred."

"Dollars? What is this, the World Series? The Yankees aren't in town, man."

"There's a holiday weekend fireworks show," says Snowman. "After the game."

Next to me, Walt shoves the butterfly into his empty Mountain Dew bottle; he screws on the lid, and offers all of us an enthusiastic thumbs-up.

Snowman eyes Walt, turns back to Beck. "Fine. Four hundred—for three tickets."

I step in front of Beck. Time to put an end to this debacle. "I'll give you a hundred for three tickets, dude. Plus three free nights at a Holiday Inn."

Snowman and Beck are both eyeballing me now.

"Long story," I mutter. Then, to Snowman, "Look, the game's already started. It's Reds versus Cubs, and I'll bet you got a stack of tickets, which in approximately two and a half hours won't be worth a nickel."

Walt pokes a stick in the bottle, torturing the poor creature.

"Make it one twenty, little lady, and you got yourself a deal."

I kneel down and unzip my bag to get the money. Above me, I hear Snowman say, "Your little lady drives a hard bargain."

I blush the blush of all blushes, grateful they can't see my face.

Tickets in hand, the three of us make our way toward the ballpark. Walt is literally skipping with excitement, an act worth every penny I just forked over.

Beck reaches out, stops us in front of a bronzed statue. "Idea. If at any point one of us gets lost, let's agree to meet back here. At this statue, okay? Sort of like a rendezvous point."

I raise my ticket. "We have these. We could just meet at our seats."

His eyes flutter toward Walt, then back to me. "I just think this might be a little . . . easier, you know? And fun. Or something."

I think back to the one Indians game I attended, and how frenzied the crowd was afterward, everyone trying to get back to their cars to beat traffic. One look at Walt—currently jabbing his butterfly, oblivious to the world around him—and I follow Beck's lead. "You know, I think that's a great idea. Walt?"

"Hey, hey," he says, not taking his eyes off the bottle. Inside, the butterfly's wings have gone from flapping to twitching.

"Walt, look at me buddy, this is important. You see this statue?" His eyes follow my index finger to the bronze baseball player. "If you get lost or separated from us, come straight here, okay? Straight to . . ." I read the name on the plaque. "Ted . . . Kluszewski."

Beck pats Walt's back. "Kluszewski is the rendezvous, Walt. Can you remember that?"

"Yes," says Walt, going back to his butterfly. "I'll remember the rendezvouski."

I smile at Beck, a wide-eyed, *can-you-believe-the-awesomeness-that-is-Walt* sort of smile. He's wearing the same one.

"I think we'll all remember the rendezvouski."

ONCE THROUGH THE gates, we follow the signs to our section. Vendors are everywhere, selling hot dogs, beer, peanuts—one guy even has a half-dozen empty beer bottles glued to his hat. Just before we reach our aisle, Walt hands Beck his bottle-slash-butterfly coffin. "Bathroom," he says. Throwing his finger in the air, he disappears into the men's room.

Beck raises the bottle to his face, flicks the plastic to see if the butterfly is alive.

"Call it," I say, grimacing.

Beck looks at his phone. "Time of death, four fifty-two."

"Poor thing never stood a chance." I kneel down to tighten the Velcro straps on my shoes; afterward, I notice Beck admiring them. *"Très chic, non?"* I say, kicking a foot up in the air.

He nods. *"Oui. Et* . . . French-for-old."

"Vieilles. And yes, they're old. I like old things, though."

He looks at me like he wants to laugh. "You like old things?"

"Sure. Frayed, worn, stringy, faded . . . It's all just proof of a life lived well."

"Or maybe it's proof of a life, well . . . *lived*."

I smile, and for the next few moments, we people-watch. I'm about to crack a joke about how crowds wouldn't be so bad if it weren't for all the people when Beck says, "Speaking of life and living it—Mim, you see this?" He points to the same gaggle of girls I'd seen out front, the ones with the ridiculous shopping bags.

Easy, Mary. Don't scare him off.

I nod—coolly, coyly, like I just noticed.

"Live your life," he chuckles, rolling his eyes. But it's no normal eye roll. It's an iris-receding, sigh-inducing, shoulder-sagging eye roll. In the history of History, no one has rolled eyes like this, and I suddenly can't remember the name of any boy I've ever known. I'm not sure what that says about me, that I can get this turned on by an eye roll. Honestly, I don't care. In the movie of my life, I jump in Beck's arms, wrap my legs around his waist, feel the slight bitterness of his tongue against my own as we kiss and the crowd goes wild. Walt—depicted by an unknown actor in an Oscar Award–winning breakout performance—is an ordained minister. He marries us then and there, right by the men's restroom. Beck is a Phoenix brother, either River (pre–Viper Room) or Joaquin (pre-bearded insanity), and I, as discussed earlier, am indie-darling Zooey Deschanel. Or . . . fine, a young, straight Ellen Page.

"Live your life. How about, *breathe your air*?" he says.

I smile at him. "Eat your food."

"Button your pants."

"Walk your dog."

"Take your shower."

"Do your work."

Beck shakes his head. "Live your life, Mim. Whatever you do, just . . . live your life, okay?"

Walt returns from the bathroom. "I've decided something important," he says. Taking his bottle from Beck, he holds it an inch from his nose. "I'm going to name him Mr. Luke Skywalker Butterfly."

Beck and I smile at each other, and as we turn toward our aisle, neither of us says a word. We don't have the heart to tell him Mr. Luke Skywalker Butterfly has gone the way of Obi-Wan.

... 27 ...

The Many Flaws of Beck Van Buren

THE CHEERING, CLAPPING Beck Van Buren best exemplifies the contagious nature of Walt's enthusiasm. The Cubs' first batter of the inning draws a walk, but from the exuberance of my friends, you'd think they'd just won the pennant. It is, truly, a thing of beauty.

I rummage through my backpack, locate the Hills Bros. can, and do some math. I started with eight hundred eighty dollars, minus one eighty for the bus ticket, then seven dollars for haircutting shears and makeup remover. Between there and Nashville, everything was covered by the Goofball Greyhound Corp. Three bucks on carnitas, five on ice cream (at the inimitable Aces Dairy Dip Mart Stop Plus), three hundred on Uncle Phil, fifty-six on gas, nineteen at Medieval Burger, one hundred twenty on these tickets, and six on my official Reds program. I have a total of one hundred eighty-four dollars.

Damn, Malone.

Still. It's not *my* money.

"I'm gonna get a pretzel," I say.

The Cubs ground into a double play, something they do often and well. Beck and Walt throw their hands in the air as if the ump got the call wrong.

"You're getting a pretzel now?" mutters Beck, leafing through the program. "It's a long game."

"Is it, Beck? Please, enlighten me about the ins and outs of this strange game." I stand, start for the aisle.

"Here, wait. Gimme your phone."

I pull my phone out of my backpack—like it's no big thing—and hand it over.

"Old-school," he says, flipping it open. "Nice."

I reach out my hand. "If you're just gonna make fun of it . . ."

He punches a few keys, then hands it back. "There. Now you have my number. Just in case."

I smile, wondering if he can actually see my heart in my throat. "You're like a little safety patrol officer, aren't you? Rendezvous points and emergency phone numbers. Are my clothes bright enough?"

He waves a hand in my face, turns back to the game. "Your pretzel awaits."

I jog up the cement stairs, unable to hold back the smile of my young adult life. This detour has already paid for itself.

THE CONCESSION LINE is about a mile long, but I don't mind. In my experience, the amount of time a person is willing to wait in line for any given thing is a pretty good barometer for how much that person wants the thing. And right now, "about a mile" is just the distance I'm willing to wait for a salty soft pretzel.

With the top half of the inning over, the Jumbotron is airing an animated race between two boy baseballs and one girl baseball (an anatomical feat in its own right). Nearby, a woman of considerable girth is holding a couple of hot dogs and a funnel cake; she's staring at the Jumbotron, cheering mightily for the girl baseball to win. Three kids stand around her, grimy, silent, eyes fixed on the food in their mother's hands. One of the kids quietly asks for a hot dog, to which the woman lets loose a slew of curses and threats about interrupting her while she's "busy."

Around us, other people keep their heads down, check watches, read programs, anything to avoid acknowledging the uncomfortable nearness of this horrible stranger.

"Hey," I say, a slave to my impulses. The woman stops screaming, and looks at me as if I just apparated right in front of her. "You know they're animated, right?" I point to the Jumbotron. "The numbered balls, I mean. *They* can't hear you." Her kids are staring now, too, their faces dirty but cute. I point to them, look the woman dead in her eyes. "But *they* can."

Before I know it, everyone in line is clapping. The woman starts to say something, then thinks better of it. I smile wide and wave at her as she storms off. I won't pretend not to be pleased by the response of those around me, but still—this woman's ridiculous behavior is exactly why I really don't care for crowds. Sheer mathematics dictates a ten-to-one ratio in favor of crazy.

The line inches forward. I keep my head down, follow the steps of the man in front of me.

Shit.

My epiglottis flutters, bottoms out.

His shoes.

Before I can get to a bathroom, or even turn my head, I vomit all over the bottom half of the guy.

"What the hell?" he says, quietly at first. Anger of this magnitude needs time to set in. "Oh—God." He turns around wild-eyed. "What the *hell*?"

Without a word, I'm gone; down the bustling walkway, into the nearest ladies' room. The mess drips down my chin, leaving a trail behind me like Hansel's white pebbles. Running straight to the sink, I finish throwing up.

Penny loafers.

I close my eyes.

I'd like to be friends, Mim.

It does no good.

You want to be friends, don't you?

All I can see are those shoes.

The glassy eyes.

What then—for the rest of my life, any time I see a man wearing penny loafers, I should expect to vomit? Lord help me should I work in a bank one day. Plenty of people wear penny loafers, and not all of them are Grade A pervs.

The mirror—caked in dust and dirt and a thin yellow layer of bathroom grime—reflects a host of curious glances.

"Are you okay, sweetheart?" asks a woman in a flowery dress.

But I don't answer. I can't. I just stare at my reflection in the mirror and wonder how long my right eye has been closed.

"WHAT TOOK SO long?" asks Beck.

"I got . . . held up."

He eyeballs me. "I thought you were getting a pretzel?"

I lean over and put my head between my legs.

"Mim? You okay?"

"I threw up."

"Are you sick?"

"What do you think?" I snap, harsher than I mean to be.

Walt turns to me with the most concerned of looks. "You're sick, Mim?"

"No, Walt." I give him a thumbs-up. "I'm fine. Just fine and dandy."

My unenthusiastic response is rewarded with a double A-OK gesture.

Beck pulls his camera out of his bag. "Mim sure is lucky to have a friend like you, Walt. Damn lucky."

Walt nods, smiling. "Damn lucky."

A cool, post-rain breeze floats from the Ohio River, a small gesture of gratitude from what has otherwise been an unforgiving climate. Beck takes some pictures, and the Cubs, as they've done so beautifully for so many decades, go down in a glorious blaze of errors, stranded runners, and missed opportunities. In the symphony of losing, the Cubs aren't just the first chair violinist—they're the conductor, the bassoonist, the entire percussion section. And Walt, bless his heart, hasn't lost one ounce of enthusiasm. He's just wild with it, actually, cheering hard on the most mediocre of plays. The game draws to a close with the Reds winning twelve to three.

A little while later, the fireworks show starts behind the center field wall.

"Ha! Oh yeah! Ooh, look, Mim! Beck! Hey, hey, that was a good one!"

Smiling, I lean sideways toward Beck. "He's like a kid on Christmas morning, huh?" I look from the explosive sky to Beck's eyes—surprisingly, there's not much difference.

"I lied," he whispers.

Careful, Mary. There's something fragile.

"Okay."

"Ahhhhhh, Beck, look at *that* one!" Walt shouts.

Around us, the congregation of fans cheer, laugh, point, each of them gleefully oblivious to all but the fireworks. Beck and I are with them, but not *with* them. It reminds me of Thanksgivings growing up, sitting at the "kids' table." The grown-ups are right there, talking about important matters at work, upgrades around the house, goings-on in the neighborhood. What they don't realize is that none of that matters. But the kids know it. God, do they ever.

"It's not just a photography pilgrimage."

"Wowwwwwweeee!" screams Walt, jumping up and down.

Beck stares blindly at the Reds program between his feet.

"Claire," I say. "The phone call?"

He nods. "She's my foster sister. Lived with us for a year in high school before she ran away. We were close, and the way things ended . . . I just need to see her again."

I say nothing. I wait, listen as the pieces take shape.

"Kaaa—boooooooom! Hey, hey, that was a good one!"

"She's near here," continues Beck. "Just across the river. After getting kicked off the Greyhound, I was just gonna hitchhike the fifteen miles, but then I heard you guys trying to buy that truck."

"Ha! Yeah, yeah! Ooooh!" Walt sounds like he's about to have a heart attack.

"That truck," I say, "has a name."

Beck smiles, a movie star smile, a smile which my left eyeball takes a picture of and sends to my brain, which in turn, directs a lightning bolt straight to my heart, which melts on the spot.

"I called her six months ago," he says. "Arranged this trip to come see her, but . . . she keeps calling back, telling me not to come. The whole thing's been a disaster." His voice is low, at once fleeting and infinite. "I don't know what to do."

For just a moment—just this one singular moment—we're the only two people at the kids' table.

I reach up and gently nudge his face toward the sky. "I think you do, Beck. And I'll help. But right now, you're missing one hell of a show."

Together, the three of us watch the sky explode.

What I would give to see these fireworks with both eyes . . .

... 28 ...

Devou Park

September 3—late at night

Dear Isabel,

I was eight.

Dad was drinking beer, working on his motorcycle. He never rode, just worked. This was one of the many missing pieces of my father, his aptitude for the unfinished. Whatever pleasure he found in the toiling means, he rarely found in the rewarding ends.

The three of us were in the garage. Mom was trying to explain how a record player worked. (I can't remember exactly how these conversations went, because, well, I was eight. So I'm paraphrasing, but you get the gist.)

"Yes, Mom, but *how* does the music get from that needle"—I pointed my chubby little finger to the record player—"to my *heart*." My earliest memories of music had nothing to do with listening, and everything in the world to do with feeling.

"Right," said Mom, blowing the dust off *The Doors*.

"That's called the stylus. And it runs along these grooves, yeah? And then something else about vibrations or something, and an amplifier I think, and then there's another thing, and then *voilà*. Music."

Dad, who was now polishing his spic-and-span motorcycle, snorted.

"Frog in your throat, love?" said Mom, setting the vinyl on the turntable.

He mumbled something I couldn't hear, sipped his beer.

"Get me one of those, will you?" said Mom.

Dad left the garage. We sat on Mom's old College Couch and listened to Jim Morrison break on through.

"This feels weird," I said. "Like he's singing crazy."

Mom nodded. "That's because he *was* crazy. A lot of famous rock stars were."

"Like who?"

"Well, remember Jimi Hendrix, the one who played *Star Spangled Banner*?"

God, did I. (Are you familiar with this particular rendition, Iz? Inspired.)

"Yes," I said. "His guitar sounded like this man's voice. Like"—I shook my head, pondering the nebulous intricacies of rock stardom, and how to wield such wildness into words—"like . . . just . . . crazy and good and *crazy good*."

Mom laughed, and it was full of the Young Fun Now. She let her head drop back against the rough plaid of her beloved couch.

"The Jimi-man went crazy, too?" I asked.

"Yeah. Jimi-man went good and crazy."

"But why?"

"Well, different reasons, Mary. Drugs and fame and I-don't-know-what . . . I guess when too many people like you all at once, it can sometimes make you go crazy."

"What are you doing?" interrupted Dad. His voice was quiet, but I remember it startled us. He was standing in the open air, just outside the raised garage door, a beer in each hand. I could see Mom wondering how long he'd been there, carefully choosing the words that followed.

"Nothing," she said. "Just talking."

Dad didn't move. "She's eight, Evie. What the hell?"

For a second, we remained still. No one said a word. Eight or not, I usually had a pretty good handle on things, but I remember being confused. I couldn't figure what it was about our conversation that had angered him.

"I don't mind," I whispered, tucking my legs underneath my bottom, trying my best to look cute. Looking cute sometimes stopped the fights before they got bad.

Dad set the beers on the ground, then walked over to the couch and picked me up in his arms. "Not everyone goes crazy, honey."

Mom stood to get her beer. "Blimey, Barry, I didn't say *everyone* went crazy."

"You said enough."

Later in life, it would occur to me how strange it was that this obsession of my father's—that something was wrong with me, serious enough to warrant serious drugs and serious doctors and a life full of serious remedies to avoid serious madness—was driving him mad in his own way. Later in life, it would occur to me that despite his actions, my father really did want what was best for his family. As to how he would accomplish that? He had no idea. Later in life, it would occur to me that this was the ultimate dichotomy: for a person to want what's best but draw from their worst. Dad did just that. It wasn't enough to help the old woman across the street. He had to produce a fucking firearm and tell her to haul ass. His methods weren't just ineffective, they were insane. Such were the fates of good men once succumbed to the madness of the world.

Later in life, I would come to realize all these things.

But just then, as he carried me from the garage, attacking my forehead with kisses, whispering sweet comforts in my ears—as if Mom had just beaten me senseless—just then, I hated him. I hated him good and hard.

Inside the house, he plopped me down on the living room floor. "You can watch TV for as long as you want, honey."

I grabbed our giant remote off the coffee table, ran to the kitchen, and placed it in the microwave. Two minutes on high did the trick.

And those were my first fireworks.

And Mom didn't come inside for hours.

Signing off,
Mary Iris Malone,
Crazy and Good

THE ONLY THING more beautiful than bright stars on a chilly night is bright stars on a chilly night with Beck and Walt.

I stuff my journal back in my bag, turn off the interior cab light (leaving the radio on), then join them in the bed of the truck. After the game, we found a spot in this nearly abandoned park overlooking the Cincinnati skyline. Beck has been taking advantage of the view, snapping photos left and right; Walt, after spending a few minutes looking at something in his old suitcase, fell asleep on his back.

I plop down in the middle of the truck bed, pull one of Walt's extra blankets over me, and stare at the sky. The radio is crackling a song about an undertaker, which the deejay classified as a "new oldie." I have no idea what that means, but under this kind of picture-perfect panorama, the song's lo-fi, starry-skied, smoky-eyed recipe is exactly what the scene calls for.

After a slew of nighttime photos (and more than a few terrorized nocturnal critters), Beck sits next to me and leans his head against the cab window. "Do you believe in God?" he asks, his breath visible in the cool night air.

"Jeez, Beck. Just like that, huh?"

He smiles. "Willy-nilly. It's the only way."

Something about these stars made the question inevitable, I guess. Clusters of them blink and shift in the sky, taking the shape of a tall bubbly-skinned man whispering pithy truths in my ear.

"You ever see a guy with a really deformed face?" I ask. "I mean like, just grossly—"

"It was a serious question," interrupts Beck.

I sit up and round on him. "Beckett? Chill. I'm going to tell a serious story, and that's going to be my serious answer. Mmkay?"

Smiling, he nods. "Continue."

I clear my throat, summoning my best Morgan Freeman narrator voice. It's no *March of the Penguins*, but it'll do. "When I was little, maybe four years old, I went with my mom to a bank. It could have been a pharmacy or a fish market, but I remember it as a bank. I held her hand in line while she talked to someone behind us. A man stood in front of us—he wore a trench coat, and was tall. Like a giant."

"You were four," says Beck.

I shake my head. "His tallness wasn't contingent on my shortness. By any standard, this guy was tall. Anyway—God, this is weird—I remember he smelled exactly like a slice of Kraft Singles. Like milky and sweet and sticky or something."

"Gross," whispers Beck. "Also, specific."

"I remember reaching up and touching the hem of his trench coat. When he turned around . . ." A shiver runs up my spine to my cortex, raising the hairs on my forearms and navel.

"What?" says Beck, sitting up.

I touch my left cheek. "This entire side of his face was just a mound of bubbling skin. Like foamy toothpaste, or a . . . pile of zeroes, or something. It was just all bubbly. I don't know how else to describe it. I remember he smiled down at me, which just made his condition worse. Like his smile was a butter knife, cutting through all those—"

"Mim!"

"Sorry. Anyway, I tried to wrap my infantile brain around what I was seeing. I compared his bubbly face to what I knew of the world, but drew a blank. It just didn't make sense. So with the tact of a four-year-old, I pointed right at his cheek and asked what happened. He smiled even bigger and said God made him that way.

"'Did he mess up?' I asked.

"'Nope,' he said, smiling like a fool. 'He just got bored.'

"I have no idea what happened the rest of the day. Mom probably jumped in, considering the guy looked like a blistered caveman."

Chuckling, Beck slides down on his back next to me.

I lower my voice to a whisper. "Ever since then I've wondered—if that's what God makes when he's bored, I'd hate to see what he makes when he's angry."

For a second, we just lie there, enjoying the specific silence of nature. The bubbly skinned constellation is gone. Hell, it probably never existed.

"So is that a yes?" asks Beck.

I consider the original question and answer the only way I know how. "Honestly, I don't know. The prospect of there being a God scares me. Almost as much as the prospect of there not being one."

The undertaker song climaxes into a final smooth chorus and draws to a close with that mystical power so many songs attempt, yet few achieve: it leaves me wanting more.

"What about you?" I ask.

"What about me?"

"Do you believe in God?"

"Oh, definitely."

Considering my own spiritual wrestling, Beck's conviction takes me off guard. I sit up on one elbow and stare him down. "How can you be so sure?"

"Did you know, at birth, our bodies have three hundred bones? Over time, they—"

"Hey," I interrupt. "I asked you a question."

He raises an eyebrow. "Mim? Chill. I'm going to tell a story, and that's going to be my answer. *Mmkay*?"

I wave a hand in front of me. "Continue."

"So. Over time, those three hundred bones fuse together into two hundred and six. Don't even get me started on how weird this is. More than *half* of those are in the hands and feet, which are four of the smallest human features. And yet, if you add up all those bones, the entire skeleton is only responsible for fourteen percent of the total body weight."

"You're a science freak."

"Possibly. Well. It's been suggested."

God, I could eat him. "So what's your point?"

"My point is this: My heart must continue beating in order to pump a red liquid called blood through tiny tubes called veins throughout this unit called a body. All my organs, in communication with my heart, must work properly for this carbon-based life-form called Beckett Van Buren to exist on this tiny spinning sphere called Earth. So many little things have to be *just so*, it's a wonder we don't just fall down dead."

"That happens, you know."

Beck *ha-has*, then puffs a breath ring into the air. "I guess I just think life is more mysterious than death."

"How very philosophical. You should write a book."

Another *ha-ha*, and I'm suddenly aware of my own sarcastic mitigation. Possibly due to the late hour, though more likely owing to my borderline-drunken fascination with Beck, I'm acting like a freshman at prom; blasé, elbowy, incapable of original thought. In an effort to steer the conversation toward higher ground, I say what I should have said the first time. "So you believe in God because you're alive?"

"Guess I should just say that next time, huh?"

The radio is playing a new song, and it's nice, but if it ended, I would be fine. Nothing like the undertaker song. That fucking tune left me ravished.

"Where was your dad?" Beck asks.

"What?"

"In your story, at the bank or fish market, or wherever. Where was your dad?"

"He was never around back then." I pause. "Actually, I don't know why I said that. He's always been around, but even when he's around, he's not . . . *around*, you know? Not present. Or at least, not since Kathy ruined everything."

Something howls in the distance.

"What do you think?" I say. "Coyote?"

"What if you're wrong?" says Beck.

"Yeah. Probably just a wild dog or something."

"Not that. About Kathy."

"What do you mean?"

Beck shuffles, uncomfortably. "Nothing."

"Uh-uh. Out with it."

"Look, I'm sure I don't know the whole story, but you've mentioned this bitch of a stepmom more than a few times, and I don't know . . . you've never really given any good reason for not liking her."

I am Mary Iris Malone and I count to ten with the best of them. A deep breath, one through ten. My face flushes, and for once, I care nothing for Beck's eyes. "You don't know what you're talking about."

"Mim, I wasn't—"

"You don't."

Somehow, I'd imagined our first fight would be different. (Something like . . . while honeymooning in Venice, we polish off a tiramisu at some world-renowned restaurant that none of the other stupid American tourists know about. We order a second bottle of Cristal, then argue about whether to open it in the gondola on the way back to Hotel Canal Grande, or wait, and open it from the hotel's rooftop balcony. Something like that.)

The second song ends. Good riddance.

"You still good with the plan for tomorrow morning?" asks Beck. "It's not too late to back out, you know."

"Beck. I need you to say it."

"Say what?"

"Say you don't know what you're talking about."

He looks away, and I honestly don't know what's coming. He nods once, then says quietly, "I don't know what I'm talking about."

If possible, I feel even worse. For a few seconds, we lie there, not talking, just taking in the sheer distance and scope of the stars. I think about how quickly things have changed for me. But that's the personality of change, isn't it? When it's slow, it's called growth; when it's fast, it's change. And God, how things change: some things, nothings, anythings, everythings . . . all the things change.

"Beck?"

"Yes?"

"Do you know what you want?"

A second's pause. "What do you mean?"

I don't answer. He knows what I mean.

"I thought I did," he says.

"Yeah."

"I mean, I thought I did."

"Yeah."

I always figured, if love was in the cards for me, I'd find it, or capture it—never did I think I'd fall into it. Falling in love is boxes of chocolates and carnations, will-he-or-won't-he, fumbly kisses, awkward pauses, zits at inopportune times, three a.m. phone conversations. In other words, not me. But listening to Walt's snores in the bed of a pickup named Phil, I can't help but think, *of course*. This is the only way it would happen for me. Imperfect. Supremely odd. *Fast*.

A love born not of growth, but of change.

Mom's voice rings in my ear. *Are you in love with him?*

I turn my head without moving my body. With my good eye,

I take in his silhouette, and begin to feel that timeless combination of jubilation, perspiration, and indigestion.

Are you, Mary?

"So," I whisper. "A junior in college. That makes you . . . what, twenty? Twenty-one?"

"Jeez, Mim. Just like that, huh?"

Too nervous, too cold, too a-thousand-things to smile, I pull the blanket up to my chin. "Willy-nilly. The only way."

He leans up on one elbow and looks at me, and . . . God, people are wrong when they say eyes are the window to the soul. Windows don't effect change, they reveal what's inside. And if Beck's eyes aren't changing me—and I mean really stirring every ounce of Mim right down to the bottom of the barrel—then I don't know a thing.

"What difference would it make?" he asks.

He knows what difference. "Don't say that. You know what difference."

Sighing, he lies on his back again, putting one hand behind his head, the other on his chest.

"You do," I say.

His breathing slows. I see it in the rhythm of his hand rising and falling. I see it in his warm breath, plunging into the night air. I watch that breath take shape, and form two short, lovely words: "I do," he says.

... 29 ...

Architectural Apathy

"FIFTY-TWO, FIFTY-FOUR, FIFTY-SIX . . . fifty-eight."

Beck turns into the driveway of 358 Cleveland Avenue and shuts off the engine. The sun has only just risen; a dim morning mist somehow adds an extra serving of strange to this heaping pile of peculiar. I rub the back of my neck, reminding myself never to sleep in the bed of a truck again.

We're in Bellevue, just across the Ohio River. On the way through town, we passed one stop light, one gas station, a Subway, and the most rundown downtown I've ever seen. All the shop windows were either boarded up or smashed in, each storefront more dank and depressing than the last.

"Okay," says Beck. "I guess, I can just—okay—I'll just . . . I'll go on and . . ."

"You want us to go with you?" I ask.

He smiles, but for the first time, it's unnatural. "No thanks. Actually, definitely not. You guys stay in the car. I'll just—go ring the doorbell and take it from there."

"Piece of cake," I say.

Beck stares through the windshield. "Piece of cake."

"Cake?" Walt lifts his head, emerging from his Rubik's fog. I swear, as much as I love the kid, sometimes I forget he's even around.

"There's no cake, Walt."

Beck laughs harder than the situation warrants. After quieting down, we sit in silence for a minute.

"Beck?"

"Yeah?"

"You have to, you know, get out of the truck, if you wanna ring the doorbell."

Wiping sweat off his forehead, he opens the door. "Wish me luck."

"Good luck," I whisper.

"Good luck!" shouts Walt.

In keeping with my detours-have-reasons theory, I'd decided after the game that helping Beck was imperative. This is his Objective. Like Arlene's box, or like my getting to Mom.

Cleveland Avenue is Beck's Cleveland.

On the front porch, he fumbles for the doorbell, finds it, rings it, waits. Number 358 is sandwiched between 356 and 360. I suppose these townhouses are economical, but this sort of cookie-cutter design just oozes architectural apathy.

"What's Beck doing?" asks Walt.

"He's checking in on an old friend."

"How old is he?"

"No, not *old*, just—never mind. It's a she, and she's probably in her twenties."

Having never seen a Claire, it's hard to know what to expect.

Typically, I hear a name and immediately know what I'm dealing with. Walt, Beck, Carl, Arlene . . . these are good people. As opposed to Ty and Kathy and Wilson. But Claire . . . Claire is a tough one. I watch from inside the truck as my first Claire opens the door, and I have to say, it doesn't bode well for the Claires of the world. She greets Beck with a frown which I understand to mean, *this isn't an especially awful day, and this isn't my especially frowny face, but I've frowned for so long, this is the face my face now makes.* Her eye sockets are sunken and dark, and I'd bet all the cash in the can (what's left anyway) that Claire is an avid smoker.

Beck disappears inside the townhouse.

I have to do something. Anything.

"Yo, Walt."

"Yes?" he asks, cubing it up big time, just *click-click-click*ing away.

"Can you do me a favor?"

"Yes?" He shakes his head no.

"I need you to stay here while I check the tires."

"The tires?"

"Yeah, I thought I heard a noise back on the interstate. I just need to make sure they're still . . . filled with air and whatnot. Can you do that? Can you stay right here?"

He throws his head in the air and mixes up the squares. "Yes."

"Good. I'll be right back. Don't go anywhere."

I hop out of the truck and jog around the back of the end unit, number 350. Hopefully Walt stays focused on those colors. Knowing him, if he sees me, he'll follow. And if he follows, I'd have a better chance at a covert operation by riding in on a moose's neck. Lucky for me, the house's lazy design is only outmatched by its diminutive size. In no time, I'm in the backyard of 358. My only real plan had included inching open a sliding glass door, or possibly just all out breaking and entering, but luck is on my side apparently. Even though it's chilly, a window is open just next to the outdoor AC unit. Crawling around a thorny thicket, I position myself under the window and listen. Beck's voice is unmistakable.

"—don't buy it. I just don't."

"Why would I lie about this?" Frowny Claire's voice sounds as sad as she looks.

"After the shit we've been through, that's a really great question."

"Beck, like I said on the phone, I'm seriously sorry."

The click of a lighter, and then—smoke. Coming in a billow out the window, just over my head.

I knew she was smoker.

"Would you like some lemonade or something?"

"What? No." The conversation comes to a brief silence. Then, Beck's damaged voice again: "I really thought—I don't know. I mean, I know it's been a while, but I thought when I got here . . . if you could just see me . . ." More silence. Then, Beck in a whisper: "You really don't remember me?"

Another billow of smoke.

"I was in a number of homes. It was a hard time for me.

My therapist says it's normal, you know, to block out the pain." Another beat, another billow. Then, Claire's voice again, this time, quieter. "Listen, I didn't . . ."

More silence, then Beck says, "Are you okay?"

"No. I mean, yes, it's just . . ."

"What?"

"It's probably nothing, but—did I make a promise or something?"

Another beat.

"Like what?" asks Beck.

"Nothing. I'm sure it's nothing. Would you like some lemonade?"

Beck sighs. "I gotta go."

Hunched over, I backtrack around the townhouses, scurry over to the truck, and start kicking the tires just as the front door opens. As Beck crosses the lawn, I stick my hands in my pockets like I've been here the whole time.

"What're you doing, Mim?" His voice is shaky.

"Just making sure the craft is seaworthy." I clear my throat and throw on my most casual, super-optimistic, non-spy smile. "So how'd it go?"

"Fine," he lies, opening the driver's door. "Let's get out of here."

Back in the truck, Walt clicks the last green square into place. "Are the tires still filled with air and whatnot, Mim?"

"Sure, Walt."

"Hey, hey, I'm Walt."

"Damn straight," whispers Beck, pulling out of the driveway.

We make our way back through downtown Bellevue in silence. I can only guess what's going through Beck's mind right now. He came all this way only to be offered lemonade—twice—by a frowny-ass-chain-smoking amnesiac. That's a shit hand right there.

In front of a boarded-up ice-cream parlor, a little boy stands alone, crying his eyes out. I can't help but think that's about the only thing a little kid can do these days. I can't help but think that's the only thing that even makes any damn sense.

… 30 …

Kung Pao Mondays

WITHOUT POMP, WITHOUT circumstance, I wipe off the war paint. There are no balloons, confetti, or plastic-wrapped roses. Even so, staring at myself in yet another grimy mirror, there is a sense of I-don't-know-what . . . nostalgia, I suppose, whirring in my heart. I've never been much of a runner, but with Cleveland mere hours away, this sure feels like the homestretch.

In all likelihood, that was my magnum opus.

Like most everything else in this restaurant, the bathroom door is constructed entirely of bamboo: the faded Berber carpet is its soil, the flowery wallpaper is its oxygen, and—behold!—the perennial evergreens of exotic Southeast Asia sprout forth like so many common weeds right here in ho-hum Northeast Ohio.

Basically, I hike back to our table through the Asian outback.

"Are you blushing?" asks Beck, gnawing on a piece of red chicken on a stick.

Damn. Even with the makeup remover, the lipstick leaves a reddish afterglow. "No," I say. But yeah, I probably am. And if I wasn't before, I am now. "Where's my duck?"

Beck chuckles. "You know you sound ridiculous, right?"

Walt, without looking up from his plate, cracks up.

I slide into the bamboo booth. "If I want duck, I'm getting duck. Anyway, I'm not the one who suggested Chinese before eleven a.m."

"You don't like Chinese food?" says Walt. Having consumed his own red chicken, he's now using the stick to stab a green bean.

"Love the food, Walt. Hate the restaurants. Well. All but one."

Beck and Walt both ordered the buffet and have now moved on to sweet and sour chicken. You gotta hand it to the Chinese; they've really perfected chicken varietals.

"Which one?" says Beck.

"What?"

"You said you only eat at *one* Chinese restaurant. Which one?"

"What difference does it make? They aren't all the same. Most are like—" I point to the buffet in the middle of the restaurant, where a line of wild-eyed, overweight white men are jockeying for position.

Beck munches a piece of broccoli. "You're quite mad, you know."

"Pardon me for preferring my food unsullied."

"Unsullied?" says Walt.

"Fresh. Untouched by gross, deformed strangers who pay five ninety-five a pop and eat enough in one sitting to last a week. A buffet is just—it's not food, see. It's a *feeding*."

"I like feedings," says Walt, just as my duck arrives. After finishing the last bite on his plate, he gets up and heads back to the buffet.

Beck watches him go, sips his water, and frowns. "I wish we could do something for him."

I take a bite. It's tough for duck, but all things considered, I don't regret my order. "What do you mean?"

"I mean—the kid is homeless. What's his endgame?"

To say I haven't considered this would only be a half-truth. I've considered Walt's endgame, just as I've considered Beck's and my own. But until now, I've only let myself consider the fantasy. In the movie of my life, Beck and Walt and I form our own weird little family, where love and honesty trump all. We take Uncle Phil and drive coast to coast, picking up odd jobs where we can find them, flipping a burger here, mowing a lawn there. We stay in remote mountainside villages, and at night, we drink in pubs, rubbing elbows with innkeepers and artisans, local farmers and woodsmen, simple folk, folk of value, the kind of folk you read about in tales. Folk. Not people. Fucking *folk*. And if, in time, Beck falls madly in love with me, so be it. That won't change anything (save the sleeping arrangements). Our love for each other would only increase our love for Walt. Under our roof, he would have fresh Mountain Dew aplenty. Under our roof, he would never miss a Cubs game. Under our roof, we would laugh and love and live our mother-effing lives. Under our roof . . .

The realities, I've spent far less time considering.

"I wonder if I could get him to Chicago," says Beck.

I stop mid-bite. "Really?"

"What do you suggest? We just drop him back off in the woods?"

I swallow the bite, suddenly tasteless. "I'm not suggesting that. God, that's—why would you even think I'd suggest that?"

Beck runs a hand through his hair. "Listen. Ultimately, you're trying to . . . I don't know . . . figure out home, right? What about *his* home?"

I say nothing.

"Mim?"

Walt rejoins the table, his plate piled high. "Hey, hey," he says, tucking in.

I feel Beck watching me. "Mim," he whispers.

"I'm not hungry," I say, pushing my plate away.

Minutes later, the waitress comes by with the check. It's on a little tray with a handful of fortune cookies.

Suddenly, I can't breathe.

I pull a twenty and a ten out of Kathy's ever-dwindling coffee can, toss the money on the table, and slide out of the booth, pulling my bag behind me.

"Mim, wait," says Beck.

I don't answer. I can't. All I can do is put one foot in front of the other, faster now, head down, trying not to faint, trying not to cry, trying not to vomit, just trying to breathe—God, just to breathe.

September 4—late morning

Dear Isabel,

Some Reasons come up and bite you in the ass when you're least expecting it. This one is odd, because while I can't quite trace *how* it's a Reason, I know it is. It's like that tiny middle piece of a puzzle, the one you know is important, if only you could find the corners first. I don't know if that makes any sense, but this Reason feels like that tiny middle piece.

Reason #8 is the tradition of Kung Pao Mondays.

Before the divorce, the move, the shit and the fan, Monday was my favorite day of the week. Mom and I would hop in her beat-up Malibu, crank Elvis, and roll down to Evergreen Asian Diner, proud purveyors of the best Kung Pao chicken this side of the Great Wall.

One Monday, Mom told me about the time she hitch-hiked from Glasgow to Dover and almost fell into the river Thames. I listened like a sponge, pretending not to have heard this one before, just happy to soak in the magic of Mondays. She finished the story, and together, we laughed the bamboo shoots off the roof. (In the history of History, no one has laughed like my mother, so fiery and thoroughly youthful.)

She cracked a fortune cookie against the side of our table like an egg, then unrolled the tiny vanilla-scented paper. I waited patiently for the celestial kitsch: the *doors to freedom* and the *dearest wishes* and the *true loves revealed by moonlight.* But her fortune wasn't nearly as fortuitous as all that.

Just then, staring at the paper, Mom did three things.

First, she stopped laughing. It was tragic, really, to watch it evaporate like that.

Second, she sipped her beer and held the fortune across the table. "Read it, Mim," she whispered. She never called me by my nickname. From her lips, it sounded strange and guttural, like a foreigner mispronouncing some simple word. I looked at her fortune, flipped it over, flipped it again. There was nothing written on it. No words of wisdom or dire predictions, just . . . nothing. A blank strip of paper.

The third thing she did was cry.

Signing off,

Mary Iris Malone,

Darling of Celestial Kitsch

... 31 ...

Liquid Good-byes

I SHUT MY journal with a *pop* and climb down off the hood of the truck. Across the parking lot, Beck and Walt exit the restaurant, and immediately, I can tell something is off. Beck has his arm around Walt, who appears to be walking gingerly.

"What happened?" I ask as they approach the truck.

Beck opens the door, helps Walt get inside. "Midway through his last plate, he just stopped. Said he was all wrong."

"I'm all wrong!" groans Walt from inside the truck.

"See?" says Beck.

I climb in on the passenger side while Beck hops behind the wheel. "What's wrong, buddy?"

"My head, my stomach, all of me. I'm all wrong."

Up close, his face is pale and clammy. I put my hand on his forehead for a few seconds. "Shit. He's burning up."

"Okay, well . . ." Beck pulls out his phone.

"What're you doing?"

"Looking for the nearest hospital." A few seconds later, he says, "We're in a town called Sunbury. Looks like there's a neighborhood clinic just down the road, except . . ."

"What?"

"It's closed. For—"

"Don't even say it."

"—Labor Day weekend."

I swipe my bangs out of my eyes. "So what, then, people are supposed to hold off on getting sick until after the holiday weekend?" Between us, Walt is moaning, rocking back and forth in his seat. "Well, we have to do something. That fucking buffet probably gave him food poisoning. He probably needs a stomach pump from all that red chicken."

"The feeding!" moans Walt.

"I think I found a place," says Beck, staring at his cell.

"Well, *let's go, man*."

Beck stuffs his phone in his jacket and revs up the engine. Walt's moaning has reached new heights, and suddenly, I realize I don't know the kid's last name. *How do I not know that? What kind of friend am I?* A hospital means paperwork, and paperwork means knowing last names. If this is something serious, we're in trouble.

A few minutes later, Beck pulls into the parking lot of a strip mall.

"Where's the hospital?" I ask.

He turns off the ignition and points through the windshield.

SUNBURY VETERINARY
Animal Care Center
(Open Holidays)

"Animal care center?"

"Come on, buddy," says Beck, ushering Walt out of the truck.

"Animal care center?" I reread the sign, just in case I got it wrong the first time. Nope. Spot-on. "Beck, you can't seriously be—"

Beck slams the door. I watch through the windshield as he throws Walt's arm over his shoulder and helps him inside the clinic. (Correction: *animal care center.* For animals.) Shaking my head, I drop down out of the truck and join them inside.

The front room reminds me of the principal's office at my school: minimal decor of maroons and browns, cheesy posters, dusty leather chairs, prehistoric magazines.

A youngish girl appears from a back room, and like that, this idea goes from bad to bullshit. Her dark hair is tied back in a bun; she's wearing a surgical uniform, which appears to have once been blue. But no longer. From head to toe, this girl is covered in blood. Liters of it.

"Hello," she says, like it's nothing, like we're locker partners, like she didn't just take a blood shower and then come out here all, *hello.*

"Umm," Beck starts. He looks to me for help. *As if.* "Right," he continues. "Well. Our friend here is sick. We think. I mean, he is, clearly. Look at him."

The vet—who I choose to believe is in the middle of surgery, and not some ritualistic sacrifice with a host of bloodthirsty minions from the bowels of hell—shifts her focus to Walt. I watch her eyes as the situation dawns on her. *Yes,* I want to say. *We come bearing humans. Please don't Sweeney-Todd us.* The looks on our faces must be obvious—she gazes down at her clothes. "Oh, I'm sorry," she laughs. "You guys have a seat. Lemme get cleaned up, I'll be right back."

The two of us ease Walt into a chair. He's still moaning, but to his credit, he's dialed it down a few notches since the truck. I sit next to Beck and stare him down.

"I saw it on an episode of *Seinfeld*," he says, avoiding eye contact.

I say nothing.

He shrugs. "Forget it, you're probably too young."

"For what, reruns? I've seen *Seinfeld*, man."

"Well, did you ever see the episode where Kramer found a dog who had a cough that sounded exactly like his?"

I tilt my head, hold back a smile, and for a second, we just look at each other. "So—I think my best course of action here is to just, you know, let the ridiculousness of that sentence marinate."

Now Beck is holding back a smile. "Ditto."

Together, we hold back smiles, marinating in the ridiculousness of our sentences.

I cross my arms. "Anyway, I'm still mad at you."

"For what?"

"*For what*?" I mimic.

A few minutes later, the vet returns, and if I was scared of her before, I'm terrified now. Her hair is down, a beautiful mocha with just the perfect amount of wave. She's turned in her surgical garb for a purple fitted blouse, with a giant bow at the neck, a black pleated skirt—not too short, but short enough—

and a pair of Tory Burch flats. Her face, free of animal blood, has that natural sort of put-togetherness only another female can see through. The outfit is complete with a dazzling smile—in Beck's direction.

"Sorry about before," she says, circling the desk. "I was doing an emergency splenectomy on a seven-year-old lab after a tumor, possibly caused by hemangiosarcoma, ruptured the spleen. Poor thing had a distended belly, pale gums, the works. Anyway, the spleen had to go, *obviously*, and sometimes, you pull that sucker out, and"—she puts her fists together, then explodes them, complete with sound effects—"blood . . . *everywhere*."

I look at Beck and remind myself to work out some secret signal for future predicaments such as this, something that means *get me the hell outta here.*

Beck stands up, reading my mind. "Well, we don't wanna interrupt or anything. Sounds like you got your hands full."

"Oh, the dog died," says the vet, tossing her hair over her shoulder. "You're golden. I'm Dr. Clark, by the way. Or just . . . Michelle, if you want."

For a beat, no one says anything. Walt's voice comes quietly, surprising us all. "Your dog died?"

Somehow, the kid is able defuse even the strangest of situations with nothing but blind innocence.

"Michelle," Beck cuts in, "this is Walt. We think he has food poisoning, or something, and the . . . people clinic is closed for Labor Day weekend."

Walt, still slightly hunched in his chair, seems frozen in this girl's presence. "You're really, really pretty," he says. He points to her shoes. "Shiny shoes." He points to her face. "Shiny teeth." He lowers his hand, nods. "I like your shininess."

Dr. Clark tilts her head, smiles, and—*curses*, even her smile is solid. Kneeling down on one knee, she puts an arm on Walt's shoulder. "That's so sweet of you, honey. I'm sorry to hear you're not feeling well. What hurts?"

Walt touches his head. "I'm not all wrong anymore, but my head is. My head hurts."

Dr. Clark looks up at Beck, as if I'm not sitting right next to her. "Vomit or diarrhea or both?" she asks.

"Umm, neither," he answers.

"Really?" She takes his pulse, then stands and helps Walt out of his seat. "Come on, honey. We'll be right back, guys. Make yourselves at home."

"You smell shiny, too," says Walt, disappearing with Dr. Clark into the back.

Beck falls into the chair next to me, leans his head back, and closes his eyes. "I'm exhausted."

"Sleeping in trucks will do that."

"Mim, I don't know what I said to upset you, but I'm sorry."

Just hearing him say it out loud makes me cringe. He's only looking out for us, which is nothing to apologize for. I think about his words at the restaurant, about how I'm trying to figure out home. And he's right, I am. But it's not just that. All my life, I've been searching for my people, and all my life, I've come up empty. At some point, and I don't know when, I accepted isolation. I curled into a ball and settled for a life of observations and theories, which really isn't a life at all. But if moments of connection with another human being are so patently rare, how is it I've connected so quickly, so deeply with Beck and Walt? How is it possible I've forged deeper relationships with them in two or three days than I ever did with anyone else in sixteen years prior? You spend your life roaming the hillsides, scouring the four corners of the earth, searching desperately for just one person to fucking *get* you. And I'm thinking, if you can find that, you've found home. Beck's words at the restaurant cut deep because . . . "I don't know how to say good-bye to you."

He opens his eyes, his head still resting on the back of the chair. "I know."

It's quiet for a moment while I try to shape these impossible words. "Maybe it doesn't have to be, like, a *solid* good-bye, you know?"

"As opposed to a liquid one?"

"Yes, actually. I much prefer liquid good-byes to solid ones."

Beck smiles, yawns, stretches. "So—I think my best course of action here is to just, you know, let the ridiculousness of that sentence marinate."

God, I could eat him. "Ditto," I say.

Closing his eyes again, Beck repositions his head on the back of his seat, and in one sure movement, reaches over and grabs my hand. Even with his eyes closed, he knew where to find me. I want to cry for a thousand reasons, laugh for a thousand others; this is my anomalous balance, the place where Beck and I can let the ridiculousness of our collective sentences marinate, and other things, too. It's a singular moment of clarity between two people, and rare or not, I'm not about to let go.

I'm done roaming hillsides.

I've scoured the corners of the earth.

And I've found my people.

God, I'm almost jealous of myself.

Holding Beck's hand in my lap, I find a courage I never knew I had and drop my head on his shoulder.

"HEY, HEY!"

I wake in a daze. Walt is standing over us, and while he doesn't look completely like himself, there's a little more color in his face. Beck lets go of my hand, sits up straight, and rubs his eyes.

"How long have we been out?" he asks.

"About ten minutes," says Dr. Clark. She's sitting behind the front desk, typing at the computer, and I may be mistaken, but she sounds a little less *Michelle* and a little more *Dr. Clark*. "I hated waking you up at all, you both looked so . . . *cozy*."

What I'm thinking: *Victory! Your giant bow, perfect hair, tiny skirt, and expensive-ass shoes are no match for the wiles, the skillz of Mim Malone, Mistress of Moxie, War-Crazed Cherokee Chieftess, Conqueror of Voodoo Vets the world over!*

What I say: "So what's the verdict, doc? We need to remove Walt's spleen?"

Dr. Clark, completely ignoring my (hilarious) joke, pulls a piece of paper from the printer and rounds the desk. She hands the paper and a box of pills to Beck.

"What's this?"

"Aspirin," she says. "May I ask—you didn't happen to eat at Ming's Buffet, did you?"

It's quiet for a second—this time, I'm the one who breaks the silence. "I fucking *told* you."

Dr. Clark smiles, but it's not sweet. "Your friend here didn't get food poisoning. He had an adverse reaction to MSG. My sister got the same thing at Ming's. You get a hankering for Chinese, you're better off driving into the city."

"We ate the same things," says Beck, eyeing the bill.

"MSG affects different people differently." Dr. Clark pats Walt on the back. "The good news is, he really just needs sleep and hydration, and he'll be good as new. In the meantime, the pills will help with the headache."

Frowning, Beck passes the bill to me. "I'm sorry," I say, reading it over. "You're charging us two hundred dollars? For aspirin?"

Dr. Clark bats her eyelashes. "A diagnosis isn't cheap."

Diagnosis. Right.

Beck and I look at each other. "I don't have it," he says.

"Me neither."

"I have a pouch," says Walt. "My father-money."

I'd completely forgotten. We've been lugging his suitcase around, and not once did I consider what was inside. He'd yet to change clothes. In fact, the only time I'd seen him open the thing was last night in the back of Uncle Phil.

"Walt," I say, glancing at Beck for some reassurance. "Are you sure?"

Walt nods, looking at Dr. Clark like he'd agree to jump

off a cliff should she give the word. I hate taking his money, although . . . it is for *his* illness.

I stand, make my way for the exit. "I'll be right back."

Outside, the sun is at its highest, radiating against the asphalt of the parking lot. I unzip my hoodie, hop in the bed of the truck, and kneel in front of Walt's suitcase. The silver hinges on either side are hot to the touch; working quickly, I snap them sideways and open the top. There's not much inside. A few ratty shirts, a couple of blankets, a Ziploc full of tinfoil, paper clips, and other shiny junk, two canned hams, the Reds program, his Rubik's Cube, of course—I smile when I see the cutoffs. Underneath the torn denim, I find a bulky leather pouch. Sticking the pouch in the pocket of my hoodie, I'm about to shut the suitcase when something under the blankets catches my good eye. It's shiny, of course. *Probably a hubcap,* I think. Pulling back the layers of fabric, I find a frame, brass and wood.

Inside the frame is a photograph. Walt is smiling his signature smile, wearing his signature Cubs cap, tilted back, like someone just flicked the bill. Behind him, a woman, probably mid-thirties, has both arms wrapped around his shoulders. She's planting a kiss right on his cheek. The two of them are standing in front of Wrigley Field, on what appears to be a glorious sunny day. This is, without a doubt, the happiest-looking photograph I've ever seen. As the knot rises in my throat, I carefully replace the photo beneath the blankets, click the suitcase shut, and walk back to the office.

Beck is right.

... 32 ...

The Homestretch

"YOU'RE LYING," SAYS Beck.

I shake my head and smile, though it's the first time I've ever found it funny. "Before they got married, her name was Kathy Sherone. I still have her old name tag from Denny's, if you don't believe me."

The rain is back, though not quite as brutal as it was in Cincinnati. Through the barrage, I make out a sign along the side of 71 north:

ASHLAND/WOOSTER—58 MILES
CLEVELAND—118 MILES

"But why hyphenate?" asks Beck.

"The woman is beyond logical comprehension."

Beck keeps his eyes on the road, shakes his head. "Kathy Sherone-Malone."

"Sherone fucking Malone," I whisper.

Between us, Walt has his suitcase in his lap, his head on his suitcase, his hat on his head. After leaving Sunbury Veterinary, he fell asleep almost instantaneously, though whether from the problem (five heaping plates of MSG), or the solution (four extra-strength aspirin), I'm not sure. Probably some combination of both.

I haven't told Beck about the photograph of Walt and his mother. I can barely think of it myself.

I stare at my shoes.

A far cry from Tory Burch.

"So," I say. "You get her digits?"

"Did I get whose whats?"

"*Michelle*. You get her digits?"

Beck sort of smiles, but not really. "No, Mim. I did not . . . *get her digits*."

I slip on Albert's aviators. It may be overcast, but sometimes it's nice, feeling like someone else. "Bush-league, Van Buren. Just think of the missed opportunities."

"Such as?"

"Well, for starters, unlimited dog spleens. Relationship pays for itself right there. Sexy bloodbaths, diagnostic dirty talk . . . She probably needs help tying those giant bows on her shirts."

"I am a dynamite bow-tier."

"Right? Plus, she's a walking malpractice suit."

"And that's a good thing?"

"For you, it could be. By her side at trial, the good husband—"

"Husband?"

"Boyfriend, whatever. Play your cards right, you might even get your own reality show."

"Damn," says Beck. "You're right. Should've gotten those digits."

"Well, it's not too late, man. Unless . . . you didn't give her a *solid* good-bye, did you? If ever there was a time for a liquid good-bye, it was with Doctor"—I toss my hair aside, as if it were three times as long—"*Michelle. Clark.*"

He sucks in, raises his eyebrows, nods slowly.

"Bush-league, Van Buren. Bush-league."

I've never been more pleased with the outcome of a conversation, nor have I been more confident in my ability to rule the mother-effing world.

Our discussion hasn't deterred Walt's sleep. If anything, his snores are louder than ever.

Beck smiles down at him. "We totally just took Walt to the vet."

"Yeaaaah, to be fair, he is kind of our pet, though."

We laugh because we love, and for the next half hour, I discover all sorts of little nuggets about Beck: he likes the smell of books more than babies; he thinks Bill Pullman sucks, but Bill Paxton is great; he likes roasted red peppers on everything *except* pizza; he hates the Rolling Stones, casseroles, and lakes; he loves the Beatles, Thai food, and oceans. And he's a great driver. In fact, his focus might rank up there with the likes of Carl L. Jackson, which is really saying something.

The conversation comes to a lull. I leaf through the Reds program, shifting my thoughts from the fantasies to the difficult realities. Walt's photograph is burned in my mind, and while I know Beck is right (we *have* to help him), I have no idea how.

"She *was* kind of sexy," mumbles Beck.

Every ounce of blood in my body races to my face. "Who?"

"Michelle."

I flip a page. "Yep."

I feel him glance at me, but don't say anything. I flip another page.

"You don't think so?" he says.

"Sure." I flip another page, wait a beat. "Probably closer in age."

Between the rain and the snores, it's not quiet, but it suddenly feels that way. It's heavy, uncomfortable, both of us buried under the weight of words. I toss the Reds program on the dashboard. "So. Out with it."

"Out with . . ."

"What did Claire promise you?"

I'm not sure who is surprised more by this question, Beck or me. After quite the internal debate this afternoon, I'd decided not to ask. But somebody had to say something just now, or we were likely to suffocate.

"I knew you were out there." Beck stares into the savage rain, slowly shaking his head. "I saw that open window, and I just knew."

"Yeah, yeah, you're brilliant and know everything. So what did she promise you?"

"Nothing," he whispers, his voice cracking. "I made a promise to her, though."

I don't say a word. I don't need to. Just like Mom taught me—tip the barrel; let the apples do the rest.

"About a year after Claire moved in, we got notice that her father had been released from prison. She was beyond happy. Started talking differently. Like, if we all went out to eat, she'd say, 'I'll sure miss this place.' Or we'd go to a movie, and if it was good, she'd say, 'I'm definitely bringing Dad to this one.' Everything revolved around her moving back in with her dad. So a few days go by, and we don't hear anything. Then weeks, then a month . . . nothing. Claire was living out of her suitcase at this point—wanted to be ready at a moment's notice. Then one morning, there was a spread in the local section of the newspaper. Her dad had been stabbed to death in a drug deal."

"Shit."

"Claire shut herself in the upstairs bathroom. We could hear her sobbing all through the house. I kicked down the door, found her in the tub. She'd slit her wrists."

"Shit, Beck."

"It didn't take, obviously. But things were different after that. She ran off. Then, like three months later, my parents split up."

From behind the safety of my sunglasses, I stare into the rain with my good eye and try to put myself in Beck's shoes. He'd wasted years on a regret that, when confronted, hadn't wasted one second on him. I picture Frowny Claire, sitting alone in that apathetic townhouse—cigarette, therapy, lemonade, rinse, repeat . . . If her habit is king, it's tyrannical.

"You ever have the feeling you lost something important, only to discover it was never there to begin with?" asks Beck.

I don't answer; it's not that kind of question.

"Before Claire ran away," he continues, "while she was still in the hospital, I looked her right in the eye and promised I'd always be there for her. But I wasn't. And now she doesn't even remember me."

I recognize this tone. *What if . . . what if . . . what if . . .* I play the *What If?* game all the time. But it's rigged, is the thing. Impossible to win. Asking *What If?* can only lead to *Maybe Things Could Have Been Different,* via *Was It My Fault?*

On February fifteenth, Dad and I went to a movie. I remember the exact date because the theater was running a post–Valentine's Day two-for-one special. After the movie, Dad insisted on a late-night breakfast. He knew I couldn't say no. (Breakfast is a primary strand in the Malone gene, and like it or not, you put bacon and eggs in front of me, I'm as Malone as they come.) He suggested Friendly's. I sighed, ever the tragic teenager, and said I preferred Denny's.

Denny's it was.

Our waitress was a struggling romance novelist; a chatty, happy-go-lucky gal, new to the food service industry. Dad ordered a Grand Slam (the metaphor of metaphors) and had three refills of coffee. As Dad rarely drank coffee at night, I found this odd, but said nothing. We ate, left, and that was that.

Only later, after all the pieces fell into place, did I begin playing the *What If?* game. What if I hadn't mentioned Denny's? Was it all my fault he met Kathy? Maybe things could have been different . . .

Checkmate.

House wins.

Every. Single. Time.

Beck drives, navigating the treacherous roads of *What If?* while I search for the right words to a thing that has none. The wiper blades, the rain, the snoring—I'm still in this I-don't-know-what . . . orchestra, I suppose. This cacophony of travel. And even though things are heavy right now, it occurs to me how happy I am just to be with my friends. Sure, I'd love to kiss-hug-marry-hold Beck, but for now, I'm happy just to be with him. Sometimes *being with* gets overlooked I think.

And there they are.

The right words.

"You showed up on her front doorstep, Beck."

He starts crying. I turn my head and watch the wild rain with my good eye. "You showed up. And that's really something."

ASHLAND, OHIO

(61 Miles to Go)

... 33 ...

Peach Gummies

September 4—evening

Dear Isabel,

I'll be honest with you, Iz, there are times when I would give just about anything to be dumb. I'm not saying I'm a genius or anything, and I know it sounds weird, but sometimes I think of how wonderful it must be to be an idiot. I could sit around all day and eat cheesy snacks and get fat while watching soap operas or Japanese sporting events in the middle of the afternoon. God, that just sounds fantastic sometimes. The best part about being dumb, I would imagine, is that you just *wouldn't care*. I could do all those things now, sure, but at the end of the day, I'd feel like a dog for not getting anything done.

(I suppose I've strayed from Reasons, haven't I? Oh well. Sometimes you gotta go with a thing.)

I met my first Claire this morning, and as a general rule I'm officially warning you to stay away from the lot of them.

Rotten, through and through. This particular Claire may not be overweight, but I'll bet she can absolutely slay some cheese puffs.

I swear, the older I get, the more I value bad examples over good ones. It's a good thing, too, because most people are egotistical, neurotic, self-absorbed peons, insistent on wearing near-sighted glasses in a far-sighted world. And it's this exact sort of myopic ignorance that has led to my groundbreaking new theory. I call it Mim's Theorem of Monkey See Monkey Don't, and what it boils down to is this: it is my belief that there are some people whose sole purpose of existence is to show the rest of us how *not* to act.

Signing off,
Mary Iris Malone,
Aspiring Idiot

THIS GAS STATION is the worst. Beck is pumping diesel, but from the way that hussy is staring, you'd think he was stripping right in front of her.

"I like your stick figure book."

"What?"

Walt points to my journal. "Your stick figure book. Coooool."

The anemic stick figure, with its ridiculous flat feet, stares up at us from my lap. The journal itself hasn't really held up too well, though it was pretty cheap to begin with. I suppose a Moleskine would have been too much to ask.

"Walt, how you feeling?"

"I'm not all wrong anymore, Mim. I'm all right."

I'd wondered about this, his talk of being all wrong. Suddenly, it makes all the sense in the world. If someone isn't all right, logically, it would follow that they're all wrong. I make a mental note to tell Beck about this killer new Walt-ism.

"You up for a Mountain Dew?"

He drops his unfinished Rubik's Cube onto the floor and smiles at me.

"Yeah, I figured. Wait here, I'll be right back."

"Okay. I'll wait here, you be right back. With Mountain Dews."

I climb out of the truck and stare scimitars at the hoochie mama pumping gas in front of us. "Beck, you want anything? I'm getting *dos* Mountain Dews."

"Make it *tres*," he says, replacing the gas cap.

Once inside, I can't help but think how much I hate greasy, smelly, damp, inexplicably dirty, undeniably horrible places, which is the same thing as saying I hate gas stations. I've never been inside a maximum-security prison, but I imagine it's probably just one big gas station behind bars. God, I'm sick of gas stations.

A hefty cashier spits tobacco into a cup, which makes me wonder about Albert and Ahab, which makes me miss Arlene. (A true dame from the old school, may she rest in peace.) Three Mountain Dews and a pack of peach gummies later, I'm standing at the checkout. "This," I say, plopping down the sodas and candy, "plus whatever we owe on the blue pickup."

"You're supposed to prepay. I could have you arrested."

"Wouldn't be the first time this week."

Hefty Cashier chuckles, punches numbers into an antique register. "That'll be eighty-three dollars and seventy-four cents."

"*What?* Okay, how much without the gummies?"

Under the heavy weight of Hefty's eyes, I pull out the last of Kathy's cash. "See you 'round, Guy."

"Not if I see you first, little lady."

I turn around and give him a professional thumbs-up with my right hand, and a decent A-OK gesture with my left, which is pretty difficult what with me doing three Dews and a bag of peach gummies, but I manage. I'm almost out the door when I pass a newspaper stand that about makes my heart stop.

Strike that.

The newspaper stand surgically removes my heart from my body, then stomps on it like it's an empty soup can.

"You okay, hon?" asks Hefty Cashier.

I nod, but no, I'm not. I am Mary Iris Malone, and I am not okay. I am shocked.

A flyer, just next to the newspaper, just by the door, just at eye level, just right in my face . . .

I always hated that picture.

Always.

"Are you going to comb your hair, Mim?" I pull my long hair around one shoulder, then swallow a bite of waffle. *"Dad. I combed it."* He stands by the toaster, waiting for his own Eggo. Long ago, we'd turned in our waffle maker for the frozen food aisle. *"Really? It looks like you just rolled out of bed. Did you blow-*

dry it?" Mom walks in the room, wearing those ratty slippers, giant bags under both eyes. I pretend not to notice. *"Mom, please explain to Dad the repercussions of me blow-drying my hair."* Mom says nothing, goes straight for the coffeepot. I look back at Dad. *"They're unfathomable, Dad. The repercussions cannot be fathomed."* At first, Dad doesn't answer. Mom's presence seems to have thrown him. I look from one to the other, wondering how many nights they can keep it up. Mom waits on the coffee. Dad turns, stomps out of the room. The second he leaves, his waffles pop up. *"Mom,"* I whisper. She looks down, opens her mouth, then whispers, *"Not now, Mary."* Dad storms back into the room and tosses a green turtleneck at me. *"What is this?"* I ask. He pulls his waffles out of the toaster. *"It's school-picture day, Mim. You have to dress to impress."* I hold up the turtleneck, a Christmas present from last year, which I'd promptly buried in my dresser. *"What does that even mean?"* He takes a bite, looks to Mom for help, finds none. *"You have to dress for who you want to be, Mim, not who you are."* I take a bite of Eggo, talk with my mouth full. *"Well, I* don't *want to be the keynote at an Amway convention. And I'm not blow-drying my fucking hair."* Mom stumbles out of the room. Dad chews his waffle, watches her leave. He turns to the cabinet and pulls out my bottle of Abilitol. *"We've tried things your way,"* he says, setting the bottle in front of me with a resounding thud. *"And watch your mouth, for Chrissake."*

The memory fades.

As I stand in that hellish gas station, staring at myself in the picture, I have the overwhelming sensation that Myself in the Picture is staring back. She's wearing the green turtleneck. Her hair is blown dry as the Sahara. And even though the black ink is faded, the words are blinding.

MISSING

MARY MALONE, 16

LAST SEEN IN JACKSON, MS, WEARING A RED HOODIE AND JEANS
IF YOU HAVE ANY INFORMATION, PLEASE CALL 601-555-6869

My epiglottis can currently be found somewhere in Earth's stratosphere.

I put my hand in my pocket and squeeze my mom's lipstick. God, this is . . . this is . . . well, it's certainly not nothing. It's certainly something. The somethingest something there ever was.

I storm out of the gas station and hop back in the truck.

Walt raises his eyebrows. "Hey, hey, where's my Dew?"

"Here," I shove the bottle into his hands and tear into the bag of peach gummies.

"You okay, Mim?" asks Beck.

(Gummy one, down.) I really hated that turtleneck.

"Mim?"

(Gummy two, down.) What has it been, like, three days? Leave it to Kathy to freak out over three days. Probably trying to prove to my dad that she cares, but seriously, a Missing Persons report?

"Mim!"

I swallow my third gummy. "Yeah?"

"Are. You. All right?"

No. I'm all wrong. "Yeah," I lie.

Beck shakes his head, brings the diesel engine to life.

"Wait," I whisper.

(Gummy four, down.) My memory of that morning was identical to a thousand others, right in the middle of the darkest of days. Mom, slippers, silence. Dad, waffles, denial. Rinse and repeat. And repeat. And repeat and repeat and repeat . . .

"May we help you?"

Walt's voice brings me back to the now. I turn in my seat, flick his cap up, and kiss him on the cheek. "Walt, my God, you are a thing of beauty."

"Hey, hey, I'm Walt!"

"Mim, what's going on?" says Beck.

"Nothing, it's just—we need to make one last detour."

Beck's eyes are searching, as if he's inside my head, walking around with a flashlight, inspecting a certain dusty corner. *Oh*, says tiny-Beck-in-my-head, *I see. Yes, we really should take care of that.*

"Where to?" he whispers, half smiling like he does.

I point back to the highway. "Next exit."

"Woooooooster," says Walt between chugs of Dew.

(Gummies five through nine, down.) "Not Wooster, buddy. Ashland."

... 34 ...

Ashland Inn

BY THE TIME we pull into Ashland, the sun is long gone. Beck suggests parking somewhere and sleeping in the back of the truck again, to which Walt says, "Uncle Phil hurts my bones," to which Beck smiles, to which a thousand metaphysical Mims do a flash dance to the tune of "Celebration" by Kool & the Gang.

Walt offers to pay for a hotel; after some discussion, Beck and I agree to use a small amount of Walt's father-money and find the cheapest motel available.

"How does thirty-three bucks sound?" asks Beck, returning from the front office of a dingy one-story called Ashland Inn.

"Bedbuggy?" I say, climbing out of the truck. "Sketchy? Murdery?"

Beck grabs his duffel and Walt's suitcase. "So, perfect, in other words."

"*Very* other words." I sling my JanSport over my shoulder and decide to keep quiet regarding my mom's theory on motels, and their subsequent place of prominence in my heart. It's best if Beck just thinks I'm a typical girl in this regard. The regard of me assuming motels are grime pits, full of vermin and sperm bunnies.

Inside, the room is cheap and small, even by cheap, small motel standards: two twin beds, one nightstand, one love seat, one tiny dresser with one TV. The carpets, a grayish maroon, have what I hope to God are coffee stains scattered every few feet. Looking up, I notice the ceiling is stained, too, which seems an interesting achievement.

Beck pokes his head in the bathroom and whistles low. Joining him in the bathroom door, the first thing I notice is the toilet: any lower, and it would be *in* the floor. The sink looks more like a porcelain salad bowl, barely deep enough to fit your hands under the faucet. But worst of all is the shower. If the outer room is small, the bathroom is comically small. And if the bathroom is comically small, the shower is oompa-loompally small.

"That could be problematic," says Beck.

"Problematic?" I raise an eyebrow. "For a hobbit, maybe. *Impossible* for us. That showerhead can't be more than four feet off the ground."

He smiles at me, tilts his head, and there it goes—the jellification of my heart, the sinking of my brain into my shoes.

"I didn't peg you for a Middle-earth gal, Mim."

"Oh, I've got game."

"So it would seem," he says, looking back at the shower. "Well. It's gonna take more than a Ringwraith to keep me outta that shower tonight. I'll just have to make it work." He joins Walt by the television, leaving me to imagine Beck Van Buren "making it work." In a shower. Showering. With the . . . water, and all the soap, and . . .

Pull it together, Malone.

We spend the next fifteen minutes watching Walt crack up at an old episode of *I Love Lucy*. Beck's phone rings, and while he goes outside to take the call, I decide to brave the shower from the Shire.

It's far from ideal, which is to say I have to hunch over the entire time, and the water isn't quite as hot as I'd like, but it's a shower, and I'm grateful. Afterward, I pull out the last of my clean clothes, including Mom's old Zeppelin tee. Slipping into my stained jeans, I peer into the foggy mirror and do what I can for my hair. After a few tussles it's not half-bad. The cut really took, it seems. More rakish than mod, maybe, but still . . . not bad. I give myself a once-over.

Things could be better: the jaw, the nose, the cheekbone, still too Picasso.

Things could be worse: people pay millions for Picasso.

Millions, Mim. You're worth millions.

By the time I open the bathroom door, I don't feel like complete shit, which is really saying something. "Have you guys thought about din—"

On the television, Lucy is stomping grapes at a vineyard, but no one is watching. The room is empty.

I cross the carpet in my bare feet (avoiding stains like landmines), and peer through the curtains. The truck is gone. Beck and Walt are gone. *They're gone.* I let the curtains fall back in place. *They're gone.* It's a heavy weight—I feel it in my shoulders first, sinking like an anchor into the depths of Mim. *They're gone.* My elbows, heavy. My hands and hips, heavy. My thighs, my knees, my feet, heavy, heavy, heavy. *They're gone.* I am sinking into myself, falling to the bottom of this immense heaviness. It's an ocean. *They're—*

The door opens.

"Hey, hey."

Walt enters, carrying a plastic bag. Beck is right behind him, holding a plastic bag of his own. Walt sits on the bed, pulls out some Combos and a Mountain Dew, and laughs as Lucy picks a fight with another lady in the grape vat.

"We got hungry," says Beck, digging around in his bag. "Went out for gas station dinners. Hope you like beef jer—" He stops when he looks up. His face changes, and while I've learned most of his looks, this one is new. "You look . . . nice, Mim."

The smile takes root in my stomach; it grows, weaving up through my chest and arms, shoulders and neck, before blooming in my face. I locate the only word between what I want to say and what I should say. "Thanks."

After our gas station dinners, Beck decides to take a shower (*gulp*), and Walt promptly falls asleep. I turn down the volume on the TV and drop on the couch as another episode of *I Love Lucy* begins. Eventually, Beck emerges from the bathroom, wearing a clean gray V-neck and jeans. His hair is wet, and while I try not to picture him in that tiny shower, all making-it-work and whatnot, I just can't help myself.

"I don't watch this show very often," says Beck, "but chick seems to be quite the troublemaker." Lucy is currently stuffing pieces of chocolate down her shirt. "I don't really get it."

"It's . . . sexy slapstick?"

Beck looks back at the screen, baffled. Lucy has her mouth full of chocolates now, like a chipmunk preparing for winter.

A *chocolate chip*munk.

"That's supposed to be sexy?" says Beck, plugging his cell phone in by the nightstand.

"Yeah, I don't get it either. I guess back in the fifties, most girls were busy, you know, balancing books on their heads and baking pies. Knees were sexy back then, too, I think."

"Knees?"

I nod. "And Lucy showed a *lot* . . . of knee."

Beck crosses the room, reaches for the light switch. "You need this?"

I shake my head, yawn, and curl my legs up on the couch. In this new darkness, Beck sits next to me, and together we watch the lost art of Lucille Ball while I try my best not to jump Beck's bones.

"You ever notice how motel rooms all smell the same?" he says.

I swear he and my mom would be friends.

"Moth's shoe," I say.

"What?"

"My mom, when she was younger, used to hitchhike through Europe."

"Wow, really?"

"She's British."

"Oh."

"Oh-nothing. It's still awesome."

"Right. I mean, sure. It is."

"Anyway, she stayed in a bunch of hostels and said they all smelled the same. Like a moth's shoe."

Beck sniffs the air. "Yep, that's it."

Walt's snores are a freight train, but we're too tired to laugh.

"Speaking of moms," says Beck, "I told mine. On the phone. Just now—or, before, I mean."

It takes me a second to put his sentence back together. "You told her what you're doing? About Claire and everything?"

He nods.

"What'd she say?"

"She said—" Walt turns over in his sleep, grunting. Beck runs his hands through his wet hair, and lowers his voice. "She said I'm making a huge mistake, dropping out of school. Said I should come home. She said a lot, actually. You know what she didn't say? *'How's Claire?'*"

His pain is visible, even in the dim light of the television. "What're you gonna do?"

"No idea." He looks at Walt for a second, shakes his head, turns back to the TV. "I saw her, you know."

"Your mom? When?"

"No, not—Never mind. It's silly."

I stare him down, wait for him to continue. He will. I know this, and so does he. After almost a full minute, he comes through.

"I saw Claire," he says. "Walk out of that bathroom at Jane's Diner."

"What?"

"Not *actual* Claire. I mean the kid looked nothing like her. But when she walked out of that bathroom, the look in her eyes was just . . ." Life, it seems, delivers the best punch lines only after we've forgotten we were part of a joke. I suddenly feel like I need to throw up. ". . . so fucking pained, you know? Crushed. By the world."

Beck's voice, along with the blue-lit room, dissolves, and I feel those things—I feel the weight of the world, I feel fucking pained.

I'll scream.

I'll tell on you.

"Mim? You okay?"

I feel his eyes on me now, trailing from my hair, down my body, lingering in places they don't belong . . .

"Mim?"

. . . for the first time in a long time, I feel like a helpless girl. "You are beautiful, you know."

"I'm not," I say, I don't know how loud.

"You're too good," he whispers, leaning his head closer.

"I'm not good," I say. "I'm no good at all, Isabel."

"Yes, Mim," says a voice, cool like a fountain, and comforting. "You are."

Nothing will happen.

"Mim, look at me."

Nothing you don't want.

"*Look* at me."

I open my eyes. Or eye. And I'm sick of things the way they are, my many oddities, my limited depth perception, as if it's not bad enough I only see half the world, but it always seems to be the wrong half.

"Mim," whispers Beck.

And I've never so loved the sound of my name.

"Hi, Beck."

His face comes into focus now, in front of a familiar stained ceiling. Somehow, I ended up on the floor, my head in his lap, his hands on the back of my neck. In his eyes, I see a look I've never seen, not in him, not in anyone. It's a recipe of fierceness, fire, and loyalty.

"I knew it," he whispers, shaking his head. "When you called him Poncho Man, I fucking knew it."

Beck holds me like that on the floor well into the night. We don't talk. We don't need to. Sleep is close, and I'm okay with that. Because among the not-knowing of sleep, I'll know Beck. At some point, he carries me to bed and lies down next to me. It isn't weird, though maybe it should be; it isn't wrong, though it definitely could be. I curl up next to him, put my head on his shoulder. He wraps an arm around me, and I swear we were once a single unit, a supercontinent divided millions of years ago—like my fifth-grade science project—now reunited into some kaleidoscopic New Pangaea.

"I'm Madagascar," I say, sleepily.

"You're what?"

"I'm Madagascar. And you're Africa."

He squeezes my shoulder, and—I think he gets it. I bet he does.

I AM WOKEN by the sharp edges of my brain, a thought more persistent than sleep. "Beck," I whisper. I have no idea what time it is, or how long we've been asleep like this. The TV is still on. The curtains are dark. "Beck. You awake?"

I feel his breath catch in his chest as he clears his throat. "Yeah."

For a moment, I am acutely aware of my youth, and the recklessness that comes with it. I am aware of the darkness, and of every possibility it offers. I am aware of our comfortable nearness, of his scent, of us *being with*. But my sharp edges are more persistent than the recklessness of youth, the possibilities of darkness, even Beck's comfortable nearness. "I thought you left me."

"What?"

"Earlier, when I came out of the shower. You were gone. You and Walt. I thought you left me."

It's quiet. Just when I'm beginning to wonder if he fell back asleep, he answers. "We wouldn't leave you, Mim. Not like that."

"Not like what?"

"Like—high and dry." He clears his throat again. "At the very least, you'd get a liquid good-bye."

And that's when I know what this is. Or rather, what it's *not*. I remember our conversation from last night, out under the stars, in the back of Uncle Phil, and I know. "This isn't a crush, you know." I say it with my head in his arm—I want him to physically *feel* my words.

"I know," he says.

"It isn't."

"I know."

Tell him, Mary.

It's deep and real and fucking old-school. It's a fortress of passion, a crash—a fatal collision of neurons and electrons and fibers, my circus of oddities coming together as one, imploding in a fiery blaze. It's . . . I-don't-know-what . . . my collection of shiny.

It's love.

I don't say any of this, but not because I'm afraid. Wrapped up in Beck, I might never know fear again. I don't say it because I don't have to. Beck sees what it is.

I feel his weight shift on the bed; he rolls sideways, toward me, his face hovering over mine. We stare at each other for a second, silent, unmoving. I drink his green eyes, shiner and all. I drink his sharp nose, his jaw covered in desert-island stubble. I drink his eyebrows, thick and just the right amount of wild.

And I sense the move before it comes.

Beck leans in, slowly, and kisses my forehead. It isn't brief, but it's gentle, and full of sadness and gladness and everything in between. The sensation of his stubble lingers long after his lips are gone. His breath is robust and pleasant, how I imagine a ski lodge might smell, or a late-night jazz club. And just as I'm wondering how it would smell-taste-feel to have his lips pressed against my own, to feel his weight on top of me, to forever reunite Madagascar with Africa—he whispers the answer to last night's question.

"I'm too old for you, Mim."

Another kiss on the forehead, lighter this time, and he's gone. He pushes himself off the bed. In the semidarkness, I watch him step over to the couch and lie down. That's that. Game over. My fortress of passion crumbles around me, the most ruined of ruins.

And then, with nothing but two soft words from across a stained room, Beck rebuilds it. "For now."

... 35 ...

Olfactory Lane

September 5—morning

Dear Isabel,

In my very first letter to you, I declared myself incapable of fluff. And it's true. On a typical day, you might even say I'm unfluffable. (Oh God, will you please?) But I'm not quite myself this morning, which is to say I'm feeling spry. Peppy. Full of morning-person stuff, and yes, even a little fluff. So, taking advantage of this rare a.m. energy, I reread some of my previous letters, and would like to, hereforthwith, attach a few amendments. I hope you don't mind. Actually . . .

Amendment, the First—In reference to these amendments, I just said, "*I hope you don't mind*." I really don't give a rip one way or the other. Until delivered, the letter belongs to the author. I will attach amendments, as it is my right to do so, and whether you mind or not. (*Le* Boom.)

Amendment, the Second—On September 1, I wrote this about pain: ". . . *I know it's the only thing between me and the most pitiful of all species—the Generics.*" While it's true that pain will keep you from becoming a Generic, I take back what I said about that particular group being "the most pitiful of all species." Make no mistake, of all the despicable qualities available to a person, trying to be something you're not is by far the most pitiful. (I would know.)

Amendment, the Third—On September 2, I wrote, "*I don't think a vivid imagination is all it's cracked up to be.*" I went even further, lamenting the burden of having such an imagination. I've thought about it, and in light of a few recent developments, would like for you to ignore everything I've written as it relates to imaginations. I wouldn't trade mine for a single ounce of practicality.

Amendment, the Fourth—In my last letter, I wrote, "*. . . most people are egotistical, neurotic, self-absorbed peons, insistent on wearing near-sighted glasses in a far-sighted world.*" Ha-ha. How very Mim of me. Chock-full of cutting cynicism and wit, no? Well. While I hold to this general sentiment, it's possible I've underrepresented a certain demographic: Good People. There are a few out there. And, okay, I promise not to go on and on about this (lest you think I'm a card-carrying member of the Generics), but if I don't tell you about one of these Good People, my head might explode. It won't be all, *dear diary, I met this boy and he's like, so totally hott, and now my life has, like, total value and stuff! Lol.*

Instant nausea, right? Right. Still though . . .

I met a boy. And he is, like, so totally hott. And stuff. Laugh out loud.

My fetching photog. My heroically flawed Knight in Navy Nylon. My New Pangaea. His name is Beck, and he's beautiful, intelligent, and kind. He challenges my spirit while comforting my everything else. Beck is teaching me how to be a better person, and when you find someone who inspires you like that, you hold on for dear life.

The last thing I'll say about him is that he's my friend. I know it sounds cheesy, but I'd rather have that than all the rest. I've made some royal mistakes in this life, but one in particular trumps the rest. The remedy for this mistake is so simple it's maddening, so important, I'm going to underline, capitalize, and cursify.

Ready?

Here it is.

DO NOT UNDERESTIMATE THE VALUE OF FRIENDS.

Any elaboration, I fear, will only serve to detract from the powerful simplicity of the statement. So we'll leave it at that for now.

Signing Off,
Mary Iris Malone,
Part-time Morning Person

*****

THERE ARE FEW things more depressing than seeing your childhood home gutted. The coffee table with a thousand ringlets of stained condensation—gone. The watercolors purchased from, literally, a scam *artiste* on the streets of Paris—gone. The stained love seat no one could remember purchasing, yet everyone insisted on keeping—gone. No furniture. No lights. No life.

"I don't think anyone's here," says Beck, shaking the digital lock attached to the doorknob.

I pull my face away from the front bay window of a darkened 18 Meadow Lane and swallow through the knot in my throat. "I mean it's a great house, what's the holdup?"

Beck walks over to the FOR SALE sign, sticks his hands in one pocket, then another. "Shit."

"What?"

He jogs up to the truck and digs around in his duffel bag. "I must have left my phone at the motel."

I pull my own phone out of my bag and walk over to the sign. "Beck, Beck, Beck. You'd lose your head if it wasn't attached."

"You mean my arm?"

We smile at each other, recalling one of our first conversations. I'd never tell Beck this, but I've come to think of that as our first date, complete with dinner (apples) and a show (Walt's Rubik's jig).

I dial the number on the sign, but no one answers. Lying over the phone is hard enough, but a voice-mail lie . . . I don't think I have that kind of prowess in me right now. I turn up the ringer and check my call log. I only cleared it once, back in Nashville. Since then, Kathy has called sixty-eight times. (Stevie Wonder must be developing inflamed throat nodules.)

Walt is humming to himself, walking around, and staring intently at the ground.

"Walt," says Beck, "you okay?"

He doesn't answer. By the driveway now, he's walking in figure eights, humming, looking down at his feet, and just when I wonder if he's sick again, he stops dead in his tracks, and throws a finger up in the air. "Got it!"

Beck and I glance at each other as Walt picks up a stone the size of a softball.

"Walt?" says Beck. "What're you doing, man?"

Suddenly, in an all-out sprint, Walt charges the front door.

"Walt, wait!"

But it's too late. In one fluid motion, he swings the rock down on the handle, knocking the digital lock, along with the doorknob, clean off. Looking back toward me with, no kidding, the winningest grin ever, he bows low to the ground, then gestures for me to enter. "Ladies first," he says.

Beck smiles at me as I pass. "Kid's full of surprises."

Inside my old house, a wave of musky familiarity rushes into my nostrils, and like that, I'm home. I feel Beck's hand in mine, and while I'm beyond grateful for his presence, his touch, I need to do this alone. As if reading my mind, he gives a little squeeze, and lets go. "We're gonna drive back to the motel real quick. See if they have my phone. You okay?"

I nod. "You'll be back?"

"Definitely." He gives me a little hug, throws his arm around Walt, and disappears out the front door.

I REMEMBER HEARING once that the section of the brain that triggers sense of smell is located next to the section where memories are stored. In this way, a person can literally smell a memory. (Maybe Beck is right. Maybe the body, in its enigmatic miraculousness, truly is of the divine.)

Standing alone in the middle of my old living room, I suddenly find myself craving cashews and bloody video games. I remember . . .

One Christmas, years ago, Mom went through something of an eighteenth-century kick and decided to decorate our Christmas tree with real candles instead of electric lights. The tree burned down, scorching the carpet and leaving behind a peculiar, not altogether unpleasant, musky pine scent. That was also the Christmas I received a new PlayStation and discovered the delicious cashew.

I push aside my bangs, then stick my hand in my pocket and grip the war paint. As an afterthought, I touch my dead eye to make sure it's open. I may not be able to see the difference, but sometimes, it's just nice to know everything is in its right place. Inhaling the musk, the tree ash, the happier times, I put my head down and let my strappy high-tops lead the way.

In the dining room now, the smell of musk gives way to a different kind of smokiness. Across the room, I open a window; my nose burns and the back of my tongue goes numb. I remember . . .

I couldn't have been more than nine years old when I discovered Dad smoking in secret. I guess Mom knew, but it was a secret from me. He was right here, blowing smoke out the window when I asked if I could try one. He held out the pack with a grin on his face. "*Sure,*" he said. I studied him suspiciously.

"What's the catch?" I asked. *"No catch. Go ahead."* I pulled out a cigarette, surprised by how light it felt in my fingers. Dad lit the end, then told me to breathe in deep. I followed his instructions and inhaled deeply, deciding Dad was way cooler than I'd given him credit for. This was immediately followed by my hacking my lungs out, then throwing up on my mother's favorite Venetian blinds. I couldn't taste anything for a week. It was my first and last cigarette.

Out on the back deck, I take in the fragrant yard: the chrysanthemums, the slight sweetness of fertilizer, the fall mastery of dying summer dirt. Instinctively, I look around for lightning bugs and feel unending loneliness. I remember . . .

Hot summer nights, at dusk, Dad would shove a Wiffle ball bat in my hands and show me how to smack the hell out of lightning bugs. A direct hit, he said, was rewarded with a splattering of neon goo. He called it Goo Ball. I always knew he wanted a son, but it was never more obvious than on Goo Ball nights. (I usually missed on purpose, poor things.)

And there—on the far right-hand side of the yard—the detached garage. I smell cheap beer and turtle wax. So many memories of my father washing and rewashing his precious, never-used motorcycle while Mom and I listened to records. And the old College Couch, which, like me, has been hauled south. I turn back to the house, thinking about the last conversation I had on that couch. I wouldn't be one bit surprised to find more mischief than cotton tucked inside those plaid cushions.

Back inside, I peer at the door to the basement: tall and weighty, like a prison gate in some medieval movie. And its lock, forever broken, hanging there like nothing ever happened. Like my whole world didn't fall apart down in that basement. Beyond that door, there will be no aromatic reminiscing.

Deep breath. And again. Now walk.

I head for the other staircase, the safe one, the one going up. Fourteen steps, just like I remember. At the top landing, I duck to avoid the slanted ceiling, pass the crawl space/storage closet (a nook I once sleep-pissed in), and walk straight into my old bedroom. I absorb the curled edges of the wallpaper, and the browned bloodstain in the corner (my first period). My unnecessary bunk bed is gone. My debauched *Titanic* poster is gone. My typewriter, my futon, my vinyl collection, my lava lamp—all the *stuff* is gone, but the essence of the room is the same. At least, to me it is. I saunter, I ponder, I inhale. The scented recipe of my room is equal parts Neutrogena, salty tears, and awkward self-discovery. I remember . . .

In eighth grade, Tommy McDougal dumped me by the tetherball pole. (The one with no tetherball.) He said I looked like a boy. He said I didn't have breasts. He said I was a nerd. He said he didn't want to go out with someone who used bigger words than he did. I said I hoped he was prepared to copulate himself for the rest of his life, which I'd hoped would work on a number of levels, but as he didn't understand the word, only worked on one: making me feel even worse. That night I locked myself in this room and sobbed, alternating between Elvis (circa *Heartbreak Hotel*) and Elliott Smith (circa *Either/Or*). I did the same thing when Erik-with-a-kay dumped me, and the same thing when the fights got loud, and the same thing when I just needed noise to drown out the factory of my insides. It's sad really. I poured out a lifetime of tears in the springtime of my life with no one but my musical anomalies to feel my pain.

Moving on.

Down the hall, I walk inside my parents' bedroom. It is potpourri. It is perfume. It is ratty slippers. Like a lost little orphan, Mom's vanity sits alone in the far corner, the only piece of furniture left in the house. Impulses screaming, I walk over and pull the war paint from my pocket.

This is it.

Ground Zero.

My mother's lipstick. My mother's bedroom. My mother's vanity.

I wonder: What would it be like if she walked in the room right now? If she found me painting my face like some politically incorrect Cherokee chieftess? What would I tell her? The truth, I hope. That in my longing for originality and relational honesty and a hundred other I-don't-know-whats, this action, while strange and socially awkward, makes more sense than just about anything else in my world. And even though it's cryptic and more than a little odd, sometimes cryptic and odd are better than lying down for the Man. Maybe I would tell her how the war paint helped get me through a time when I felt like no one else cared about what I wanted, or who I was. Maybe I could muster the courage to speak those words so few people are able to say: *I don't know why I do the things I do. It's like that sometimes.*

Maybe.

I twist the last bit of lipstick from the tube and stare at the reflection of my mother's room behind me. In my mind, the dream is still fresh: our old feet crossing the room slow as a freighter; our lipstick the paint, our face the canvas, we get to work; time and time again, we draw, but nothing sticks. Nothing except the war paint. Our only color.

It's a narrow place, where Mom ends and Mim begins.

Only a single letter's difference.

"How fitting," I say aloud, raising the war paint to my left cheek. The two-sided arrow is first, headed straight for the bridge of my nose.

At that moment, from the depths of his canvas tomb, Stevie Wonder interrupts my proceedings with a wail. I pull the cell phone out of my bag and silence the ringer. "Give it up, my man. It's unrequited."

I return to the mirror, ready for the stroke across my forehead, the bridge connecting both arr—

"I thought I might find you here."

Hand to face, I am frozen. "What are you doing?"

A phone slaps shut. "Mim, I'm—"

"What the *hell* are you doing here?"

"Nice, Mim. Real nice."

Motion returns. Without bothering to remove my unfinished war paint, I spin around and face my stepmother head-on. Actually, the war paint makes perfect sense.

"Fuck you, Kathy."

She smiles, and her eyes fill with tears. With one hand, she rubs circles across the very slight bulge in her stomach, up and down, round and round. I can't help but wonder if little Isabel can feel her do this. Minding her own business, swimming along in the muck of her pre-birth—does she know there's a whole world outside, just waiting to love her, ruin her, disgust and admire her, disappoint and awe her? Does she know about us? Probably not, seeing as how she's about the size of a mango. God, if only she could plant those tiny little feet in there, just grab hold of Kathy's uterus with all her might, and make *that* her home sweet home. I'm sure it's tight quarters, but blimey, it's not much better out here.

"Mim, I can't imagine how you must feel. But you have to understand—your father and I have been *out of our minds*." She steps into the room now, closer to me. "I know you blame me. But—"

"You're not my mother."

I state this calmly, as a matter of fact, as if we're in court, and Kathy is trying to prove otherwise. She starts crying, and the thing she says next is a silver bullet.

"I don't have to be your mother to care about you."

She's close enough to smell now: her recipe is equal parts sanitizer, tacos, and pigheaded denial. I remember . . .

... 36 ...
BREAKING NEWS

"MIM, WHY DON'T you have a seat?" said Dad.

"Why don't you drop dead?"

His signature sigh. Then, "Mary, sit. Your mothe—Kathy and I have something to tell you."

"Oh my shit, Dad. Really?"

"God, Mim, language."

I pointed at Kathy who looked like she was on the verge of tears. "That woman is not my mother. And I'm not Mary, not to you."

"We have news, would you like to hear it, or not?"

"Barry . . ." Kathy started, then thought better of it.

"Fine, whatever." I plopped down on Mom's old College Couch, the setting of so many vinyl-spinning memories. (Back in Ashland, after Mom left, Dad said he didn't want the couch anymore. Said it wouldn't match any of "our things." I asked him who he meant by "our." He said nothing. I said I would literally jump off the roof while simultaneously swallowing a bottle of sleeping pills before I'd go to Mississippi without this damn couch. That pretty much ended the conversation.) Before I knew it, Dad and Kathy were on the couch, too, wedging me in the middle. In the peripheral of my good eye, I saw them holding hands behind my head, and for a second, I tried to command my misplaced epiglottis into action. God, that would have been a vomit for the ages.

Kathy spoke first. Two words, simple enough on their own, but whose combined forces conjured a catastrophic pandemic of madness.

"I'm pregnant," she whispered. Blushing, she traded smiles with my dad, then looked back at me. "Mim, you're going to have a baby sister."

I knew my reaction was being carefully studied, as if, at any moment, I might jump through a closed window. Actually, that wasn't a bad idea.

"What are you, kidding?" I looked from one to the other. "You guys just got married, like, yesterday."

Their smiles, already forced and nervous, grew downright twitchy. They looked at each other, then back at me, and before either could say a word, I knew the inevitable ending of this horrible story. It was just too damn predictable. I studied Kathy: for the first time, I noticed that yes, in fact, her breasts were slightly bigger; and yes, in fact, she had put on quite a few pounds since the wedding; and yes, in fact, her face looked a little reddish and inflated. Tears gathered in her eyes as she watched me figure it out.

I blinked.

The divorce had barely been finalized when they got married.

I breathed.

The wedding had been beyond quick, everyone said so. The move south, even quicker.

I was Mary Iris Malone, and I was not okay.

"How pregnant are you?" I whispered.

Dad put his hand on my knee. The same hand that polished and repolished a never-used motorcycle. The same hand that put distance between a golf ball and its hole so I could win. The same hand that, as a small child, spanked and fed me, the ultimate personification of a villainous hero.

And wow, had my hero *fucked. up.*

I met Dad's eyes for the first time in weeks, shocked at how sad they were. "You cheated on her?" I whispered.

He tried to say something but choked on the word.

I was crying, too, but the words came out just fine. "You cheated on Mom?"

"Mary," he said, "this is—"

"Don't ever call me that again."

I sat there frozen, wondering if this icy truth could ever melt, if the madness of the world could ever be cured.

In the back den, someone had left the TV on . . .

". . . no way to know how many soldiers are missing or whether they're even alive. Sources close to the Pentagon are, as usual, keeping quiet. In these moments of uncertainty, one can only pray for their families and loved ones. Back to you, Brian.

"Thanks, Debbie. That's Debbie Franklin in Kabul. Once again, for those who are just tuning in, BREAKING NEWS from Afghanistan . . ."

I sunk into my mother's old couch and let my breaking news wash over me. Like some giant jigsaw puzzle, a thousand separate things took the shape of one whole thing, ugly and shameful.

"We're calling her Isabel," said Kathy through tears.

"What?"

"Your sister. We're naming her after your aunt. We're calling her Isabel."

Of course they are, I thought. But I said nothing.

Dad pulled a small paper sack out of nowhere and set it on my lap. It had a big red ribbon tied haphazardly around the top.

"What the fuck is this?" I was intent on cursing as frequently and offensively as possible.

"It's a journal," said Kathy. As if that explained everything. As if a journal was fair exchange for my dad cheating with, and impregnating, a replacement mother.

"What the fuck do I need a journal for?"

Kathy cleared her throat, looked at Dad.

"So you can write letters to your sister," he whispered.

I looked down at the bag, but only to avoid eye contact.

"I read about it," he continued, "and thought this might be something you'd like to try. This way, you can talk to her before she gets here. And, I don't know—it might help you process things. Or something."

I unwrapped the ribbon, the paper, held the journal in my hands. It wasn't leather-bound or anything, and some of the corners were already beginning to fray. *He's apologizing,* I thought. *This is his apology.* But it was cheap in every way imaginable. A real apology cost something, because you had to stand there like an idiot and say it out loud for all the world to hear—*I'M SORRY.* And the world, as always, would respond with a resounding,

"Yes. Yes, you are." Dad wasn't going there; I wasn't sure he could. That kind of humility required a depth of love he had never been proven to possess.

"Of course, if you do plan on giving it to her one day, maybe you could avoid topics of, you know, tragic substance. Or at least despair."

I looked up at him, wondering how it was possible I could be a product of this man's loins. "And how do you propose I do that, Dad, seeing as how our family is prone to substantial desperation?"

He rolled his eyes and flared his nostrils. "I was kidding, Mim. Trying to lighten the tension a little. Of course, write what you want. Tell little Iz all about the atrocities of life. I just hope you'll remember some of the good stuff, too."

I looked at the journal and suddenly remembered that day long ago, reading a book at Aunt Isabel's feet. "I can round off the sharp edges of my brain," I said.

Only it wasn't supposed to be out loud. Dad and Kathy looked at each other, their concern thick in the air. Suffocating, actually. Still holding the journal, I stood from the couch.

"Oh, wait," said Kathy. "I got tacos."

I looked at her, wondering what she'd actually said. Surely it wasn't *I got tacos*. Surely, even she could understand how *I got tacos* was not the thing to say at the foot of this colossal conversation. Surely . . .

"You what?"

She blinked. "From the Taco Hole. I thought we could have dinner and . . . talk."

Nope, I was wrong. She didn't understand. She never would. I turned, walked from the room.

"Honey, where are you going?" asked Dad.

The real question wasn't *where,* but *when* and *how*. I knew the where, because I'd already looked it up.

Nine hundred forty-seven miles away, I thought to myself. *Nine hundred forty-seven miles . . .*

CLEVELAND, OHIO

(947 Miles from Mosquitoland)

… 37 …
Best for Her

"FOR REAL THOUGH, you have to show me how you did that."

I will ignore her. For all of eternity, if possible.

"Your haircut, I mean," says Kathy. "You really pull it off."

From my bag, I grab the makeup remover and wipe the war paint from my face. Beck and Walt are following behind us in Uncle Phil. Their trip back to Ashland Inn had turned up nothing. Beck's phone was officially missing, most likely stolen by some disgruntled maid or maintenance worker. They'd arrived back at the house just as Kathy and I were exiting. I'd give a pinky toe to be with them instead, but leave it to Kathy to suck the fun out of a thing. Her one condition for allowing us to continue to Cleveland was that she would drive me the rest of the way.

"Still wearing those shoes," she says. It's her last-ditch effort to get me to talk, and I have to say, a rather predictable move. I don't bite.

"You know—" she starts, then shakes her head. "Never mind."

"I'm so sick of people doing that." Honest to God, I had every intention of not speaking to her, but this is just too much.

"What?" she says.

"Starting a sentence, and then saying 'never mind.' Like it's really possible for me to not sit here and try to figure out what you were *gonna* say, before you thought better of it."

"Well, what I was *gonna* say was really not my place."

"Ha! Right. Okay. Well, how about we go back in time so you can apply the same set of scrupulous principles to basically every decision you've made in the last six months."

She takes a deep breath and rubs her belly, which seems to have grown considerably over the last five days. "You're mad. I get it."

"Mad? Kathy, my life was fine before you. It wasn't perfect, but it was good. And then you came along and suddenly home wasn't home anymore, it was part-time, like a hostel or something. Dad wasn't Dad, he was Part-time Dad. Mom wasn't Mom, do you know what she was? *Gone.* Along with my life, both of which *you* took from me, leaving this I-don't-know-what . . . part-time shadow of myself in its place. Now you and my part-time dad are having a full-time kid. And you want me to be, what, part of the family? Thanks, I'll pass."

Kathy takes the next exit, and navigates a back road. For a moment, we sit in silence, avoiding the uncomfortable nearness of one another. "Whether you like it or not, Mim, this family needs you. Now more than ever. Izzie's going to need a big sister. She's going to—"

"I read the letters, you know. The ones Mom sent you, asking for help."

Kathy stops talking, which is half the battle. The other half is to shame the shit out of her.

"She's sick, right?" I say. "Is she dying?"

Silence.

I shake my head. "Whatever it is, she asked you for help. The least you could've done was put a damn TV in her room."

"Do you still have them?" Kathy asks quietly. "The letters?"

"I could ask you the same question."

Kathy glances sideways at me. *The look of guilt.*

"I'm not sure what you mean by that, Mim."

"I mean three weeks ago, I stopped getting letters. Quite suddenly, actually. And wouldn't you know it, every time I get home from school the mailbox is empty."

"What are you suggesting, that I'm . . . *hiding letters* from your mother? Mim, I would never do that."

"Right, okay. Just like you would never suggest I should stop calling her. Or keep me from visiting her."

Kathy is shaking her head now, a look of confusion on her face, and I have to give it to her, I hadn't expected such high-caliber acting. I pull out the sixth letter, the only survivor, and hold it up like an Olympic flame. "Look familiar? Here, let me refresh your memory." I unfold the wrinkled paper, smooth it out in my lap, and clear my throat. "'Think of whats best for her. Please reconsider.'"

My epiglottis is a hummingbird, my heart matching it beat for beat.

I suddenly remember Beck's *hmm* the first day I met him. He saw the envelope with my mother's PO Box address; then he saw this note and said *"Hmm."*

Looking closer, the scrawl of this letter is so different from my mother's familiar handwriting . . . I recall the first line of the first letter, the core of my epistolary snowball. *In response to your last letter, the answer is no.* I stare at the letter in my hands, as if seeing it for the first time: *Think of whats best for her. Please reconsider.*

"You wrote this," I whisper. It comes out inadvertently, in a breath. Kathy is staring through the windshield, into the horizon, her mouth half-open. Her eyes are wet, and I don't care. I want to hurt her, to punch her, to reach across the car and stick my fingers in her eye sockets.

"We asked if you could visit," says Kathy. "When Eve said no, I was so mad I couldn't even write straight."

"But that doesn't make sense," I say. Terrified as I am to complete this puzzle, I have to see it through. "Why would you still have a letter you wrote *to* someone?"

She's all out bawling now, rubbing her burgeoning stomach. "Oh, honey."

And suddenly, I know the answer. "Say it, Kathy. Why would you have a note you sent to someone else?"

I need to hear it out loud. This thing won't be a thing until I hear it.

Kathy wipes her face and puts a hand on my leg. "We love you so much, dear. You have to believe that."

"Fucking *say* it."

She pulls her hand away, wipes old tears as new ones come. "She sent it back, Mim. Eve sent that letter back."

All the air in my body escapes. At once, the crippling effects of my week's diet and sleeping habits hit me fully. I am, 100 percent, exhausted. I'm beat. No, I'm beaten.

"It doesn't matter," I say, a lie. I lean my head against the cool-paned window. "It doesn't change anything."

The interstate is long gone. We ride in silence through a winding labyrinth of back roads, staring idly at the tall Ohio corn. I focus on the only thing that might keep me from bashing my head against the dashboard: my friends. In the side mirror, I watch Beck's lips moving. Walt is focused on something in his lap. I can't even see his face, just his Cubs hat. He's probably working out his Rubik's Cube for the bazillionth time. God, I miss those two. It's bizarre when I think about it. A girl can go her entire life without missing a person, and then, three days later—boom—she can't imagine life without them.

"That's what I meant about friends, Iz."

Kathy looks at me quizzically. "What?"

My cheeks flush. Shit. "Nothing," I say, staring out the window.

But it's something, Iz. It's a huge something.

… 38 …
Stick Figure Redemption

MAGNOLIAS!

Of all trees in all places at all times, it had to be magnolias, here, now. And in droves. Lined in perfect symmetry on either side of the lengthy driveway, the Mississippi state trees stand tall like a hundred marines at attention. Kathy's PT Cruiser rolls between them; through the passenger window, I observe the immaculate lawn, an abundant deep green, each blade trimmed with purpose and care. Like an arrow, the driveway leads straight and true, its tip piercing the heart of an old stone mansion. Or manor, rather. A stately manor: no shutters, no gutters, simple angles. This place would fit nicely in some boring BBC period piece. In fact, I wouldn't be one bit surprised to see Keira Knightley frolicking around in the fields, wrapped in a shawl, crying a little too passionately for the death of her sister's husband. (They were secret lovers, see. God, Keira, just give it a break.)

We pass a sign written in colorful rainbow:

SUNRISE MOUNTAIN

REHABILITATION CENTER:

HOLISTIC CARE FOR SUBSTANCE ABUSE AND DEPRESSION

My misplaced epiglottis suddenly seems more misplaced than usual. "What are we doing here?"

Pulling into a wide parking space, Kathy shuts off the engine. "You wanted to see your mother." She checks her makeup in the rearview mirror, then opens her door and slides out. "You coming?"

I flinch as the door slams. For a moment, I consider just living in the belly of the PT Cruiser. I could eat here, sleep here, raise a family. Anything to avoid stepping outside, facing this scene.

Suddenly, Kathy's words from Principal Schwartz's office ring in my ears: *She'll beat this disease. Eve's a fighter.*

I am a child. I know nothing about anything. And even less about everything.

Walt raps on the passenger-side window, grinning like a maniac, pressing the Reds program against the glass.

"Look!" he yells. "Just like your stick figure book!"

In something reminiscent of a preschooler's homework, Walt has drawn the most glorious stick figure diagram in the history of stick figures, or diagrams, or basically anything ever. It's a thousand times better than my "stick figure book." Not one bit anemic. Three figures stand in front of explosive fireworks. Each one has multiple arrows pointing to various objects on, or around, their bodies. The figure on the left is taller than the others. He's standing next to a truck, and has something draped around his neck. Above his head, written in all caps, it says MY

FRIND BEK. Little arrows indicate the truck is UNKLE FILL, and the object around his neck is CAMRA. The figure on the right has giant muscles. Above his head, it says WALTER. An oblong object in his right hand is labeled MOWNTAN DO, and a square in his left hand is marked COLOURFUL CUBE. The figure in the middle is me. Above my head, it says MY FRIND MIM. I have crazy big shoes, labeled SHOOS (X-TRA STRAPS). I'm wearing sunglasses, labeled accordingly, and a backpack, labeled BAKPAK. On the ground next to me, there's a stick labeled MIM'S SHINY—my lipstick.

We're holding hands, smiling from stick ear to stick ear.

I read once that the Greek language has four words for the word *love*, depending on the context. But as I step out of the PT Cruiser and tumble into Walt's perfectly huggable arms, I think the Greeks got it wrong. Because my love for Walt is something new, unnamed, something crazy-wild, youthful, and enthusiastic. And while I don't know what this new love has to offer, I do know what it demands: grateful tears.

I cry hard.

Then harder.

Then hardest.

Behind me, Beck's voice is a salve. "Hi," he says. "I'm Beck, and we tell each other stuff."

I pull back from Walt, wipe my eyes. "What?"

"Umm. Hello? She's *pregnant*?"

I grip my backpack, and tilt my head, and—damn it, there's my cute face again. It will be my undoing. "Oh yeah. That."

"Oh. Yeah. That. Mim, that is *pertinent* fucking info. Also, it explains a lot."

"Such as?"

He looks up at the top of the mansion's high stairs, where Kathy has just walked through the double-door entrance. "Such as a certain disdain for a certain stepmother, for which a certain someone snapped at a certain someone else when that certain someone else brought it up in the back of a certain truck. You know of which certain instance I'm referring to, certainly?"

I hold back a smile. "You know—I think my best course of action is to just let the ridiculousness of that sentence marinate."

He throws one arm around me, one around Walt, and leads the way toward the stairs. It's a communal walk, full of life, love, and the pursuit of Young Fun Now. I am—north to south, east to west—globally slain.

"So you like the drawing, Mim?" Walt asks, cradling the program like a newborn.

Beck leans into my ear. "He worked on it the whole way over here. Kid was beyond pumped to show you."

This Walt-Mim-Beck mobile sandwich makes me wonder if there's some kind of reverse Siamese twin operation. Or . . . triplets, as it were. "Walt, it's an absolute masterpiece. I love it. Every twiggy inch."

We're forced to let go of each other, as simultaneous stair-climbing is basically impossible, not at all conducive to Siamese triplets.

"So," says Beck. "Brother or sister?"

I don't answer at first. I can't. I've written the word, probably said it hundreds of times in other contexts. But never out loud, as it applied to me. I look Beck in the eye, and say it. "Sister."

"Nice. They have a name picked out?"

"Isabel."

Beck stops three steps short of the landing. I look back at him, and see something lighter than a shadow pass over his eyes. "What?"

"Nothing."

"Uh-uh. Out with it, Van Buren."

He takes one more step, pauses, runs his hand through his hair. "Last night, at the hotel—you may have mentioned her name."

"What?" I look to Walt, as if he might offer some assistance. And by assistance, I mean resuscitation. CPR. The Heimlich. Those electric pads that literally shock your life back into its skin. Walt has his head buried in the Reds program. Probably not the best candidate for electric shock, come to think of it. "When?"

"During your . . . I don't know what to call it . . . episode?"

Sometimes my brain hurts. Not a headache. A brainache. Chalk it up as just another in a long line of Mim's medical mysteries, but right now, my brain hurts like hell. I take the last three steps, imagining my blackout and the host of private thoughts I might have announced: internal monologues, theories meant for no one but me, words that put the utterance of my unborn sister's name to shame.

And then Beck's hand is in mine, and my brainache subsides. (In place of the pain, curtains rise on a lavish Broadway song and dance, Rodgers and Hammerstein in their prime.)

At the top of the stairs, we are greeted by a rainbow-colored sign next to the entrance.

THIS IS YOUR NEW BEGINNING
PLEASE CHECK ALL NEGATIVITY AND SELF-DOUBT HERE, AS YOU WILL HAVE NO NEED FOR THEM INSIDE. FROM THIS POINT ON, YOU WILL LIVE *YOUR* LIFE.

"What a shame they didn't remind me to breathe my air," says Beck, opening the door with a half smile. But it's not his signature half smile, all cute and coy. This one is different, lackluster. Supremely lacking in luster. "Mim," he starts. And suddenly, my arms are around him, because I don't want him to finish that sentence.

They aren't coming inside, because this isn't for them.

This is my wooden box.

It's a deep, powerful hug, and Walt turns around, because even he understands there's nothing romantic or funny about it. My mouth, just inches from Beck's ear, whispers the familiar line on its own.

Beck kisses me on the cheek, and responds beautifully, simply, "Yes, Mim. You are."

And I think of all the times I thought I wasn't okay, and all the times maybe I could have been, if only I'd had a Beck Van Buren around to tell me otherwise.

He steps back now, throws an arm around Walt. "We'll be

starting a New Beginning when you get back. Right, Walt?"

"Hey, hey, I'm Walt."

"Damn straight," says Beck, winking at me.

An image: my two best friends with their arms around each other, so different and so alike, colorful and puzzling and alive, clicked into place like Walt's cube. I tighten my backpack, wondering if I'll ever again have friends like these.

"Damn straight."

… 39 …

Sunrise Mountain

SUNRISE MOUNTAIN REHAB slaps me in the face with its unapologetic frontier motif. Standing between a butter churn and a rodeo saddle, I'm thinking it should apologize—to me, yes, but not exclusively. This place owes an apology to all those who have had the misfortune of setting foot inside its hellish doors.

On a throw rug a bald eagle soars atop snow-capped mountains; it is majestic, patriotic, and above all, obnoxious. Beyond the mountains, a purple sun sets on my electro-fuchsia shoes. A large bust of Daniel Boone stands tall in the corner, leading an army of oil paintings like a brigadier general: a wild lynx, an impossibly gorgeous horizon, a diagram of birds in their natural habitats—each painting in impeccable formation, awaits the trumpeting charge of their courageous General Boone (*sic*).

It is this: ridiculousness magnified.

Locating the nearest ladies' room, I run inside and slam the door behind me. But there's no escaping the resiliency of the eagles. They've soared their way in here as well, at least a hundred of them, flapping their wings for freedom, hovering, circling, diving, intent on breaking out of their embroidered wallpaper prison. An Aztec tapestry hangs on the wall above the toilet, adding a certain I-don't-know-what . . . turquoiseness to the mix. A miniature cactus sits in a pot on the sink, crooked and lonely.

I drop to my knees, lean over the toilet, yank back the seat, and heave.

She's here. In this awful, kitschy, eagle-soaring hellhole.

It pours out of me . . .

Lonely.

All the semi-digested contents of my stomach . . .

Lost.

God, it stinks in here.

She's here.

Sometimes, when it gets bad like this, I imagine my heart, my stomach, my liver, kidneys, and spleen, all the innards of Mary Iris Malone, pouring out of me like a hose, leaving behind a sagging skin–shell, a deflated air mattress, a soft mannequin. I'd be Born-Again Mim. A fresh start. One hell of a New Beginning.

I collapse on the bath mat (an altogether hideous depiction of cowboys and Indians, complete with stampeding buffalo and six-shooters) and try to catch my breath. A minute later, there's a knock on the door.

"Mim? You okay?"

I sit up, take a long pull of paper towels and wipe my mouth. "Be right out!"

Above the toilet, a sign reads:

USE TRASH CAN FOR PAPER TOWELS

AND FEMININE PRODUCTS

DO NOT FLUSH

And like dominoes, the memories tumble; a yellow-tinted bathroom knocks over the most Carlish Carl, knocks over Arlene, knocks over old wisdom, knocks over youthful innocence, knocks over, knocks over, knocks over . . .

Looking at the handle on the toilet, I smile. Young Mim of Not So Long Ago, upon discovering the well of friendship to be completely tapped, found new friends, an ensemble cast of saviors.

Mom is here, in this stinking place. But this time, there are no Carls or Arlenes or Pale Whales or Karate Kids or Fabulous Walts or Consummate Beck Van Burens to save the day. There is only Our Heroine, and once again, she is on her own.

At the sink, I splash water on my face and rinse my mouth. There is no mirror, so I stare at the droopy cactus.

Lonely.

Crooked.

A trash can sits in the corner, boasting perfect trajectory. With precision, with skill, with lionhearted determination, I swipe the potted cactus across the room and into the trash can—hole in one. I wipe my hands on my jeans, exiting the Southwestern ladies' room forever and ever, and good riddance.

Down the hall, Kathy is talking to a guy at the reception desk. He's tall, attractive, a few years older than me. As I approach, my stepmom straightens up. "You okay?"

I nod, then smile at the receptionist, who, upon closer inspection, really isn't good-looking at all. Like a connoisseur of fine wines lost in a hack's vineyard, I have been spoiled rotten by the beauty of Beck Van Buren.

"You must be Mim," he says through crooked teeth. "And how are you today?"

"Swell. Listen, I just chunked in your ladies' room, so you might wanna spritz something piney in there. Or floral. Whatever you have in stock. It should be strong though. Weighty, you know?"

He gapes at me, growing uglier by the minute. "I'm sorry, you . . . you what?"

"I ralphed."

He tilts his head.

"Drove the porcelain bus?" I say. "Ate in reverse? Buicked my Kia?"

Now they're both staring.

"I vomited in your bathroom, man. And now the place stinks to high heavens."

They're still staring, but with completely different looks on their faces.

"Also, can I get a Mountain Dew?" I ask, smacking my lips. "It's like I just chewed a tube of wood glue or something."

The receptionist gives Kathy a look that I interpret to mean *Is she serious?* Kathy's eyes respond with *Deadly.* Mildly Attractive Male Receptionist scurries off, presumably after a Mountain Dew.

"Come on," says Kathy, starting down the hallway.

"What about my drink?"

"You wanna spend any more time here than you have to?"

Next to me, Daniel Boone's bust is wearing a *who, me?* smile.

I jog to catch up with Kathy, noticing, not for the first time, what a curious walk she has. It's equal parts sass, *z*-snap, and street smarts. Her earrings jangle, her artificial curls bob, her too-tight jeans ride, her acrylic nails click, her bedazzled belt sparkles, her pregger boobs bounce—in this moment, I must applaud Kathy, and all the delusional fashionistas before her, clinging just as fiercely to their lost youth as they are their fake Louis Vuittons.

She hands me a slip of paper with the number 22 written in a mildly attractive handwriting. As we pass room 11, sweat beads across my forehead. I feel—and hear—my heart pounding against its adjacent innards, sending vibrations through my rib cage, my recently emptied stomach, my skin, my Zeppelin tee, my red hoodie.

Room 17 passes in a blur. God, we're walking fast.

The narrow hallway is consistent in design with the rest of the place: nature-y oil paintings, plush carpeting, flowery wallpaper with a bunch of ridiculous eag—

"You ready?" whispers Kathy.

"What?"

She points to the door: room 22. On the other side, I hear the clear, deep baritone of a man who has lived his life.

...40...

The Drive Back

September 6—noon

Dear Isabel,

I write to you with the strongest of urges. I write of substance, and of despair. I write to teach and learn, purge and fill. I write to speak, and I write to listen. I write to tell the fucking truth, Iz.

To that end . . .

I was six when Aunt Isabel hung herself in our basement.

She was visiting from Boston at the time. I remember, the day before she killed herself, she sat in our living room and suggested I write a letter to her when she got back to Boston. But I was as impulsive back then as I am now. I decided I couldn't wait that long. So the next day, I sat in my room and wrote a letter about nothing . . . just a letter. And then I went to find her. I searched high and low, every room of our house. Finally, and as a last resort, I tried the door to our basement. It was one of those ancient, heavy doors that creaked when you opened it. So you can imagine, as a young child, how this frightened me. Also, it had a big brass lock on it, but for as long as anyone could remember the lock had been broken. (I've often wondered how differently my life would have turned out had that lock been fixed, or had I been too scared to go down there. But it was broken, and I was brave, and 'twas always thus.) I made my way down the dark stairs, calling out for Aunt Isabel the whole way. Needless to say, she didn't answer.

Nor would she ever again.

I found her hanging there, her feet dangling inches from the floor—inches from life. Later on, I would piece things together: Aunt Isabel was sick in the head; she came off her meds; at her doctor's behest, she went to stay with family; she wrote letters (of serious substance and despair, I would imagine) to her doctor; and, ultimately, she decided her life wasn't worth a damn.

There can be no question that our father blames himself, both for the suicide of his sister, as well as the ensuing shock brought upon his daughter (me, not you). There can be no question that this has fed his suspicions as to my own illness, that he thinks he could have done more to save Aunt Isabel, that maybe he could have done more to save me from *finding* Aunt Isabel. That maybe he can do more now to keep me from *becoming* Aunt Isabel. But I'm not her, and I never have been. One day, I hope he sees this truth.

So. The elephant in the room. They're naming you after her. Yeah. Ha. Ha. Ha. Hilarious, right? Or, if not funny, counterintuitive. I mean, Isabel is a great name, don't get me wrong. But blimey, that's a heavy-handed welcome to a world full of weak hands.

So why'd they do it? Why name you after the most tragic figure in our family? I'll tell you, but when you read what I'm about to write, remember what we determined about Reasons. They're hard. Damn near impossible sometimes.

Okay, then, here it is: I was supposed to be Isabel.

(Boom, right?)

So you're probably wondering what happened. Why am I *not* Isabel? Why am I Mary Iris Malone? (Why, indeed?)

It begins with a promise.

Before you and I were born, our grandmother, Mary Ray Malone, died of lung cancer. On her deathbed, or so the story goes, she asked Dad and Aunt Isabel to carry on her mother's name (Isabel) should they one day have a daughter of their own.

They agreed.

Enter Eve Durham (my mother), the firecracker from Across the Pond. Shortly after they were married, Eve informed Barry that she was pregnant, to which Barry informed her that should the baby be a girl, her name would be Isabel, to which Eve informed Barry that she hated the name Isabel. Barry pushed. Eve pushed harder. In the end, he gave in, on the one condition that they use his mother's name—Mary. Mom said, fine, but she wanted some kind of flower in the name.

BARRY MALONE'S FACE

(Upon Hearing the News That His Wife Wanted a Fucking Flower in Their Daughter's Name)

And so I was born, the improbable Mary Iris Malone, kaleidoscopic anomaly from the word *go*.

Mim was a quick nickname. Only occasionally has Dad called me Mary, and then, only by accident. But I can't blame him. My name—my existence—is a constant reminder of his broken promise to his mother.

That's where you come in, Isabel. You get to make Dad whole. Through you, he gets redemption. He gets to keep his promise. In fact, I make a prediction: Dad will never call you anything other than Isabel. You will have no nicknames.

God, I envy you.

Anyway . . .

I'm with your mom now, riding back to Mississippi. Mosquitoland. That's what I've been calling it. It's catty, I know, but how else does one kick an entire state in the balls? I've chosen mockery.

The truth is, Mississippi doesn't feel like home. Not yet.

Until yesterday, I thought home was in Cleveland with my mom, but God, did I have that wrong.

Home is hard.

Harder than Reasons.

It's more than a storage unit for your life and its collections. It's more than an address, or even the house you grew up in. People say home is where the heart is, but I think maybe home *is* the heart. Not a place or a time, but an organ, pumping life into my life. There may be more mosquitos and stepmothers than I imagined, but it's still my heart. My home.

A real kaleidoscopic New Pangaea.

My hope for you, Isabel, is that your home will be easy. Obvious. Desirable. My guess is it will be none of these things. My guess is you'll have your own Mosquitoland to deal with. Good effing luck.

I haven't decided whether I'll continue writing to you after you're born, or if my Book of Reasons is more of a prenatal correspondence log. Part of me thinks it would be a great way to offer up a lifetime of advice, and tell my stories as they come, rather than wait for you to grow up to hear them. By then, you probably won't care anyway. Or I might forget them all, because I'll be old. Or dead. That's the thing about life—you don't know how long you have until you're dead, and by then, you don't know much of anything at all.

Maybe I will. Keep writing, I mean. It does make me feel okay. And feeling okay is at a premium these days.

Anyway, I suppose you'd like to hear my ninth and final

Reason. The thing of Things, the gemstone talisman, the last layer in my Giant Onion of Reasons. Are you ready? Here it is:

Isabel Sherone-Malone, *you* are Reason #9.

And if I'm honest with myself, you were the only Reason that ever really mattered. My dad wanted to divorce my mom? Fine. He wanted to marry another woman? Fine. He wanted the three of us to move way the hell away from my mom, my life, my world? Fucking *fine*. But he and the new wife were having a kid together?

Peace out.

And then yesterday happened. Sunrise Mountain happened. I walked into a room, and my life changed. (You should be ready for this. Sometimes you walk into a room one person, and when you come out the other side, you're someone else altogether.) My Objective, once achieved, turned out to be something else entirely. Your mother was a big part of this. She pulled back a dusty curtain to reveal oh-so-many truths. Someday we'll talk about it more. I'll give these letters to you and fill in the gaps as best I can. You'll probably have questions, and that's fine. I will provide honest answers. Because even though honesty is hard, you really have to murder people with it if you expect to be a person of any value at all. Remember that, Iz. Be a kid of honesty. Wave it like a banner for all to see. Also, while I'm thinking about it—be a kid who loves surprises. Squeal with delight over puppies and cupcakes and birthday parties. Be curious, but content. Be loyal, but independent. Be kind. To everyone. Treat every day like you're making waffles. Don't settle for the first guy (or girl) unless he's the right guy (or girl). Live your effing life. Do so with gusto, because my God, there's nothing sorrier than a gusto-less existence. Know yourself. Love yourself. Be a good friend. Be a kid of hope and substance. Be a kid of appetite, Iz. You know what I mean, don't you? (Of course you do. You're a Malone.)

Okay, that's all for now. Catch you on the flip side.

Blimey, get ready.

Signing off,
Mary Iris Malone,
Your Big Sister

... 41 ...
Behind the Curtain

AS I WALK into room 22, Mom's silhouette commands my attention, as it did that fateful Labor Day, one year ago exactly. She's sitting in an easy chair with her back to me, facing the window. Outside, the sun is setting. Its gentle glow casts my mother in an ominous light, made even more so as it seems to affect nothing else in the room. Next to her, a CD player sits on a coffee table. As the song comes to an end, the CD whizzes and hums, and the song begins again.

Elvis on repeat.

Shit.

It's bad.

"What are you doing here?" she asks without turning around. Her voice sounds beyond repair. I don't have to try hard to remember the last time I saw her. The night she sat next to Dad. The night of the one-line speech. My mouth freezes, my forehead melts, my hands tighten; I am 110 percent unprepared for this. My only response is so elementary, even I wince.

"Happy Labor Day, Mom."

My Goodwill shoes carry me toward her. The shades turn as I

walk, from brown to blue, lighter, then darker, then lighter again.

"Mary, you can't be here."

"Eve . . ." Kathy's voice comes out of nowhere. It had only taken seconds for me to forget she was in the room. "She came a long way to see you. You have no idea—"

Mom turns her head and interrupts Kathy with a look. And in this, my moment of Moments, I see my stepmother's face, and realize how wrong I've been about her.

Mom turns her head back to the window and whispers, much too low for me to hear. I twist her lipstick in my pocket, even closer now, close enough to rest a hand on her shoulder. She looks into my eyes, fully, finally, and for the first time, I see her—God, I see her for what she is, was, and will be. I see a million miles of life, a million lives in one, a million headaches, heartaches, and brainaches, a million ingredients in her eyes. The recipe is this: natural joy and learned sorrow; love found and love lost; fireworks, fortune cookies, famous rock stars, empty bottles, true compassion, false starts, staying up late, moonlight, sunlight, being a wife, being betrayed, being in my corner, being my mother, being, being, being.

"I was lovely once, but he never loved me once."

I nod and lose my shit. From my gut to my heart to the sockets of my eyes—one dead, one alive—tears don't discriminate. I am overcome by the urge to tell her about the Great Blinding Eclipse, and how I've been half-blind for two years, and how I've never told anyone. I want her to be the first to know. I want her to know everything about my trip, all the people I've met along the way. I want her to know about Beck and Walt. I want her to know about Arlene and the extra Carlness of Carl. I want her to know about Mosquitoland and our horrible house bought for the low, low price of Everything I've Ever Known to Be True. Because right now, looking at this shell that I once called Mom, it seems nothing could ever be true again. I miss Kung Pao Mondays and teaming up against Dad. I miss the mutinous cul-de-sac and giving money to Reggie. I miss the way things used to be.

I miss *home.*

I want to tell her all these things, but I don't. I can't. It's like running a marathon, then stopping one foot before the finish line. So I stand. Thinking.

I think of a decade-old conversation. From the deformed mouth of a bubbly-skinned man, in line at a bank or a pharmacy or a fish market, it doesn't matter. The conversation travels through a black hole of time and space, beyond every star and moon and sun in every galaxy of the universe; for its final destination, it arrives at Planet Earth, USA, Ohio, Cleveland, Sunrise Mountain Rehab, Room 22, Mim's Ears.

"Did God mess up?" I asked.

"Nope," said Bubbly Skinned Man, smiling like a fool. *"He just got bored."*

From that moment to this, I've pondered the peculiarities of an angry Almighty. And now I know. I see it in the medicated drool dripping from the face of my once youthful mother. I see it in the slew of trained specialists assigned to her keeping. I see it in the Southwestern motif, from floor to ceiling of this nightmare called Sunrise Rehab, and I know what God makes when He's angry: a person with the capacity for emptiness. But not the always-emptiness of Dustin or Caleb or Poncho Man. A drained emptiness. A person who was once full. A person who lived and dreamed, and above all, a person who cared for something—for *someone.* And within that person, he places the possibility of *poof*—gone—done—to be replaced by a Great Empty Nothingness. I know this is true, because right now, a Great Empty Nothingness is staring me right in the fucking face.

"Mary," it whispers.

I hold her hand for the first time since that fateful Labor Day, somewhere between mutiny and mediocrity. Crying, I look out the window, hoping like hell she doesn't say what I know she's going to say.

"I'm so sorry," she whispers between sobs. "I never wanted you to see me like this. I'm just so sorry."

"It's okay, Mom." My words pour out in ugly, nasal globs, and I hug her as hard as I've hugged anyone. "It's okay," I say again, because if I keep saying it, maybe it will be true. *It's okay it's okay it's okay it's okay.* I rest my head on her shoulder and gaze out the shaded window half expecting fireworks to go off in the distance. God, wouldn't that just be the thing of Things? There are none, but it's okay. It's still Labor Day. Just a different kind of mutiny.

And now Kathy is pulling my hand. "It's time to go," she whispers, motioning toward the door.

I nod and kiss Mom's forehead. Turning, I notice a vanity—not *the* vanity, but one similar—standing just next to her bed.

It's a dark wood, rife with the ornate vine etchings so popular in its day. Though the top of the vanity stands waist-high, a mirror attached to the back rises all the way to the ceiling, standing tall like it owns the place. I cross the room, noticing a hairline crack running the length of the mirror, from top to bottom. When I position myself in the middle, one half of my face is on either side of the crack.

Right Side Mim and Left Side Mim.

Split in half.

My reflection is a throwaway recipe of expired ingredients: gaunt, unfamiliar, worldly, homesick, aged, exhausted, to name more than a few. On one side of the crack, my right eye is almost closed. The zipper from my hoodie follows the crack in the mirror, down, down; I notice the red cloth is deeper, dirtier, a thicker shade of blood.

An image: Right Side Mim turning to Left Side Mim, asking oh-so-many questions. One hand on the vanity, I recall the dream I'd had only months ago: the old feet, the low whispers, the reflection of *our* faces. Her makeup tray isn't here, but her makeup is: the perfumes, blushes, eyeliners, and concealers. All of it, save one item.

I pull the war paint from my jeans pocket, and twirl it in my hands. Like me, it's different now, well-traveled, a little longer in the tooth. Having never finished my last application, there's still a little left. And I know just how to use it.

In even strides, I cross the room, stepping between my mother and her shaded windows. Head down, I see her feet in those same old ratty slippers—right next to my feet in those same old ratty shoes. So many similarities . . .

I twist the tube of lipstick, and like a phoenix rising from the ashes, so too it rises ready for work. Kathy stands silently by the door; she doesn't try to stop or rush me.

"You look different," my mother whispers. It takes me off guard, because for some reason, she didn't look like a person who was going to say something.

I raise my eyes to meet hers. "I cut my hair."

Mom shakes her head and leans into my ear. "You look like my Mary."

The tears become a flood. And I have a new image now: my unopened bottle of Abilitol, the truest talisman of disappointment, snug in the bottom of my backpack. It's been days since I bowed to the king of habit, and yet, I feel more Mim than ever before.

I wipe my eyes, place one hand on my mother's shoulder, grip the lipstick between my thumb and forefinger, and lean in. "Let me show you a thing or two."

She smiles a little, and so do I, recalling my first and last makeover. I paint her lips evenly, careful not to miss those elusive corners, careful not to go outside the lines. She's staring at me, her eyes full of I-don't-know-what . . . wonder, appreciation, embarrassment, love. All of it, and all at once.

Finished with the makeover, I step back and admire my handiwork. Still a shadow of her former self, there is something there, something absent only minutes ago—a glimmer of youth, or a little light behind the eyes. It's not much, but it's something.

"Look at you," I whisper, smiling, crying. "Lovely."

I kiss my mother's forehead and nod at Kathy. Before walking out of room 22, I set Mom's empty tube of lipstick on her new vanity, back where it belongs.

… 42 …
New Beginnings

I FOLLOW KATHY out the front doors of Sunrise Mountain and slip on Albert's aviators.

"I didn't even notice how dark it was in there," says Kathy.

Metaphor is the word I'm thinking.

"You wanna get some Chinese or something, Mim? I'm starving."

The image of a blank fortune crosses my mind, but before I can say *thanks, but no thanks,* something far more important occurs to me. "You see Beck or Walt anywhere?" I ask, looking around.

Kathy is digging in her giant purse. "Damn it. I think I left my keys back at the desk. Wait here a minute?"

She goes back inside while I squint across the lawn. A quick glance in the parking lot, and my poor heart—after beating its tail off in room 22—is performing backflips. Uncle Phil, the trusty, rusty blue pickup, is gone.

I pull my phone out of my bag to call Beck, before I remember . . . *his phone.* These memories don't tumble, they crash down: a lost phone knocks over Ashland Inn, knocks over *I Love Lucy,* knocks over an empty parking space, knocks over, knocks over, knocks over.

We'll be starting a New Beginning when you get back. Right, Walt?

I put my hand on my chest, feel my heart beating . . .

Hey, hey, I'm Walt.

beating . . .

Damn straight.

beating . . .

I feel the camera zoom in on my eyes.

And what about the voices, Mim? Have you had any episodes lately?

I feel the audience watching.

Symptoms of psychosis, Mr. Malone, are not themselves psychoses.

I feel the audience waiting.

I am Mim Malone. I am Mim Alone. I'm alone.

I feel the red hoodie, the pool on a roof, the untouched bottle of Abilitol.

I'm not crazy.

I feel the empty parking spot.

You ever have the feeling you lost something important, only to discover it was never there to begin with?

I feel all my sharp edges.

I feel . . . a force, heavy, pulling me like an undertow, pulling me out to sea, the Sea of Trees, dragging me down to the bottom. It's a strange lot down here: plants and animals, a secret society of creatures, a life of struggle and survival and the struggle for survival. The landscape is blurred, but the ground is firm. I watch myself, Aqua-Mim, as if through a lens: shadowy, blue, naked under the water, pushing against the current, holding her breath. She swims right up to a rainbow-colored plant, a plant urging her to live her life, a plant offering the possibility of a New Beginning. She grabs hold, feels the weight begin to rise until her head breaks above water and . . .

I breathe.

Taped right in the middle of the New Beginnings sign is my life preserver. A stick figure masterpiece. The Reds program. In Sharpie—fucking physical and permanent proof of reality—my name is written across the front. I pull it off the board, ripping traces of indigo, violet, and yellow from the sanguine palette. Fumbling through the pages of the program, I see Walt's precious diagram, and somehow, I know there's more. On the next page, across the Cubs' depleted scorecard, the script of my fellow stick figures:

Hay hay mim! Ha. Beck told me wee're going, so we are going but I miss you sooper big already. Doing the do, and oh i thought about the time we first met under that brige and how funny you look when you sleep maybe I nevr told you. but Also pritty. You looked pritty. so I will miss you while wee're away but he says we can see you at the game, so thats what we will do. See you then cant wait!

Sinsearly yours forever and ever.

Walter

I didn't think I could cry anymore. I was wrong.

Flipping to the next page, I see Beck's reckless penmanship, scrawled across the picture of some top prospect. Even through my tears, I laugh at the salutation.

DEAR MADAGASCAR—

"I don't know how to say good-bye to you," said Mim, staring into the devastatingly handsome eyes of Beck Van Buren.

"I know," said Beck, in a devastatingly handsome tone.

How do you like it so far, Mim? It's for my memoir, The Devastatingly True Story of the Handsome Beckett Van Buren. Too writerly? Okay, how about this . . .

"I don't know how to say good-bye to you," she said.

"I know," he said.

And I don't, Mim. God. I really don't.

But I had a thought . . .

On the way over here, Walt showed me a photograph. He's with his mom in front of Wrigley Field, and I don't know if you've seen it, but Mim, the kid looks 100% happy. Like, lifetime-supply-of-Mountain-Dew happy, and maybe his mom died, but what if she didn't? Either way, if Walt has family somewhere, I intend to find them. Chicago is quite a drive, but I think Uncle Phil is up to the challenge. You found your home. It's Walt's turn.

Last night, I promised not to leave you high & dry.

Please believe me when I say—I kept this promise. And while I still don't know how to say good-bye to you, I know a certain devastatingly handsome character who would like another shot. So here goes:

"I don't know how to say good-bye to you," she said.

"I know," he said.

They sit together, trying to locate the impossible words. She finds them first. "Maybe it doesn't have to be, like, a solid good-bye, you know?"

He looks at her, wondering how he got to be so lucky. "As opposed to a liquid one?"

"Yes, actually. I much prefer liquid good-byes to solid ones."

"Fair enough," he said, kissing her lightly on the forehead. "When the day comes, you shall have your liquid good-bye."

THE END

LOVE,
AFRICA

P.S.—I'm sure you've put this together by now, but I've basically stolen your truck. I feel like an ass, just so you know. Please don't press charges. I'll reimburse you at the game. Which brings me to . . .

P.P.S.—Flip the page for your liquid good-bye . . .

Barely able to breathe, I turn to the next page in the program. It's a schedule for the following year's slate of Reds games. One game in particular is circled: Opening Day. Reds v. Cubs. Then, next to it, three words in red: *"Remember the rendezvouski!"*

I imagine Walt with a butterfly in his bottle, and Beck with the camera around his neck, and together, we stand around the statue of some old baseball player turned rendezvous point. Opening Day is early April, and suddenly, spring can't get here soon enough.

"You okay, Mim?"

I look up, wondering how long Kathy's been standing there. "Yeah," I say, stuffing the Reds program in my bag. "You find your keys?"

She holds up the key ring, gives it a shake. "It was in my purse the whole time. So. How about that Chinese food?"

I hook my thumbs in the straps of my backpack, and follow her down the stone steps to the parking lot. "Could we do Mexican instead?"

"Honestly, I don't really care what we eat so long as we do it soon." She pushes a dyed curl out of her face. "Izzie's starving. Which reminds me, we'll probably have to split up the trip—half today, half tomorrow. I get tired quick these days."

Kathy rubs her stomach, and again, I wonder if my sister can feel her mother's touch. I hope so. And I hope she knows that kind of love is not nothing. It's a huge something, maybe the biggest of all. It's a mini-golf kind of love, the kind of love people like Claire and Caleb never experienced. Maybe those two never really got a fair shake. Maybe if they had fathers who let them win at meaningless games—or mothers who rubbed their pregnant bellies, reassuring Fetus Claire and Fetus Caleb that yes, even though the world was fucked up beyond measure, there was beauty to be had and it was waiting for them—maybe then, Claire and Caleb would've turned out differently.

I watch Kathy walk toward the car, and I think about Dad—how his sister and first wife were both incredibly complicated women prone to topics of substance and despair. No wonder he wanted me to avoid those particular subjects with Baby Isabel. And no wonder he ended up with Kathy Sherone-Malone, she of the Grand Slam breakfast and glue-on nails, a wholly uncomplicated woman prone to topics of pop-culture and cheer.

From the passenger-side door, I look at Kathy over the top of the PT Cruiser. "So this is why you didn't want me to call her," I say. "And why she stopped writing. This is why Dad moved us cross-country. So I wouldn't have to see her like this. So we could all have a . . . whatever . . . a fresh start."

"Maybe. But then, we wanted you to visit, so . . ." She puts her keys in the door, pauses. "Let's not do this, okay?"

"Do what?"

"This. This thing where we talk the hell out of it until there's nothing left to just . . . think about, you know?"

The funny thing is, I do know. I know exactly.

Inside the car, Kathy turns on the radio. Wonder of wonders, it's Stevie effing Wonder, telling all of us why he called.

"Sorry," says Kathy, blushing. She turns the dial.

Against every bone in my body, I switch the station back to Stevie. Then, pulling Kathy's Hills Bros. can from my bag, I hand it over. "Here. Also, sorry. Also, I'll pay you back."

She takes the can, shrugs, tosses it in the back seat. "You teach me how to cut hair like that, and we'll call it even."

"Deal."

"Listen, Mim"—her head tilts and she sighs, and I know, whatever she was going to say, she just decided not to say it—"you ready to go home?" she asks.

A montage rolls through my head, and like a curtain call, the characters of my trip take a bow . . .

Carl is driving a Greyhound to Anywhere, USA, summoning extra Carlness as a semi passes in the pouring rain. Arlene's tombstone, a shining beacon of hope in the Land of Autonomy reads *Here lies Arlene, a Grande Dame from the Old School, if ever there was one.* Claire is frowning a new frown, pouring herself a glass of lemonade in her appropriately apathetic townhouse. Ahab and the Pale Whale are pumping gas, kicking ass, swimming and sunbathing. Officer Randy, like Doctor Wilson before him, is inventing new ways to furrow, wrinkle, shake, sigh, and doubt. Dr. Michelle Clark, with her blood, bows, and perfect teeth, would like to say hello.

The villains of this odyssey—Poncho Man and Caleb (aka "Shadow Kid")—are humming a sad song behind bars, staring ten to twenty in the face. And though it is a well-deserved end, I am reminded of a certain Amazon Blonde being helped through the wreckage of a bus by the unlikeliest of hands. And I am reminded of two distinct voices in the woods, one of which might even be considered sadly sympathetic. And I wonder at the virtues of the villain.

And what of the heroes? My dearest Walt, Rubik's Cube

aficionado and doer of the Dew, is sitting in the passenger seat of the beloved Uncle Phil, laughing a laugh for the ages. And Beck, my Knight in Navy Nylon, with that smell (everything good in the world), that smile (ditto), and those deep green eyes, rolls down the window and lets the wind hit him in the face. And though it is a well-deserved end, I am reminded of a certain someone's inclination toward the theft of shiny things. And I am reminded of a firework-infused confession of dishonesty. And I wonder at the faults of the hero.

Maybe there is some black and white, though. In our choices. In *my* choices.

Smiling, I add Our Heroine to the curtain call. She is riding with Beck and Walt, laughing at some singular, lovely thing Walt said, and now we're discussing the Cubs, and New Beginnings, and oh my God, is it Opening Day yet?

I miss them beyond belief. Way, way beyond.

"Mim?"

"Yeah," I say. "Let's go home."

Kathy's PT Cruiser, fueled by the smooth tunes of Stevie Wonder, rolls between perfectly angled magnolias. From behind the aviators, my good eye dares the bright sun to finish what it started, to take the rest of my sight. But the sun doesn't, because I don't mean it, not really.

On a whim, I dig around in my bag for the Abilitol, pull it out, study it. For the first time, I notice the corner of the label is starting to peel back. I pull it off the rest of the way, revealing a slew of warnings, including the risks associated with taking the drug.

"... common side effects reported by users of Aripapilazone may include headache, fatigue, inner sense of restlessness, extreme nausea ..."

Extreme nausea.

A dark corner of my brain shakes off its thick coat of dust and comes alive in the hopes of redemption. Could it be? Could my misplaced epiglottis be no more than a misprescribed drug? I see another list, this one related to the side effects of withdrawal.

"... possible symptoms of sudden discontinuation of Aripapilazone may include emesis, lightheadedness, extreme nausea, diaphoresis ..."

Extreme nausea: a side effect of both taking the pill and not taking the pill. Like the virtuous villain, or the blemished hero, Abilitol is just another in a long line of grays.

I stare ahead, and, admiring the well-kept lawn, consider the madness of the world. Beck and Dad both blame themselves for what happened to their sisters. And they've spent years trying not to make the same mistake twice. But Dad is searching for something inside of me that may not have been there to begin with. And if he's right—if there is some dark thing down there—I need someone on my team who understands the fictional side of life. Someone who understands the difference between suites and concertos. I need a bear in the office, not a snake in the grass.

I need a Makundi.

I unscrew the childproof lid, roll down my window, and hold out the bottle. I'm sure there are people out there who rely on

Abilitol to get through the day. Hell, it's probably saved lives. But thinking back to the last place I swallowed a full dose, bowing to the kings of habit on that empty bus in Jackson, I'll say this: I'm seeing things much more clearly these days.

Slowly, surely, I tip the bottle upside down, emptying the pills right there in front of the militant magnolias. It may be difficult for a while; I may even go through withdrawal. I may need to call the Irish-in-hiding himself, the good Dr. Makundi, for a referral. But it'll be worth it. Because this is my life, the only one I get. And if it's a choice between a life Abilitoled, or a life full of Life . . . well, that's really not a choice at all.

At the end of the long driveway, Kathy turns on the blinker and looks out her window. "Let me know when it's clear on your end, Mim."

God, that sky is a perfect cobalt blue. A natural, pure, new blue. I've never noticed how beautiful that blue is until now.

"Is it clear?" asks Kathy, still staring out the driver-side window.

I turn sideways in my seat, look at the back of her head, and realize—my stepmother is a complete stranger. I don't know the first thing about her, not really. And I've never told her anything about myself, for that matter.

"Mim? We clear?"

I am Mary Iris Malone, and I see all things new.

"I'm blind," I whisper. "In my right eye."

Because sometimes a thing's not a thing until you say it out loud.

ACKNOWLEDGMENTS

Thanks to Mom and Dad, for, among other things, showing me a functional family well enough to write a dysfunctional one. To the entire Arnold and Wingate clan—I would be lost without your patience and support all these years. I have the best family in the history of families.

Heartfelt thanks to my agent, Dan Lazar, whose editorial eye and literary prowess are unrivaled. To Torie Doherty Munro, Cecilia de la Campa, Angharad Kowal, Chelsey Heller, and my entire family at Writers House, I am forever indebted to you for breathing life into Mim.

Ken Wright, you are my "ideal editor." This book would be a mess without your wise counsel and guidance. Alex Ulyett, a thousand thank-yous for the use of your brilliant brain. I owe you both more than you know. To Theresa Evangelista and Andrew Fairclough, for producing the work of art that is this cover; Eileen Savage, for both the interior design as well as Mim's fabulous illustrations; and Tricia Callahan, Abigail Powers, and Janet Pascal, for copyediting—and everyone at Viking/Penguin who made my first publishing experience an absolute joy—THANK YOU!

Writing community > Writing. And so I thank my Greater Than: my critique group—Ashley Schwartau, Josh Bledsoe, and Erica Rodgers—for making this book what it is; my good friend and critique partner, Courtney Stevens, for I-don't-even-know-where-to-start (CYB!); Jessica Young, Lauren Thoman, Kurt Hampe, and Tiffany Russell, each of whom graciously offered help and whose fingerprints are all over these pages; Ruta Sepetys for her early read and support (I got Ruta'd!); Becky Albertalli, Jasmine Warga, and Adam Silvera, for the 1,000,000,000 emails, the Oreos, the roll-out beds, and for joining me in this canoe without a paddle (#beckminavidera 4-life); Rae Ann

Parker, Kristin O'Donnell Tubb, Sharon Cameron, CJ Schooler, Victoria Schwab, Genetta Adair, Daniel Lee, Steven Knudson, Dawn Wyant, Sarah Brown, Helene Dunbar, Paige Crutcher, Patsi Trollinger, and my entire SCBWI Midsouth family.

Special thanks to: my Champion brothers across the world (champions unite!); my sister-in-law, Michelle, for the veterinary terms and general YA awesomeness; Rachel Smith and Smitty's House of Pain, and all the crazy ladies at Glen Leven; Mim Brumley (because duh); Carl Meier (a true-blue Carl) and all at Black Abbey for the "inspiration"; Daniel Meigs for his photo skillz; Stephanie Appell and all at Parnassus Books; Amanda Connor at Joseph-Beth Booksellers in Lexington; Jeremy and Tiffany Lee; Seth Worley; Stephanie McGuire, LMSW, and Sarah Hummel, LCSW, for their nonpareil professional guidance. A HUGE thank-you to the Society of Children's Book Writers and Illustrators, whose Work-in-Progress grant, wisdom, and community shaped me as a writer. And a bajillion thanks to you, the reader, without whom none of this would matter.

Elliott Smith provided more than a soundtrack while writing—he taught me that an honest voice is more compelling than a pretty one. I also owe Alexandre Desplat, Slowreader, Bon Iver, Nick Drake, M. Ward, and Jon Brion a debt of gratitude for creating the perfect notes for Mim. And a special thank-you to the legendary David Byrne for permitting me to use his words where mine simply would not do.

Thanks to my son, Winn, who was, unwittingly, the catalyst behind this entire book.

Lastly, to my wife, Stephanie: I am 110 percent positive that some mad scientist created you in a lab to perfectly compliment the specifications of a David Wesley Arnold. You have loved me real.

Boy21

Matthew Quick

It's never been easy for Finley, particularly at home. But two things keep him going: his place on the basketball team and his girlfriend, Erin – the light in even the darkest of his days.

Then Russ arrives. He answers only to Boy21, claims to be from outer space, and also has a past he wants to escape. He's one of the best high-school basketball players in the country and threatens to steal Finley's starting position.

Against all the odds, Russ and Finley become friends. Russ could change everything for Finley, both for better and for worse. But sometimes the person you least expect can give you the courage to face what's gone before . . . and work out where you're going next.

Praise for Matthew Quick:

'Beautiful . . . a first-rate work of art' *New York Times*

'Transfixed me from the opening line to the last' Annabel Pitcher

'Dark and intense yet funny: compelling stuff' *Fabulous*

978 1 4722 1290 0

headline

Hello, Goodbye, and Everything In Between

Jennifer E. Smith

One night. A life-changing decision. And a list . . .

Of course Clare made a list. She creates lists for everything. That's just how she is.

But tonight is Clare and Aidan's last night before college and this list will decide their future, together or apart.

It takes them on a rollercoaster ride through their past – from the first hello in science class to the first conversation at a pizza joint, their first kiss at the beach and their first dance in a darkened gymnasium – all the way up to tonight.

A night of laughs, fresh hurts, last-minute kisses and an inevitable goodbye.

But will it be goodbye forever or goodbye for now?

Praise for Jennifer E. Smith:

'That whole fresh, dizzy, gorgeousness of first love is there . . . Highly recommended!' Carmen Reid

'Packed with fun and romance, this uplifting *You've Got Mail*-style story is totally charming' *Closer*

'A sweet story of summer love with all its myriad complications' *Sunday Express*

978 1 4722 2103 2

headline